DAUGHTER
OF THE ENEMY

A Unique Historic Novel

SELLIPALAYAM R. PERUMAL

PARTRIDGE
A Penguin Company

ISBN: Hardcover   978-1-4828-1032-5
               Softcover   978-1-4828-1031-8
               Ebook   978-1-4828-1030-1

Partridge books may be ordered through booksellers or by contacting:

Partridge India
Penguin Books India Pvt.Ltd
11, Community Centre, Panchsheel Park, New Delhi 110017
India
www.partridgepublishing.com
Phone: 000.800.10062.62

This book is dedicated to Malala Yousafzai and
the woman of Pakistan.

CONTENTS

PROLOGUE

Pakistan is a paradise for novel writers. The military dictatorship, power hungry corrupt politicians, militants, feudalism, fundamentalism and Taliban offer a fertile ground for writers to spin stories around them. There is no dearth of action and thrill. Everyday something interesting happens in Pakistan. It is always a newsworthy nation.

The author has chosen to spin a story with real characters and real events. Fictional hero and heroin were introduced. They interacted with the real characters in the story and took part in politics and wars.

The story began in Kuwait in 1985. An Indian Brahmin girl by force of circumstances married a Pakistani Muslim and lived a happy life. But in 1990 Iraq invaded Kuwait, and they were forced to return to Pakistan. Santhi (Brahmin girl) the heroin, faced many hurdles in her life in Pakistan. She got over them successfully. When things got settled she returned back to Kuwait. But her husband had to come back to Pakistan during Iraqi invasion by USA in 2003. His interest in social services drew him in to politics. He wanted to make Pakistan as a secular state. He couldn't find a single party which subscribes to his idea. Therefore he started his own party. Santhi gave moral support to her husband and helped him to formulate the policies.

In 2018 general election the party started by the hero and heroin swept the poll in National Assembly and Provincial Assemblies in Pakistan. But the hero, before he was sworn in as the Prime Minister was assassinated by Taliban. There was a tussle for the post of Prime Minister. But the party cadre and women of Pakistan forced the Members of National Assembly to elect Santhi as their parliamentary leader. Santhi faced a legal hurdle before taking oath as P.M.

She overcame the hurdle by converting herself as a Muslim. She brought military under her control by appointing a women as Chief of the Army Staff. With the help of India she successfully achieved troupe reduction along the border. She successfully disarmed the militants and eradicated terrorism from Pakisatan soil. She took military action against Taliban and decimated them. She successfully brought entire Pakistan under the full control of the civilian government. Under her rule foreign relations and trade with neighbors improved. She gave top priority to women's education and empowerment. She empowered the women to take their rightful place in the government. She became popular not only in Pakistan but also in the whole world. She wanted to achieve more. She mooted the idea of forming a UNITED SOUTH ASIAN REPUBLICS in short form USAR. She convinced India, Afghanistan, Sri Lanka, Myanmar and Bangladesh to join the federation. A Summit of the heads of states of South Asian countries was planned and a treaty among the USAR Countries known as "Dacca Treaty" was to be signed by them. Did the summit take place and the treaty signed? Read the book.

1

KUWAIT (1985)

Salmiya was one of the oldest parts of Kuwait city. Indians and Pakistanis lived in large numbers in Salmia where number of Indian restaurants and few Pakistani restaurants were doing brisk business. Choola Restaurant was one among them. It did only 'take away' business of selling chicken kebabs. The restaurant was known for its delicious hot chicken kebabs. It had number of Indians and Pakistanis as its regular customers. In the evening people used to stand in the que to get kebabs.

Ram, a vegetarian by birth is a regular customer of the restaurant. He couldn't take non-vegetarian food at home. Not that he was afraid of his wife because he was unmarried. His sister Santhi was very strict vegetarian and she never allowed non-vegetarian food to be cooked in the house. Out of love for her brother she tolerated her brother eating non-vegetarian food in the restaurants. Ram was sitting in a chair inside the restaurant waiting for the kebab. It was summer month. Kuwait is notorious for its scorching summer. A young man in his early twenties entered the restaurant and ordered for some kebab and sat beside Ram. He looked gloomy. He was silent. Ram broke the ice to kill the boredom.

"Hi! I am Ram. I am working in KNPC as Computer Engineer. I hope you are a Pakistani. Why do you look so sad? Is there any problem back home?" enquired Ram to the young man in a sympathetic tone. This made him to open up his mind.

"I am in real trouble. I lost my job. I have to go back to Pakistan. A dead body would get a better welcome than a live Pakistani returning home without a job."

"What is your name and what do you do in Kuwait?" Ram enquired

"My name is Mansoor Ali Khan. You can call me Mansoor. You do your national profession and I do my national profession."

"I don't get you! Indian's national profession is computer Engineer. O.K! But what is the national profession of Pakistanis?"

"Driver!" Mansoor replied without any hesitation.

Ram laughed. Mansoor didn't.

"If you think that an Indian can help a Pakistani to solve his problem please tell me"

"Indians are the root cause of my problem. No harm in telling you"

"Normally Indians are busy causing problems to themselves. They have no time to cause problems to other nationalities." Ram said jokingly.

"I work as a light vehicle driver in Al Khandari trading and Contracting Co. First I came to Kuwait as a labour. I learnt driving and got my driving license in Kuwait. Both Indians and Pakistanis work in our company. Some of my Indian friends helped me to get the driving license and the job as driver. So, I developed friendship with them. Some of my Pakistani friends didn't like my friendship with Indians. Few of them were religious fanatics. They made some blasphemous allegations against me to my owner. Initially my owner ignored them. But they brought pressure on him through the Qaji of the place. He was compelled to terminate my services. Here I stand terminated and I can stay here for a month." Mansoor narrated his story.

"How many years did you serve your company?" asked Ram.

"More than five" replied Mansoor.

"What is your age?"

"Twenty four. I came to Kuwait when I completed 18 years."

Ram used the telephone in the restaurant to contact somebody. After finishing the conversation he turned to his friend and said,

"You need not go back to Pakistan. Tomorrow go to this address and meet this gentleman. He will arrange for a job. The moment you get your appointment order give me a call. My phone number is in this piece of paper." He gave a piece of paper with address and phone number.

*   *   *

Santhi came out of Salmiya Sultan center carrying her bags with provisions and vegetables. She went to the parking area and opened her car dick and dumped the bag and gunned the engine. When she moved the car, she realized that there was something wrong with her car. She got down the car and found that one of the tires punctured. She checked the spare tire. It was in a deflated condition. She did not know what to do. She looked for known face for help. She couldn't find any. She saw a young Pakistani walking towards her.

"May I help you Madam!" Mansoor offered to help her. She hesitated to accept the help from a Pakistani. But she had no option.

"Give me the key Madam. Transfer your things to my car. I will drop you at your home. I will fix the car and deliver it in the evening. I don't need anything other than a "Thank You" from you" Mansoor talked to her as if she was known to him. She hesitated for a while. But she decided to accept his help.

Mansoor drove his car at a steady speed of 100kmph in the Arabian Gulf Street. All of a sudden the traffic started slowing down. Yes, there was security check. A policeman asked Mansoor to show his papers. He showed the R.C.Blue card and his driving license. Then Santhi showed her ID to the police. He checked the I,D and asked,

"Madam! You are an Indian How come an Indian girl traveling with a Pakistani guy! There is something wrong. Give your papers. Go to Salmiya Police Station. Get back your papers after answering the questions by the police." The policeman took the papers away. They drove to the police station and met the chief.

"So, what is going on between India and Pakistan?" the chief asked sarcastically.

"Nothing as you think Chief!. My car was flat. He offered to drop me at home" Santhi explained. But the Chief refused to believe her.

"It is the job of a police to suspect. Please give some proof to prove your story" asked the chief.

"May I use your telephone with your permission?" she requested the chief and dialed her brother's number.

"Ram! I am in trouble. Please save me from an embarassing situation" she spoke in Tamil and explained the problem in Tamil.

The telephone rang. Some Kuwaiti spoke to the chief.

"Madam! I am very sorry! Had you told me that you are the sister of KNPC computer engineer I would have let you off?" He gave back all the papers with an apology.

While driving to the residence Mansoor told her how her brother helped him.

"I owe my life to him. If I have to give my life to save him I will not hesitate even for a moment. Any way Allah gave me an opportunity to help his beautiful sister" he told her with a wink in his eyes.

"Stop that non-sense! I never expected you to call me beautiful" she showed a mild anger in her eyes.

"I feel sorry to speak the truth. I will call you ugly if it will make you happy." He answered with a mischievous smile.

"Better stick with your original. Don't play with words" she laughed. Residence arrived. She got down and went in to her apartment saying "Remember to bring the car in the evening. I need it for attending my evening computer class".

*   *   *

It was Ram's apartment in Salmiya. Dinner was ready. Santhi invited Ram,

"Annaa! Set the table for dinner!"

There was no response from the drawing room. She got annoyed.

"I know where he has gone!. That retched Choola restaurant! I told him many times not to eat that kebabs. His cholesterol level is way ahead of permissible limit. His B.P. is not a thing to be happy with. Let him come back I will give him a piece of my mind" she spoke to herself and waited for him to come back.

The calling bell rang. She opened the door. She was about to shower her brother with some chosen decent abuses. But she controlled herself after seeing Mansoor with him.

She wore an artificial smile and welcomed him,

"How on earth you meet each other?" she wanted to know.

"I came to Choola to buy some kebabs. I met Ram. He compelled me to accompany him." Mansoor tried to explain his visit.

"I know he brought you as his protective shield. He knows that I am going to blast him" Santhi said with irritation.

"I just went to buy the butter milk. But I saw Mansoor in Choola. I bought some kebabs for Mansoor" Ram tried to explain.

"I know you. You always find an excuse to eat that retched kebabs" Santhi exploded.

"Cool down Madam! Why are you trying to impose your will on him? Let him relish what he wants."

"You don't know his health condition. Doctor has advised him not to touch anything that has something to do with meat. He is only twenty-eight. He has cardiac problem and hypertension. His taste buds are his enemies. I have no one but my brother. He is my father and

4

brother and I am his mother and sister" as she said this she broke down and started sobbing. Mansoor got embarassed and wanted to take leave.

"No! No! You have come as guest for the first time. You have to take food with us. Don't worry about this quarrel. This is a routine thing for us" she calmed down and showed her hospitality.

They sat for the dinner and did not talk much. After the dinner, Santhi started washing the dishes; the friends started chatting about various subjects.

"Why don't you learn some computer skills? If you do I can get a decent job" Ram suggested.

"Computers are for people like you with brains. It will not suit the people who eat the brains like me" Mansoor said politely.

"No! No! Computers are not as difficult as you think. You can do it. Some may learn faster. Others may be slow in learning. Computer is nothing but an extension of the brain as the car is the extension of your legs" Ram explained in a language that he could understand.

"It is expensive. I can't afford. I have to send some money every month to my parents which I will not stop come what may" Mansoor explained his financial position.

"I really appreciate your frankness and dedication to your parents which is rarely seen among the youngsters nowadays. Money is not a problem. If you are really interested I will pay for you as a loan. You can pay me back when you get a better salary" as Ram said this Mansoor could not control his emotion.

"I really don't know how to express my gratitude. I already owe you so much that I do not know how I am going to repay my debts?" he was choked with emotion. At this moment Santhi interrupted their conversation with two cups of coffee.

Mansoor sipped the coffee and said,

"I have tasted coffee in many restaurants in Kuwait and Pakistan. None could match this taste. What is the secret of this taste?" he was sincere in his comment.

"This is the secret of the South Indian coffee. We buy raw Pea berry coffee beans, roast them, grind it as and when required and prepare the decoction in a coffee filter. We use coffee mate to get the real taste" she narrated the recipe.

"I would rather drive to your home than taking all these troubles to prepare a cup of coffee" Mansoor said jokingly and continued "It is time for me leave". The day changed his life forever.

*   *   *

One day Santhi received a call from KNPC that her brother was having chest pain. She wanted to drive to KNPC refinery to bring her brother. She felt that taking another person's help was wiser. She called Mansoor and explained. She asked him to pick her and then bring her brother home. He obliged instantly. While driving home, Ram developed severe chest pain. Mansoor drove straight in to Adan Hospital emergency ward. He was immediately admitted in to ICU. They provided the emergency medication and conducted all the required tests. Mansoor and Santhi waited anxiously. After few hours the doctor called them in to his cabin. The doctor was Indian hailing from Tamilnadu. He was very frank about Ram's condition.

"Today Ram had his first encounter with Yama (the god of death). He might have failed today. But you cannot take chances with him. As a doctor and as a friend I would advise you to take him to Madras at the earliest. He needs treatment. You can get the best treatment at Dr. Cherian's hospital. I will discharge him tomorrow. By that time I will make the file ready" said the doctor. The doctor's advice really shocked her in disbelief.

Next day Ram was discharged and at his residence they discussed about his Madras medical trip.

"Anna! Apply for thirty-day vacation. Mansoor will handover your application in your office. I will arrange for two return air tickets to Madras at the earliest available flight" Santhi revealed her plan.

"Santhi! You have your exams next week. If you miss them you will loose one year. Think about it" Ram protested.

'My study is not important. Your health is more important to me" Santhi defended

"I have better idea. I will accompany Ram. It is an opportunity for me to visit India. I hope that both of you will accept my proposal" Mansoor intervened and suggested.

"What about the Indian Visa for Mansoor?" Santhi interrupted.

"The letter from the doctor will expedite the matter" Ram explained.

Both of them reluctantly agreed as they had no choice. Santhi arranged the trip for Ram and Mansoor with the help of the family friends. AIR INDIA flight landed safely at Madras airport.

2

MADRAS-1987

Ram was admitted in Dr.Cheriyan Hospital. By-pass surgery was conducted using angioplasty technique. Normally he could have been discharged within few days. But the doctor wanted Ram to stay in the hospital as inpatient during the convalescence period. He was admitted in a special room. Mansoor stayed with him round the clock.

After the by-pass Ram felt much better. He could take normal food within few days. They started their conversation while having the 'idli' for their breakfast.

"I really like this stuff. The chutney and sambar provided, as side dish is really fantastic. I never tasted such tasty 'idli' in Kuwait." Mansoor praised the breakfast.

"I want to make a phone call to my sister" said Ram and dialed the number.

"Hello! Ram here! I am perfectly healthy. We will return to Kuwait in two weeks. How did you do your exams?" he enquired his sister.

"I am happy to hear that you are o.k. I will get through my exams. I could have done better if you were here. I miss you annaa! Please give the receiver to your friend"

Ram gave the receiver to Mansoor.

She continued,

"Thank you for all that you have done"

"Not necessary to thank me. I have done my duty. Don't worry about us. Ram was never better" Mansoor assured and replaced the receiver.

"Would you mind if I ask some personal questions?" Mansoor turned to Ram and asked

"Not at all! Please shoot"

"This is your native place. Why didn't you inform any of your relatives about your illness? The least you could have done is to inform them after the operation. I couldn't understand why?"

"You need to know my full story to understand me. My father was a Mechanical Engineer. He worked in a British oil company. They brought him to Kuwait for oil exploration in the late fifties. At that time Indian rupee was the legal tender in Kuwait and all the essential supplies came from India. In 1980 I completed my degree in Electronics and communications from a university in U. S.A. In the same year my parents died in a car accident. My sister is eight years younger to me. I was given a job in K.O.C.and then transfeed to KNPC. They sent me to U.S.A for training in instrumentation. Since the time of the death of my parents, I took care of my sister as a father, mother and brother. This is the first time in her life to be away from me. My parents used to visit Chennai every two years and met our close relatives. After their death we lost touch with them. For all the practical purposes I have nobody in Chennai. I hope that I answered your questions." Ram stopped his narration for a pause.

"I have yet to see a brother and sister like you and Santhi. Now I understand why?" Mansoor exalted.

"I am everything for her. I have done a great injustice to her by spoiling my health. Now I have decided to obey her orders whatever it may be" Ram said in a choking voice.

"You are old enough to get married. What stops you? Is it your sister?" Mansoor enquired.

"Not exactly! I want my sister to get a decent job and get married. Only then I can think about my marriage if I am alive" When Ram said this Mansoor cupped his mouth with his hand saying,

"Don't talk non-sense I will see that you are alive to see your great grand children." Mansoor consoled him.

"To be frank with you I would have gladly made my sister as your wife if you were a Hindu. Not that I am a religious fanatic. I am a practical person. I know your attachment to your family and they would not accept a Hindu girl as their daughter-in-law. I would never put my sister's life in trouble." Ram showed his mind for the first time.

"I understand your feeling. Marrying your sister is the last thing in my mind. Our friendship matters more than anything in this world" Mansoor expressed his feelings.

At that moment the chief doctor knocked the door and came in.

"How are you Ram? Did you have good sleep? What did you have for your breakfast?" doctor asked.

"I feel much better. I had my normal breakfast. I want to know when I can travel back to Kuwait"

"Don't be in a hurry. I will discharge you within a week if you show good progress. You had a providential escape from the stroke. You should not test your luck again. Wait reduction and diet control will make you to see your grand children. Control your tongue. If not, no doctor could help you. Never touch any fried things and junk foods. Say no to non-vegetarian foods. Eat only fruits, vegetables, whole grains, pulses and green salads. Walk five kilometers every day without fail. The last but not the least don't get emotional. Nobody can predict what emotions would do. Please take your medicines regularly. Take things easy. See you tomorrow" doctor finished his checking while talking. Ram had enough talking for the day. He started reading a book till he felt sleepy.

Next day they picked up their conversation where they left during breakfast. But they decided not to talk about personal matters. Mansoor knew that Ram was well read and knowledgeable. He decided to get some knowledge about India and Hinduism.

"I don"t understand why cow is worshipped as god in India" he opened the topic for discussion.

"There are many reasons. Before the advent of agriculture, Aryans were nomads tending cattle especially cows for their livelihood. When they got settled and practiced agriculture, cows helped the farmers in many ways. Cow, among the domesticated animals is the most intelligent, useful and obedient. Without the cow's milk human race could not have flourished. I would put it this way. Cow is a very efficient machine that converts grass and fodder in to useful food products for human-beings. Its urine and dung are useful by-products used as fertilizer and insecticide. It served the humans by supplying animal power. In whatever way you look at, humans are indebted to cow. There is poetic justice in worshipping cow. If you look at the cow as a live beef weighing two hundred kilograms, you may fail to understand why it is worshipped." Ram gave longer than expected explanation. Mansoor stopped asking further questions lest it may affect Ram mentally.

The topic of discussion between Ram and Mansoor turned towards India and Indian culture. Mansoor was fascinated when he learnt many things about India. He started asking many questions.

"I do not know much about religions. I learnt Holy Quran in my school and heard speeches after Friday prayers. I never took interest to know more about other religions. Tell me in a nutshell about Hinduism and other eastern religions.

"If I have to answer your question in a nut-shell, I need a nut of the size of the moon. I will try my best to answer the question in a simple and easy to understand language. Hinduism is not an organized religion. The Europeans coined the word "Hinduism" from the word "Hindi" a Persian word to refer the people who lived on the eastern side of the river Sind. S in Sanskrit becomes H in Persian language. For example Asura in Sanscrit became Ahura Mazda. (the god of the Zoroastrians)

During the Vedic period the way of life (the path) practiced by those who believed in Vedas was known as "Sanathana Dharma" It was not that everybody in India believed and practiced Sanathana Dharma. Almost every village in India had their own deities, belief and cultures. The common man never practiced Sanathana Dharma. Vedas was kept as secret and that was the reason why Vedas were never a popular scripture among the common man. In fact many Vedic scholars believed that Vedas should be taught only to the select few and the common man should follow them without understanding them. Those who understood and practiced Vedas were known as Brahma rishi, Maharishi, Rishi, Muni, Sathus and the prohits (priests) depending on their level of knowledge. The common man was expected to accept whatever interpretation given by these people. The priest class became selfish and utilized the knowledge for their selfish purpose. They never took efforts to spread the message contained in Vedas. This was the reason why Vedas were never understood by many till the twentieth century." Ram stopped and paused. Mansoor understood his mental strain and asked,

"It is enough for the day. We will continue this some other day".

Ram accepted and laid on the bed to take rest.

Next day was the repeat of the previous day. After the breakfast the duty doctor visited for his check up. Ram started reading a book after the doctor's visit. Mansoor looked at the title and its author. The title was "The secrets of Veda" authored by Sri Aurobindo. Ram looked very calm and happy. Mansoor took courage to interfere his reading.

"May I ask few questions about your religion?"

"Why not? The child that cries gets milk and the person who asks questions becomes learned" Ram replied with a smile.

"Muslims have Quran as their scripture and the Christians the Bible. Which is the scripture for Hinduism?"

"Most people in the world think that Baghavad Gita is our scripture. It is not true. It is only part of the scriptures. Our scriptures are created not by any individual nor are they about the life and teaching of an individual. Since Baghavad Gita is popularized by the Europeans (as its philosophy suits them) it became a well-known Hindu scripture. If a book is to be accepted as a scripture it has to satisfy certain conditions. Bagavad Gita is incapable of satisfying all the conditions. It cannot pass the test of full-fledged scripture. At the best it can be described as one of the important Upanishads. Not even the Vedas satisfy all the conditions. This is my view. Many Hindu scholars may not agree with me."

Mansoor couldn't believe his words and asked,

"Hindus couldn't come to an agreement even about their scripture. This is strange."

"That is the essence of Hinduism. It has a place even for an atheist" Ram continued,

"There are scholars, who think that Vedas are revelation from the god to the Rishis who heard them and remembered. That is why they are known as "Sruthis"(means what is heard). There are four Vedas namely Rik, Yajur, Sama and Atharvana. Aryans brought with them the first three and the fourth one was evolved in fusion with the Dravidian philosophy, tradition and beliefs. Veda means book of knowledge. Veda is derived from the root word 'vid'(to learn, educate, dig).

In the opinion of European scholars Rik is the only Veda. It is the most ancient book in the world. There are people who believe that it was revealed to the Rishis at the time of creation of this world. But the scholars believe that this is at least six thousand years old. It has 1028 hymns. It is verbally and unerringly authoritative. Rishis have succeeded in transmitting the Sanskrit text in its original form with very few distortions or insertions compared to other scriptures. It is a near miracle that a book could survive more than six thousand years without much distortion. One of the verses, the well known Gayathri mantra is still recited by the orthodox Brahmins every day.(it is a prayer addressed to the sun).

Rik Veda is collection of prayers and praises addressed towards seventy-six natural objects or power. Sun, sky, moon, wind, fire, dawn, earth and rain are some of them. Some of the major deities mentioned are Indra, Varuna, Agni, Surya, Aswin, Vishnu and Rudra. Some European scholars consider these rhymes as sacrificial compositions by the primitive, barbarous and materialistic Aryans. They are ceremonial and propitiatory in character. Only the later Atharvana Veda has the philosophical contents derived from the Dravidian philosophy and traditions. This view is enforced by the interpretation of Vedas by Sayana, later Vedic scholar. But modern day Vedic scholars do not agree with this view.

They are of the opinion that the obvious meaning of the hymns is materialistic in content and lacks deeper psychological and moral ideas. But the same is case with the songs composed by Sidhars of the Dravidian culture. Their songs were couched in a language that gives a transparent meaning to a common man and completely a different mystic meaning to the learned wise people. In the same way only the sages and Rishis could understand the hidden meaning of the verses. Scholars feel that the secrets contained in Vedas are yet to be deciphered in full by the human being.

Brahmanas, the first interpretation of Vedas represents the priestly Hinduism. It contains the description of elaborate ceremonies, material offerings, animal sacrifices, directions for prescribed sacrifices and the details of various types of sacrifices. It propagates the "Varnashram" system of caste system.(the division of the people as Brahmin, Chatriya, Vaisya and Soothra according to their nature of profession)

Upanishads present the philosophical face of the Hinduism. Their basis is no doubt Vedas. But its contents derive excessively from the philosophical contents found in Dravidian culture, traditions and literatures. Upanishads did to Vedas what the New Testament did to the Old Testament. Upanishads are known as Vedanta. The literal meaning of Vedanta is at the "end of Vedas". It gives the philosophical contents of Vedas in allegorical and the discussion, question and answer form. They are rich in literary content. They are 108 in number. But only ten are major ones. Some were pre-Buddhist and some were post-Buddhists The most important contribution of the Upanishads is the concept of a single Supreme-being "BRAHMAM" which is absolute, infinite, eternal, omnipresent, omniscient, omnipotent, impersonal, indescribable, incomparable and unique without any parallel. The monotheism proposed by Upanishad supersedes the pantheism or polytheism propagated by Vedas. Unlike Brahmanas they are indifferent to the sacredness of Vedas. They denounce the external Vedic practices. They recognize only one god who alone creates, preserves and destroys. Vishnu, Shiva and Brahma are the manifestations of the single supreme-being "Brahman".

Manu, Yagna Vakya and Barathwaja composed the smirithis (remembered) which provide the ethical code for the individuals to follow in the public and private life. Manu is the renowned 'Law giver" to the Hindus.

The well-known "Bagawad Gita" is the scripture that shows the path to the devotees to reach the God. As per Bagavad Gita there are many paths that lead to the God as all rivers reach the ocean. It gives four-fold path namely Karma Yoga, Gnana Yoga, Bakthi Yoga and Sanyasa Yoga.(to reach the god through action, knowledge, devotion and renouncement).

The common man was not expected to understand the Vedas and Upanishads. To illustrate the teachings of Vedas and Upanishads two Rishis namely Valmiki and Vyasar composed the two most renowned epics in the world Ramayan and Mahabharath. Ramayan is the oldest epic in the world. This epic is enacted as drama in countries like Thailand, Malaysia, Indonesia, and Russia for thousands of years. Mahabharath is the greatest epic on the earth ever composed by an individual. Its magnificence is illustrated not only by its size and complexity but also its ability to dwell in to all aspects of human emotions, which nobody else ever attempted. It is the story of the seven generations of Bharath dynasty with hundreds of small stories intertwined with the main story. These two great epics are no doubt fictions based on historical events. That is why they are known as Ithihasam (happened like this).

To spread the spiritual message to the common man, the idol worship and Puranas (mythology) were created. The idol worship created divisions among the Hindus. After the fifth century Hinduism got divided in to six schools of thought namely Ganapathiyam (those who worshiped Vinayaka) Vaishnavites (those who follow Vishnu as their Deity), Saivites (those who accept Shiva as their Supreme god), Saktham(those who worship Sakthi), Koumaram (those who worship Skanda or Kumara or Kanda as their god), Sankyam (those who believe in rituals and worship the sun). Very few Hindus were fanatic about their sects. Generally most of the Hindus accepted all the sects as part of Hinduism.

Modern Hindus have no sects. But they stand divided by the languages, cultures and castes. They have no time to quarrel about the deities or philosophies. Modern Hindus who are supposed to believe in Bagavad Gita do not practice its most important concept "Nishkama karmam"(Action for the sake of action not for its benefits). They are as materialistic as any other people in the world." Ram stopped his narration and paused. Mansoor felt that Ram talked too much and he needs rest. He asked Ram to stop and take rest.

"I have to stop. I have given an overview of the Hinduism. My knowledge of Hinduism is limited. If you want to know more about any aspect of Hinduism or if you have any doubt about what I said, please wait for an opportunity to meet some scholars. They will be in a position to throw more light on the subject. Now I will take rest. We will talk about our program tomorrow" Ram concluded.

After the breakfast the chief doctor came to check up. He was satisfied with the progress made by Ram.

"You are fit enough to be kicked out of this hospital. Wait for a day more to complete the formalities. Don't be in hurry to hop in to the plane and land on your desk to clear your pending work. You have to convalesce for a period of fifteen days. This hospital is neither the best place nor your home in Kuwait. I suggest you to go on a honeymoon trip to some nice place with your friend as your companion because your health will not permit a lady companion. I think that Tamilnadu is blessed with some if you care to find out" the chief told jokingly. It showed that his popularity is not only due to his medical skill but also his jovial nature.

As soon as the doctor left, Ram jumped in to action. He dug in to telephone directory to get the telephone number of a good travel agent. He arranged for a chauffer driven tourist taxi and hotel accommodation in Madurai and Coimbatore.

"We are leaving this place to Madurai tomorrow. We will stay there for five days and then go to Coimbatore. We will go to Bombay from Coimbatore and then go to Kuwait. I have asked the travel agent to make airline booking accordingly. Be ready to move out in the morning. Better go to the nearby police station and inform about our tour program. Being a Pakistani you have the duty to do so. In case of any problem our Chief Doctor would help you" Ram unfolded his tour plan to Mansoor. He was very happy to hear the cheerful words from Ram.

At Madurai They stayed in Hotel Meenakshi. It was a three star grade hotel. The hotel was not luxurious yet it was comfortable. As they had their chaffer driven car they did not have any problem for the transport. On the first day they visited Meenakshi Sundareshwarar temple. Mansoor, on seeing the temple couldn't believe his eyes. He was wonder struck with awe and grandeur.

"I never imagined that a temple complex could be as large as a small township. Please fill me with some background details about this temple." said Mansoor in a tone that showed his amazement.

"This city is two thousand five hundred years old. The existing temple was built in the sixth century. But it was damaged by the Muslim invasion in the fourteenth century. The present structure of this temple was built by Naik dynasty in the sixteenth century. The Naik dynasty came from Maratta, the present Maharastra. This temple complex houses the twin shrines Meenakshi and Sundareshwarar temples. It has twelve gopuram (tower), twenty mandapam (halls), one tank and four gates. Besides it houses the shops and other commercial establishments. The area of this complex is more than sixty five thousand square meters. No doubt it aspires to be included as one of the wonders of the world" Ram reeled out the statistics, which he read from the tourist brochure supplied by the tourist department.

The ayiramkaal mandapam (literally means hall of the thousand pillars) is having nearly one thousand pillars decorated with sculptures and painting. It is an architectural marvel. In any angle of view the pillars are seen in a straight line. The outer corridor has musical pillars carved out of stones that give the seven musical notes if tapped.

Another wonder in Madurai is the Thirumalainayak Mahal. The king Thirumalainayakkar constructed this in the year 1636. It is brick and mortar construction of the dimension 75M by 52 M without any support in between or rafter or girder. It is standing proof for the technological skill of the Tamils that existed before the British rule.

They visited the Vaigai River and Azhagar temple in the banks of Vaigai.

They took a decision to go to Coimbatore via Kodaikanal, an important hill station in the Western Ghats. While traveling in the ghat road they enjoyed the nature, which was not spoiled by the humans as happened with other hill stations. On their way they saw the waterfalls and the orchards. Mansoor who saw only the desert sand in Kuwait felt exhilarated on seeing the flora and fauna of the hill station. He could not control his admiration to the nature's beauty.

"When I saw the tall buildings, super markets, modern wide roads, flyovers and well-maintained parks in Kuwait, I felt sad whether our country would ever have such things. But my feeling has changed. May be the gulf countries blessed with oil wealth are in a position to convert their oil wealth in to a concrete jungle with the help of the technology. But their wealth is nothing before the natural wealth blessed by the god to countries like India and Pakistan. With the all their wealth, the oil rich countries can never acquire even a fraction what India has" Mansoor expressed his astonishment.

"I couldn't agree more with you. We do not know how long the oil wealth would last. But India possessed this wealth for millions of years and would continue to possess as long as the world exists" Ram concurred with the views expressed by Mansoor.

They reached Kodaikanal. It is situated 2233 meters above mean sea level. It is an important hill station in the Palani Hill range of the Western ghat. They visited Kodai Lake which is man-made lake. It is situated in picturesque surroundings. Boating in this lake is an enjoyment. However Ram and Mansoor did not have enough time to enjoy the luxury. They went around various places guided by a guide. In the evening they climbed down from the hills to reach Palani Temple.

They stopped their car at Palani for the evening tea. While waiting for the tea to be served Mansoor asked,

"This temple looks like a popular temple. Please tell me something about this temple"

"This is one of the six hill top Murugan temples. The presiding deity is Dhandayuthapani Swamy (the god with the weapon in his hand). The statue here depicts his renounced posture yet carrying his weapon (a spear headed staff called "vel" in Tamil). This temple is situated at 1500 ft above msl. There are two ways to reach the top. One is climbing 697 steps and the other is traveling by an electric winch. The temple was built by a Chera king (Kerala) in the sixth century. It was further improved in the seventeenth century by Nayak kings and Pandya kings. Lord Murugan is mentioned as Skanda in Vedas. He is considered as Tamil god. In the Dravidian culture each type of land had its own deity. Kurinji (tribal) land had Kumaran as their deity. He is known by various names such as Murugan, Kanthan, Karthikeyan, Arumugan etc. He is very popular god not only in Tamilnadu but also in Kerala, Malaysia, Singapore, Australia and West Bengal.

I am not supposed to climb up the hill as per medical advice and you are not supposed to go up the hill as per the advice of your religion. Let us the drop the idea of getting an appointment with Lord Muruga." Ram finished his talk along with his tea. They reached Coimbatore for their night dinner at Woodlands Hotel. It was located in the heart of the city.

Next day morning they visited the Natarajar temple at Perur. The presiding deity is Patteeswarar. This temple is situated on the banks of River Noyyal only 5 kiolmeters away from the heart of the city. Lord Shiva and his consort Pachai Nayaki are the Deities. This temple was built 1500 years ago by Karikaala Cholan. Kings of Hoysala and Vijayanagar dynasty contributed to the architecture. This temple has long pillared corridor with exquisite granite carvings and huge sculptures. This temple causes awe and admiration like other temples in Tamilnadu. This temple is small in size but otherwise grandeur compared to other temples.

This city is a leading industrial city. It is full of industries small and medium in size. It is situated in Palghat pass in the western ghat. Even during the pre-christian era Tamilnadu had trade links with Rome and Greek. There was a trade route from Calicut (in Kerala where St.Thomas landed.) to Karur via Coimbatore.

The most important biosphere in the South India is the Nilagiri biosphere which is the meeting place between the Western and Eastern Ghats. Coimbatore is located at the shades of western and Nilagiri ranges. There are number of tourist and picnic spot in and around Coimbatore. There are two wild life sanctuaries (Anaimali amd Mudumalai) situated only hundred kilometers from Coimbatore. Ram and Mansoor visited the nearby hill stations Ooty, Koonur and Kothegiri. They enjoyed the cool and pleasant atmosphere. They visited the Sims Park at cunnoor, which is the home for more than hundred fruit trees. The pleasant stay at Coimbatore made them forget their life at Kuwait. When the date of departure arrived suddenly they realized where they belong. They boarded the Coimbatore-Bombay flight and reached Kuwait safely. Santhi was waiting with her car to receive her brother

3

KUWAIT 1987

Ram was driving his car in Fahaheel highway no100 at a steady speed of 100kmph. It was the usual early morning traffic that was moving towards the refineries and power stations at Mina-Al-Ahmadi, Shuaiba and Mina-Al—Abdulla. When he was 15km away from Mina-Al-Ahmadi he saw a huge fire and smoke that was visible at the refinery at Mina-Al-Ahmadi. After few minutes he experienced an unusual traffic jam. The traffic police informed the drivers not to proceed further as there was huge fire at the Mina-Al—Ahmadi refinery. Therefore every body started taking U turn. Ram returned home and tried to get some information about the fire accident. The information available was sketchy. The telephone of the local newspaper was jammed. He tuned to BBC Radio.

"There was huge bomb explosion at Mina-Al-Ahmadi refinery in Kuwait. Sabotage by Palestinian terrorist is suspected. One of the petrol storage tank with a capacity of half million liters is in flames. The fire fighting service is fighting to contain the fire from spreading to other storage tanks. The fire fighting experts from Netherlands are flown in to help them" the BBC newsreader announced. He further continued, "Incase the fire spreads there could be a catastrophe and the nearby residential areas were given a warning to evacuate at any moment" the news reader concluded.

Everybody in Kuwait sat in front of the T.V to get the latest news. An hour later there was flash news "The fire in the refinery was contained with the help of the Holland experts. However the fire is expected to last for a month. Normal operation of the refinery cannot be restored at least for a month" the commentator informed.

Next day more information about the blast came from the private source. It was Ramadan period. Normally the KNPC supplied subsidized food to its employees working in shifts. But during the Ramadan period they were allowed to bring some special food to end their fasting. The previous night a Palestinian employee brought a full roasted chest piece of a goat. He cleverly concealed the bomb in side goat piece. He planted the bomb near the fuel storage tank. He made his escape to Saudi Arabia within a few hours. When the explosion took place somebody noted his absence and informed the police. The police found out about his departure to Saudi Arabia from Passport control office at the airport. They informed the Saudi authorities. They could arrest him at the airport and promptly deported him to Kuwait.

Mansoor visited Ram in the evening. He was very curious to know what happened and why it happened. There was lot of rumor circulating around Kuwait. He wanted to know the correct news. He felt that Ram was the best source.

"There were few car bomb explosions recently in the Kuwait. I do not know why this is happening. The suspicion points towards Palestinians. I don't know why they should consider Kuwait as their enemy. Kuwait is providing employment to half a million Palestinians and they contribute liberally to PLO. Yet they explode bombs. Can you make a guess why they are doing this Ram?" His question made Ram to think for a while and he started explaining his theory.

"My theory is only speculation. Some Palestinian organization other than PLO asked for funds from Kuwait. Probably it did not want to support any organization other than PLO. This might have annoyed them and induced them to threaten Kuwait Government. I am not giving this news as an authoritative source. I am telling this only as my opinion" Ram took some pain to explain his speculation.

"It is quiet possible. Some Palestinian organizations think that they are justified in blackmailing even their friends in to submission." Mansoor agreed with Ram's perception.

At that moment Santhi brought some sweets in a plate.

"What is the cause of celebration? I am sure you don't celebrate the bomb blast!" Mansoor teased.

"I have completed my BSc degree from Kuwait University in first class. Only one piece is for Ram and the rest is for you" she gave the plate to Mansoor.

"Mubarak Madam! What are going to do next?" asked Mansoor.

"Whatever my annaa says" replied Santhi.

"It is very difficult to get a job in KNPC. But I can easily get a job in a private company" Ram replied.

"I want to give a dance program in the drama festival conducted by The Indian Fine Arts Association. Please allow me some time to take up a job in a private company" Santhi pleaded with her brother.

He readily agreed with her as he always did.

* * *

It was the month of April. It was springtime in Kuwait. The climate was very pleasant. Even the desert was blooming. The gardens in Kuwait were full of flowers. People started discarding their winter clothing. Indian fine Arts Association has arranged a month long cultural programs on weekends in the Indian Arts circle at Funatees. There were classical dance, drama, music, folk dances and dinners in the evenings on Thursdays and Fridays. Local cultural talents were given an opportunity to exhibit their talents. Attractive prizes were given out and encouraging gifts were distributed to all participants. This created a festival mood among the Indians living in Kuwait.

Santhi was given the prime time slot 8-9pm on a Thursday for her dance program. On that day the auditorium was fully packed. People were standing wherever they could find a place. However Ram and Mansoor were assured of their seats in the front row meant for VIPs. Ram was very happy to watch his sister's program. Mansoor was really excited because he never watched a Bharatha Natyam Dance program in his life. He heard about it as the symbol of Indian culture. He wanted to know more about Bharatha Natyam.

"It was the cosmic dance performed by Lord Shiva and his consort Parvathi. The dance derived its name from the Sage Bharath Muni who codified its aspects, rules and disciplines two thousand years ago. Bharath Muni codified every aspect of the dance. Even now it is the manual for all Bharatha Natyam dancers" Ram explained.

"I have seen some dances in the Hindi films. Is it same as Bharatha Natyam" Mansoor raised his doubt.

"Rarely can you see a classical Bharatha Natyam dance in Hindi films. You could see some in Tamil films" Ram replied.

"I have not seen any Tamil movie. One day I would like to see one" Mansoor expressed his wish.

Ram looked at his watch. It was 8pm sharp. The curtain was raised. The silence that prevailed kindled the curiosity of the audience. Suddenly there was music of the Salangai (anklet made of tiny bells). Santhi appeared in stunningly beautiful costume.

She started with the program called 'Alarippu". It depicts the sixty-four steps involved in Bharatha Natyam. It is the fundamental required for any Bharatha Natyam dancer. This program went on for about half an hour. Then she did a dance for a song written by National Poet Bharathi. Then the conductor of the program made an announcement.

"Next item of the program is dance based on a song composed by the dancer herself. The song is in Tamil. There is no necessity for the audience to understand the language. The song depicts the affection of a sister towards her brother. She will convey the meaning of the song through her expressions. That is Bharatha Natyam at its best. I do not want to delay the program by my talking. The dance starts now!" the commentator concluded. The throbbing music started.

Thaayai ariyaen thanthaiyai ariyaen
Thanayanae unnai nanarvaen
Enakkul iraivan neeyae
Maraththukku uyiraana aanivaer neeyae
Azhuthirukkiraen unnai adiththikiraen
Kadithirikiraen kaalai uthar adam pidithirikiraen
Anaiththaiyum poruththu ennai anaitthirukiraay
Thai pol ennai thaallatinai thanthai pol enakku arivu thanthaay
Thozhi pol enakku thondu seithaay
En sugam karuthi thannai maranthaay
Enna thavam seithae unnudan pirakka
Mannulla varai maravaen unnai
Mangai naanum manamudiyaen
Annan saevaiyil uyir vazhvaen
Marupiraviyulum un thangaiyaay pirappaen
The meaning of the song in English
Know not father or mother
I know only my brother
He is the god within me
He is like the principal root for a tree
I cried and beat you
Yet you never lost your patience

You fed me like a mother and
Taught me like a father
Gave company like a friend
You sacrificed all your pleasure for my sake
I cannot forget you till my death
I will not get married lest I may forget you

Mansoor was deeply immersed in the song. He was trying to understand the meaning of the song from her expressions. He wanted to get some clarifications from Ram. He turned towards Ram. He was shocked to see his condition. Sweat was flooding on his face. He was gasping for breath. He was holding his chest with his hands. His face expressed that he was in great pains. Tears were flowing from his eyes. He got up and lifted him like a child and rushed to his car. He knew Ram's health condition. He understood what happened to him. Santhi virtually killed him by her emotional song. He was taken to the emergency ward in Adan Hospital. He was admitted in ICU immediately. Doctors were rushed in. They found his heart stopped beating and his pulse almost collapsed. They tried their best to revive his heart by artificial respiratory techniques. It was too late. Doctors gave up and declared him dead.

Mansoor couldn't believe what he heard from the doctors. He did not dare to look at Santhi. He went to a corner and sat alone. He tried to control his tears. When Santhi heard the news while she was trying to remove her make-up she fainted and was carried away to the hospital. She too was admitted in ICU. Doctors fought all the way to save her life. But for the timely admission and the valiant fight by the doctors, she would have accompanied her brother. Doctors succeeded in saving her life.

When she was discharged from the hospital after a week, she looked like a skeleton. Mansoor came with his car and picked her. Santhi's neighbors were kind people. Yet they had their own problem. Nobody was prepared to take care of Santhi. Mansoor was left with no option. He stayed with Santhi and took care of her.

A month passed. The time and Mansoor's care restored her body to some extent. But she remained in her shocked condition. Mansoor treated her like a child. He cooked, fed and changed her clothes. He virtually fought a lone battle to bring her back to life. He succeeded after three months.

*   *   *

Santhi was sitting on the sofa and Mansoor sat in front of her.

"Time and work are the best healers of all the wounds. Time has done its work on you. Now you need work to keep your mind busy and forget the tragedy. I enquired through my friends. They say that you have a good chance to get job in KNPC on compassionate grounds. Please write an application to KNPC and I will take care of the rest through Ram's friends. Ram was such a nice person, his friends are ready to do anything for him" Mansoor encouraged her to take up a job.

"I don't know what would have happened to me without you. I have to accept whatever you say" Santhi accepted his suggestion.

Within a week Santhi received an interview call from KNPC. She proved that she was the sister of Ram. He had a good reputation in KNPC. She found her interview was more about her brother than about her knowledge. She was made personal secretary to the General Superintendent of the refinery. She joined duty immediately. A busy mind cures everything. She got over the tragedy. She learnt to live a life without her brother. Yet she could not decide about her future. She consulted one of her brother's friends whom she considered as a wise man.

"Mansoor lived with you for more than four months. Whole Kuwait knows about it. I understand that it was an extraordinary circumstance that made him to live with you. It is not a good idea to marry someone else. It may create problems for you in future. I sincerely advise you to marry Mansoor. Religion may be a problem but it is not a hindrance for happy married life if both of you have good understanding. I know that there are problems. But you can get over them. Talk to Mansoor and get his views. Then we will discuss the matter" he concluded.

Santhi raised the topic of her marriage with Mansoor.

"I consulted a wise man. He is of the opinion that it is better that we get married. Tell me frankly your opinion. Whatever may be your opinion I will not misunderstand you"

"I will be the happiest person to marry you. Your qualification as the sister of my friend is more than enough for me to marry you. I know you have more than that. The only problem with me is that my family will not accept a Hindu girl as their daughter-in-law. We have to find a solution to that problem" He clarified his position.

"Do you suggest that I should become a Muslim to marry you?" Santhi raised her doubt.

"Not at all! I want you to remain as you are. Even if you were to agree for conversion I am not for it. I don't believe in conversion as Ram always used to tell me. If I insist on conversion of the sister of Ram I will do a great injustice to him. It is worse than refusing to marry you. Today I make a solemn promise that I will not allow you to get converted" Mansoor was forthright in his conviction.

"We can invite your parents here. Let them judge me. I hope that they will accept me. In case they reject me we will try our best to convince them" Santhi suggested.

"It is a mature approach. Let us give it a try" Mansoor accepted.

Next day he wrote a detailed letter explaining everything to them. He invited them to come to Kuwait to see and approve their future daughter-in-law. He received the reply within a fortnight. They readily agreed to visit Kuwait. He got two visit visas for his parents and sent them through a friend.

*   *   *

It was the month of November. The summer came to an end. The weather was pleasant. Yet the daytime reminded the summer heat. Mansoor drove his car with Santhi by his side to the airport to receive his parents. He parked his car and they waited at the exit gate. When he saw his parents coming out he rushed and hugged his mother and she said "Allah bless you!" Then he hugged his father and he said the same thing. It was the turn of Santhi to respect the elders. Mansoor did not tutor her about their culture. She was bit confused what to do. But her instinct came to her aid. She bent and touched their feet with reverence. It made them very happy. They know very well how a Hindu girl respects the elders. That was what they expected from her. They blessed by saying "Allah will keep you always happy".

They reached home. The dishes were already prepared and kept in hot packs. Santhi prepared some hot rice and chappathi and placed on the dining table. They all enjoyed their dinner. Mansoor relaxed and he was confident that his parents would approve Santhi. But Santhi was not sure. She did not want to get disappointed later. She was cautiously optimistic in her hope. Mansoor slept peacefully on that night. Santhi was bit anxious and she could not get peaceful sleep. Next day she prepared some nice Aluparothas (made out potato and wheat flower) which she knew Punjabis like it.

"This aluparotha has Madrasi flavor. Any way it is very nice. The last night dinner was superb. We are happy that our son need not go to restaurants to eat nice Indian foods" his father hinted his approval.

"Your father loves eating. But food is not everything in life. There is something more" his mother was guarded in her comment.

Santhi was kept in suspense. Mansoor asked his mother what she feels about Santhi.

"A woman understands another woman better. She is the best 'bahu' I can get for my son. She is beautiful. She is more educated than you. Yet she is polite and shows respect to elders. She manages the house nicely. What else you can expect from a Bahu (daughter-in-law). I am fully satisfied. You can go ahead and arrange for the marriage. It is not good to live together without marriage" she expressed her opinion without any hesitation.

"Your mother has summed up my feeling. But I have something to add. Our community would not understand you. They will look through the religious glass. I may have to enact a small drama to satisfy them. I will pretend as if I am not happy with this marriage. After few years, once you have few children everybody would forget the religion. So keep a low profile for few years and do not visit Pakistan till you have two children" his father was wise enough to give his approval with riders attached.

Santhi and Mansoor got relieved from the anxiety after hearing the approval from his parents.

*   *   *

Mansoor applied to the Embassy of Pakistan to get the marriage registered. They refused his application on the ground that the bride was a non-Muslim Indian girl. Mansoor tried his best without success. Therefore Santhi made her application to Indian Embassy to get the marriage registered. There was no problem with the Indian Embassy. They did not even ask about the religion of the bride and bridegroom. They asked about the nationality of the groom. They wanted an affidavit to be filed by Santhi that Mansoor is not already married. She enclosed the passport copy and other evidences as proof. A notice was displayed in the Embassy notice board. After a month they got married at Indian embassy and the marriage was registered.

A celebration buffet dinner was arranged at Massilah Beach Hotel. Their friends and well wishers were invited. When an Indian girl got married to a Pakistani without any religious conversion it was news. Many people talked about the marriage. Mansoor's parents left Kuwait next day as the visit visa was expiring.

On the day the dinner was arranged it was a hectic day. They received lot of gifts. They dumped them in a room. They were tired so much they didn't even talk about the dinner or about the guests. They retired to their bedrooms and slept as usual. Next day they made preparations to celebrate their first night as husband and wife. Their bed was decorated with flowers. Sweets, nuts and fruits were arranged. They eagerly waited for the night to arrive to get the thrilling experience.

One of her friends helped Santhi to do the bridal make up. Every thing was arranged in their bedroom. At 8 p.m sharp their friends took leave of the couple.

First Mansoor entered the bedroom and waited for her to arrive as the custom dictated. She completed her chores in the kitchen, switched of the T.V and unplugged the telephone. She checked her makeup in the mirror and was satisfied with the work done by her friends. As she entered the room Mansoor eagerly came forward to receive her.

"Don't be in a hurry! There is a tradition for everything. Please stand erect near the bed" she requested. He readily obeyed. She knelt on her knees on the floor and bent to touch his foot. He didn't know what to say to her. She said

"I will not get up till you say something"

"Please tell me what I should say to you"

"If I tutor you it will be mechanical. The words should come from the heart. Say whatever you want to say. Simply say some thing" she exhorted him.

"From now on my honor, pleasure and glory are in your hands. Whether we raise or fall let us be together till death separate us" saying this he lifted her and made her to sit on the bed comfortably. He took few steps backwards and stared at her. She was sitting on the bed with her face down looking at the ground. He always looked at her as the sister of his friend. He never looked her as a beautiful woman. Now he studied her from head to tow. She shampooed her hair. He could smell the fragrance of the shampoo. She did not do any hair do. The long flowing thick hair was combed and let loose. The tip of her hair was tied with a band. She decorated her hair with sewed jasmine flowers. The natural fragrance emanated from the flowers made him sexually crazy. Her face did not wear heavy make up. The skin was natural with slight coating of Yardly talcum powder. On the forehead and between the eyebrows she planted a red circle dot with bindi powder (a powder made by mixing turmeric powder with lemon juice). She looked like an angel decorated with a red sun on her forehead. It was typical Indian married woman's face. She was wearing a Kanjeewaram silk sari with a blouse of the same material presented by one of her friends bought from India. The red color sari gave her the beauty with grace. It covered her body well while revealing enough of her body to raise the erotic feeling in any man. Mansoor's feeling got aroused. He said,

"Today you look like a different woman to me. I never thought that you could be sexually appealing. But today you look like a sexual god to me. Your silk blouse reveals more than it conceals. The poor thing tries to cover your breast but failed. Well shaped firm breasts are trying to burst and come out to show its beauty to me. Your moist lips are inviting me to taste them. Your hip below your breasts is bare and invites me to pinch. But I restrained because your eyes may shed tears due to pain.

Your sari is so beautiful that I hesitate to touch them lest it may get crumpled. I like the sari be saved from torture. More over you may feel hot with the sari on your body. Why don't you free yourself from the clutches of this sari and blouse? Let our body enjoy the cool breeze". He would have continued talking but for her interruption.

"I know what you want. But I will teach how to go about the business of love making" she taught him like a teacher.

She pulled his head and laid it on her thighs. She gave a deep kiss that lasted many minutes. Both wanted to kiss till morning. But when the nipple of her breast touched his chest he could not control himself. He got up and hugged her tightly. The air between their body got completely squeezed out. Her blouse got burst and opened. She was left with no alternative but to remove it. When he saw her breast he was annoyed with her bras, which was partly covering them. He hurriedly removed the bra and looked at the bare breasts and admired. She slowly guided him how to proceed. Her hand switched off the light. They entered through the gates of heaven. They did not sleep till the early morning. They didn't know when they slept.

*   *   *

4

KUWAIT 1989

Mansoor parked his car at the parking area of KOC hospital at Ahmadi. It was visiting time for the hospital. He walked in to the maternity ward without any hindrance. He rushed and caught hold of the hands of Santhi and enquired,

"Are you O.K! How is my son? I really wanted a daughter like you. But Ram never wanted to leave our home. He made a successful come back. Look at him. He smiles exactly like Ram. He is talking to me. I can hear him" Mansoor became emotional when he remembered Ram more than Santhi. She became a well-settled housewife cum career woman. She got over the sorrow caused by the untimely death of her brother. She was really happy with her husband. He was understanding, caring and always respected her as a well-educated lady. The prenatal care provided by him made her delivery easy and natural. The boy delivered by her was really handsome. Both were very proud of the child. When Mansoor's parents heard the arrival of their grand son, their joy found no limit. They bought all the sweets available in the shops and distributed them to everybody in their village.

Santhi was discharged from the hospital and she had three-month maternity leave. She enjoyed every moment of her life with the child. Mansoor named the child as Ram Ali Khan. Probably he was the first Muslim boy named as Ram. When Santhi hesitated to name the boy as Ram, Mansoor did not hesitate even for a moment. He felt as if he got back his friend. He never used to return from the work in time. Being a driver he had to oblige friends and colleagues whenever they needed some personal transport. But after the arrival of his son he stopped obliging. As soon as the office was closed he was at the parking lot to start his car. The moment he entered his residence he proceeded straight to the bedroom to see his son. Usually he saw his son sleeping. Never mind! He used kiss him and say "How are you my son? Have you troubled your mum?" These were his usual words. Santhi used to watch this scene every day with amusement. One day she told him,

"Ram ki Pappa! Why don't you understand that he is only a month old? He can't understand what you talk to him. Why don't you make some funny noises which he can hear and enjoy" she kidded him.

"Hey! Don't interfere with my conversation with my friend Ram. He understands me well" he protested. She smiled and said,

"O.K! Go ahead with your babble, which only your friend would understand. I have chores to do in the kitchen" She laughed and left. Both of them enjoyed their every moment of their married life. The arrival of their son made them forget the world.

Friday was a holiday. Mansoor went to mosque to pray. When the prayer and the Friday sermon were over he walked towards his car. He saw two Pakistani youngsters talking while walking slowly. He heard them uttering the words like "jihad", "India", "Hindus". He became curious. He walked towards them pretending to search something lost. He could listen to their conversation.

"Have you heard the speaker describing the atrocities committed against Muslims in Bombay. We should do something to take revenge" one man said.

"Oh! Yes! Let us contact our leader and ask him what contribution we can make to the jihad in India" said the other man.

"I think we should go back to Pakistan on vacation to get some training in making bombs and IEDs." suggested the first.

"It is better to get friendship of an Indian Muslim in Kuwait. We can discuss with him and work out a plan of action" the second man proposed.

"O.K. Let us meet our leader "Chota Bhai" in the evening in his camp" they decided and moved away in Toyota Pick up. Mansoor followed them to their flat. He noted their building number and the street number. He found out their flat number from the watchman. He drove straight to the nearby Police station.

"I want to meet the chief. I have some sensitive information, which I can reveal only to a high-ranking Police officer" he informed the cop present there. The policeman immediately contacted his boss. He in turn contacted a high-ranking Police officer. He called and asked Mansoor "Tell me who are you? What is that sensitive information you want to convey?"

"My name is Mansoor. I am a Pakistani working as driver in a private company. My wife is an Indian working as secretary to the General Superintendent of KNPC refinery. The information I have is very sensitive and confidential. I can't reveal it over the phone. I can reveal it to you in person" Mansoor finished his talk.

"O.K!Wait for me in the police station. I will be there in twenty minutes" the Police chief informed him.

Exactly after twenty minutes the police chief arrived in his car and greeted Mansoor "Salaam Alaikkum! Please get in to my car. We will talk" The chief opened the car door.

Mansoor entered in to his car and started talking.

"Sir! I am a Pakistani and a Muslim. Yet I am a human being. I can't condone the actions of Pakistani Jihads just because they happened to be Muslims. There are some Pakistanis living in Kuwait who use this country as a base for their Jihad activities. To day I happened to listen to the conversation of two Pakistanis. I learnt that they have a boss in Kuwait. They are planning to go back to Pakistan to get training in terrorist attack. After the training they are planning a terrorist attack in India. I do not have their names. I have their residential address in this piece of paper. They are planning to meet their boss today evening. Please do something. My intension is not to hurt them. I want to stop the terrorist attack in India." Mansoor concluded his talk.

"Did you develop this love towards India because your wife happens to be an Indian" Police chief provoked him to see his reaction.

"Not the least Chief! I would have done this whatever may be the circumstances. I never want innocent persons killed whatever may be the justification" Mansoor reacted.

"Don't take it seriously! I just provoked you to see you reaction. Don't worry! I will take care of the situation and see that they do not carry out any terrorist attack. I can't tell more than this. Any way I thank you a lot for conveying this information. Good bye! Take care! Never reveal this to anybody. Otherwise you will be in danger" the police concluded and dropped him near his car.

Next day a news item was carried by KUWAIT TIMES. It read like this.

"Half dozen Pakistanis were rounded up by the Police. They were found carrying out activities, which are not related to the work they were supposed to do. They were taken to the airport and promptly deported to Pakistan. The government spokesman refused to reveal further information about them. Enquiries revealed that they were part of the terrorist group. Further enquiries reveal that some Pakistani tipped off about them to the Police. It is tight lipped about the informer"

When Mansoor read this news he was happy that the police took prompt action but at the same time he was worried that the terrorist may attempt to find out the identity of the informer. He did not mention about this incident even to his wife.

*   *   *

It was summer in Kuwait. As Friday happened to be holiday "Al-Jahra" labor camp looked deserted. The sun was scorching outside. It was 5'o clock in the evening. All the inmates in the camp were inside their rooms either sleeping or watching T.V.

In one of the rooms there were six young men, three of them were Pakistanis and the rest Indian Muslims. They were sitting on two beds watching a Hindi movie in the T.V through a VCR.

"Sukkar Allah! The police did not get any information about us from the arrested boys. Otherwise we can't sit like this here" one of the men opened the conversation.

"It is a surprise who could have tipped the police. Never such things happened in the past. We should be very careful in the future while talking to each other. May be that Indian Intelligence agency has planted their men in Kuwait" another raised a doubt.

"We should find who that informer is. We should enquire the watchman of the building, where the arrested people lived. We may get some information about the informer" one of them made suggestion. All the six agreed.

Two of them Shoukat and Azeez visited the building where the arrested men lived. They met the Egyptian watchman and asked him whether there was any vacant flat available for rent.

"Yes! We have. But we do not rent it to bachelors" replied the watchman.

"We heard that flats are rented to the bachelors in this building"

"What you heard is true. Last week two bachelors who were staying here were arrested by the police and deported. Therefore our owner of this building decided not to rent out the flats to bachelors" the watchman clarified.

"In fact we are looking out for a flat for our friend who wish to bring his wife from Pakistan" Shoukat uttered a lie.

"In that case I do not mind showing the flat to you. The rent is one hundred Dinar a month. There is no water charge. You have to pay the electricity charges. Rent should be paid during the first week of every month. You have to bring copy of the civil ID of the tenant and visa details of his wife" he explained the terms and conditions and took them inside to show the flat.

"We too read about the arrest. They were staying in this building. You may know something about the incident. How the police came to know about them?. Did you inform to the police?" Shoukat provoked the watchman. He got annoyed and retorted,

"Why should I inform the police? It is none of my business. A Pakistani who came on that day might have informed"

"How do say that?"

"He noted down the building number and got the flat number from me. That is why I suspect him"

"Do you know anything about him?"

"I do not know anything about him except that he is a Pakistani aged about thirty and drove in a Toyota car. I remember to have seen the name "Al-Kandari Contracting and Trading Co" written on his car. Why do you ask this?" watchman questioned.

"We are not interested. Out of curiosity we asked. We will come back with the documents of our friend" saying this they departed.

*　　*　　*

Three month maternity leave got exhausted. They appointed a nanny to take care of the baby. Santhi was given special permission to return her home to feed the baby during the lunch break. The lunch break was one hour. But she was allowed one and half as a consideration to a lactating mother. When the work was not urgent her boss permitted her to stay back after lunch.

It was a working day. Mansoor returned from his office at five thirty evening. He sat down to watch a Tamil movie in the T.V. Santhi was in the kitchen preparing some snacks and coffee.

"It is really a good movie. Tamil films depict family sentiments better than any other film. I wish I could understand Tamil. I could have enjoyed the film better" Commented Mansoor.

"Better enjoy talking to your son rather than seeing these trash Tamil movies" teased Santhi.

At that time the calling bell rang. Mansoor got up and opened the door. Two Pakistanis standing outside tried to push the door forcibly. Mansoor sensed the danger. He was very strong man. He resisted them by trying to close the door. The struggle lasted for about thirty seconds. Suddenly they heard the police siren approaching the house.

"Police is coming! Let us get away from this place" saying these words they ran away. Mansoor heard their footsteps. He closed the door and rushed to the window to look at the street. He saw the two guys speeding in a car. He released a sigh of relief. He turned back and saw Santhi standing with a spray gun ready to attack.

"We heard the police siren. Where is the police car?" Mansoor wondered.

"Here it is." Santhi showed a tape recorder fixed on to the wall.

"Your presence of mind is really great. Where did you get this tape recorder and spray? You did not tell me about this" Mansoor asked inquisitively.

"I expected this attack. Last week the Police chief called on me and explained that the terrorists are planning to attack us. He told me about you informing the police. They provided me with this spray and tape recorder. They gave me the training. They conducted a mock attack to give me practical training. Thank god! It worked. They were lucky to escape. Had they entered the house in spite of the siren I would have paralyzed them with this spray" Santhi cleared his doubt. Mansoor really felt happy to be alive.

"Why did you decide to keep this information with you? You could have told this to me" he raised his doubt.

"I could have told you. It would have made you nervous and probably you would have applied for a long vacation. The attack was not certain. The police told me that the probability of an attack was remote. Only as a precautionary measure, they equipped me" saying this she dialed the police chief to thank him. She explained him the incident

"Allah saved you this time. Every time you can't trust Allah to save you. I advise you to move to KNPC rented buildings where the security provided is foolproof. I will make my recommendation to your boss" Police chief gave a sensible advice. His recommendation worked. Santhi got a flat in KNPC rented building in Abuhalifa. Sometimes a bitter incident leads to a better result.

5

OCCUPATION OF KUWAIT BY IRAQ

1989 passed off peacefully for the family of Santhi. 1990 was a year of happiness for them. Indians in Kuwait celebrated spring festivals. Padma subramaniam (Bharatha natyam exponent) and Hema Malini (Famous cinema actor and Bharatha natyam dancer) were invited to give performances in Indian Arts Circle. The sponsors of the program have introduced Santhi to them.

"She is the local Bharatha natyam exponent Few years back she gave a wonderful performance that it became a turning point in her life" the sponsor commented.

"For the worse" Santhi remembered her brother's death, "Now I am a mother and career woman. I can't dance any more" she explained her position.

"We can't accept this excuse. Indians in Kuwait need entertainment during festivals. People like you should not shirk their responsibility. I hope that you realize. You will waste your talent if you do not practice. You do not know! One day your dancing skill may change your life. When I visit Kuwait next time I wish to see your program" Padma Subramaniam encouraged Santhi to practice and perform. She couldn't say no to an eminent personality. She accepted her advice half-heartedly.

"You look so beautiful with a slim figure I couldn't believe that you are a mother. Please do not visit India. I may loose my position" Hema Malini flattered her. Santhi was no dumb to believe these words.

When two glamorous ladies left the place Mansoor approached and encouraged Santhi to practice.

"All the time I was encouraging you to practice dancing. You ignored me. Now you can't ignore those icons of Bharatha Natyam art. You have to dance" he said happily. He was very eager to see his wife's dance.

"Whenever I think of the dance I remember my brother and make me sad" Santhi explained.

"I do not remember Ram because I never forgot. Now I see him as my son. Please get over your sentiments. Do things that will please Ram. He would be too happy to see you dancing" Mansoor tried to convince her.

"Let me try. I am not sure whether I will succeed" she concluded.

Bharathi Kalai Manram organised a dance competition in the month of May 1990. Mansoor was very anxious that Santhi should take part in the competition. He persuaded her to give her name. She started practicing her dance every day in the evening. She wanted to dance for her own lyric. Therefore she wrote a lyric in Tamil.

Porul thaedi poovulahengum pokinravarkalae!
Makilchi enpathu intha manalilaa kidaikkirathu!
Mannil kidaippathu mannum ennaiyumae!
Ponnai virumpum poonguzhal makkalae!
Ennaip paarungal ponnaethum illai!
Kan niraintha kanavanaik kaipidikka vaendum!
Annaiyum appavum aananthikka vaendum!
Kannan pol oru kaikuzhanthai vaendum!
Ennai pol oru pen kuzhanthai vaendu!
Naan enra akanthai akal vaendum!
Anaiththum avanenra ennam vaendum!
Naam pirantha mannaiyum panpaiyum maranthidaathae!
Nammai vazhvikkum nalam tharu Kuwait!
Naalum valarum kali manramae!
Ummai vananguvaen uyirullavarai

Mansoor used to watch her practicing the dance. He wanted to know the meaning of the song. She translated the song.

Oh! Brothers roaming the world in search of wealth!
Happiness is not in dollars and Dinars!
Oh! Women of India who love flowers and gold!
Look at me! I wear no gold or diamond!
Yet I live happily with my loving husband!
Serve the parents as you serve the god!

Aspire for a son with look of baby Krishna!
Aspire for a dream girl as your daughter!
Remember! Ego is your enemy number one!
Everything happens at the will of God!
Never forget your motherland and culture!
Be loyal to Kuwait that provides everything!
Hail Barathi kalai manram that nourishes the arts!

When Mansoor read the translation he felt a humble feeling that how lucky he was to get married to such a wife. He started believing in Karma theory that he got his wife because he did something very good in the previous birth. He expressed his feelings.

"I do not know that you are such a wonderful poet. God is too much partial to you. He has given so many good things to you. I do not know whether I am one of them"

"Sure! You are one of the best boon that god bestowed on me! I will try my best to deserve the gift" she expressed with gratitude.

*   *   *

On the second Saturday May 1990 Santhi gave her Baratha Natyam performance between 8-9pm. When the program was in progress, the canteen, which served to the audience, wore a deserted look. Nobody came out of the auditorium even for coffee. Some of the audiences had wet eyes on listening to the songs. At the end of the competition the president of Bharathi Kalai Manram declared that the first prize went to Santhi Mansoor Khan. It was not surprise. In fact it was a surprise to Mansoor who did not understand the intricacies of the dance. He felt happier than Santhi. When the president distributed the prize he commented,

"Santhi is holding a very important position in KNPC. Yet she took off her time to practice and perform the dance. We should appreciate her love for the art and India. She composed the song for which she danced. The meaning of the song is very much relevant to the expats and Kuwaitis. People of this country whether they are locals or foreigners, should know that the wealth bestowed on this country is not permanent. It should not make them lose the good values. The youngsters of Kuwait do not know the hardship undergone by their forefathers. They should not think that they would live in prosperity forever. God do test the people with hardship. Those who are blessed with wealth should be compassionate towards the poor and the unfortunate. That is one of the teachings of Islam. Let us pray god for the prosperity of our country and everlasting friendship between India and Kuwait."

There was a big ovation for his speech. Many congratulated Santhi for her performance. The festival ended on a very happy note.

*   *   *

Summer started earlier than usual in the firs week of June. There were few sand storms. People kept themselves in the indoor unless their service was required. In the KNPC refinery too very few people were seen inside the plant. Most of the people shut themselves inside their air-conditioned offices. The general Superintendent had his breakfast at 9'o clock. Few of his friends came to chat with him. One among them was a British, another a Kuwaiti and the third was American. The conversation turned towards the hot topics of the day ie Saddam Hussain's relation with Kuwait.

"Saddam declared that he won the war against Iran. Celebrations were going on for weeks. When celebrations were over Saddam realized that his country owes eighty billion dollars to other nations. Even a poor country like India claimed that five billion dollars was due to them. Kuwait and Saudi Arabia offered to write off their loan given to Iraq. But Saddam was not satisfied. He claimed that he fought the war on behalf of Arabs against Persians. He described the war as conflict between Shia and Sunni sects. He demanded that Arab world was morally bound to help Iraq. The debate between him and other Arab nations was getting hot as the mercury soared in the deserts" the British friend described the situation in a nutshell.

"Bush helped Saddam because he considered him as secular and a good counter balance against Islamic Republic of Iran." the American friend tried to explain the conduct of U.S.A.

"Don't bush-shit rather bullshit my friend! The Americans knew which side of bread was buttered. The defense industry, which controls the American presidency, was very much interested in conflicts between nations who have the capacity to pay for the weapons. That's it. Saudis and Kuwaitis were paying for the weapons bought by Saddam. Iraq's soldiers were dying. But American defense industry was kept busy counting dollars all these eight years. Now the conflict is between Saddam and his neighbors. Americans are watching the show with keen interest. The only country really concerned about the conflict is Egypt. It tries its best to avoid the showdown between Saddam and his neighbors" Kuwaiti friend gave his sensible analysis.

At that moment Santhi entered her boss' room without knocking.

"Sorry gentlemen! I couldn't knock the door as I was carrying trays on my hands" Santhi apologized for her bad manners and placed the trays containing biscuits and coffee.

"How do you like your coffee? Indian? British? Or Turkish:" she asked

"Turkish" the Kuwaitis said, "British" said the British friend and the American said "Indian"

"Never mind! Poor Indian creature! She is harmless. We can carry on our conversation" her boss joked.

"That is what Americans thought about Indira Gandhi in 1971 and she treated the seventh fleet as an intruding fishing boat" the American friend passed his comment sarcastically.

"Very poor diplomacy by the Americans! Don't forget! India is the land of Bhagavad Gita! Their god taught the art of war few thousand years before the birth of your nation!" the British friend mocked at him.

Santhi served coffee as per their wishes and politely asked whether she can offer her comments on the conflict.

"Oh! Sure! Let us have the benefit of Indian Wisdom. Please go ahead" encouraged her boss.

"We have a saying in India. We can choose everything except our parents and neighbors. The ancient diplomat Chanakya said when your enemy is stronger then it is better to compromise with your enemy rather than depending on the support of dubious friends. If the conflict escalates and the Kuwaiti army is asked to fight against Iraqi army they may say that the job may be given to a contractor. In my opinion it is wiser for Kuwait to be liberal with Saddam than opening their purse to Americans. Kuwait being a small country has to live with the support of somebody. It is better with Saddam?" Santhi posed the question.

"I know that Indians always have a soft corner for Iraq and the same with Iraqis" commented the Kuwaiti friend.

"Santhi! Don't be wild in your imagination. Iraq is our brotherly nation. It will not attack Kuwait. Neighbors never do such things in the Arab world" the General Superintendent said with confidence.

"Pardon me sir to differ with you. You can depend on an enemy. But you can't depend on your poor brother. He will be ever ready to cut your throat out of jealousy. Do you know one thing chief! Saddam can order one hundred fighter planes to land on the motorways during night and capture Kuwait in thirty minutes. If Saddam knows how to plan an aggression he can trap Kuwait like a rat by landing helicopters on the borders and seal them. He can capture every thing in Kuwait leisurely. I am sure that there will be no resistance to the occupation if he takes care to treat the Kuwaitis well" Santhi gave her expert opinion. All of them were stunned to hear her military expertise.

"Thank God that Santhi is not working for Saddam. Let us hope that good sense prevail with our leaders to avert a conflict" G.S. concluded. It was lunchtime. She was in a hurry to leave to feed her baby. G.S.understood her and said,

"Santhi! You proceed. I will take care of my friends". Santhi left the place in a hurry towards the parking area.

*   *   *

July is the hottest month in Kuwait. Temperature occasionally crossed fifty degree Celsius. On a Monday it crossed fifty. Holiday was declared. All headed towards their home. When Santhi reached home she saw Mansoor playing with his son.

Ram was then ten months old. He started walking. It was really a great pleasure for parents to watch their son taking his first step. It was like seeing Armstrong taking his first step on the moon.

"I wish that the mercury strikes fifty every day and I get an opportunity to play with Ram" Masoor said jokingly.

"Don't be selfish! You may get a holiday. Think of the people who are out doing essential work. They may die due to heatstroke" Santhi reminded him.

"We can handle this heat. But Kuwait finds it difficult to handle Saddam. During the last eight years, Iraq was busy fighting a war with Iran. But Kuwait was busy sucking out crude from the no-man's land between Kuwait and Iraq. Sometimes they sucked the oil from the Iraqi territory through slant drilling. As the conflict was over, Saddam woke up and demanded compensation for the oil stolen by Kuwait. Kuwait was not ready to own the mischief. Few day before I saw the Iraqi channel. Saddam roared that he knew how to take money from Kuwaitis. On July 25th American ambassador made a statement that America would not like to interfere in the dispute between two Arab countries and it was for the

Arab league to resolve the dispute. This statement emboldened Saddam Hussain to assume threatening posture towards Kuwait" Mansoor shared his political knowledge with his wife.

She brought some snacks and coffee from the kitchen and placed them on the tray. Mansoor started eating. But she didn't.

"Why don't you take something" asked Mansoor casually.

"I do not feel like eating anything" Santhi complained.

"What is wrong with you? Tell me" Mansoor enquired her with concern.

"It is nothing! I will be alright tomorrow" she consoled him.

"No! No! You have to eat something. If I eat alone Ram will kick me" he compelled her to eat the snacks.

The moment she ate something she rushed to the washbasin and vomited out everything. Mansoor was really worried.

"I know a doctor friend living nearby. Let us go and check with her" he said and lifted his son and his car keys. She changed her clothes and locked the door.

*　　*　　*

"Congratulation! Santhi! You will be mother again. When was your last day of the period?" the lady doctor enquired. Only then Santhi remembered "I forgot that I missed my period" she felt shy to look at the doctor.

"I know it is embarassing to get pregnant even before the first birth day of your son. We can't help. Family planning methods are prohibited in Kuwait. Be happy that you are going to get another three maternity leave after eight months. You will have enough work to do at home for another ten years" the doctor jovially commented.

Mansoor really felt happy and said "I will take care of the children. I will resign my job if necessary" he assured his worried wife. "God will find out a way out. I am not worried. I behaved like an illiterate woman. I could have spaced the children if I was careful. Any way birth and death are not in our hands. Let us accept and be happy" she said and took leave.

*　　*　　*

On July 31st Arab league meeting was held in Jeddah due to the initiative taken by Egypt. The main agenda of the meeting was the dispute between Iraq and Kuwait. The meeting started in the late evening. (The Arabs always hold meetings late in the evening and night)

Saudi delegate took the chair and opened the discussion.

"We understand the debt problem faced by Iraq. All the Arab nations are ready to write off their debts. We cannot speak for other nations. It is for Iraq to take up the matter with other governments to reduce or cancel the debts. OPEC is ready to give unlimited quota to Iraq till the debts are cleared. Iraq is having enough oil reserves to clear all the debts within few years. Iraq should be happy with these conditions. I hope that all the members of Arab league will agree with this statement"

Iraqi delegate got up and started speaking,

"Our country is not a beggar to beg other countries to write off the debts. We want compensation for the oil stolen by Kuwait in our side of Rumaila oil field. It is flooding the oil market with over production and depressed the market at the instance of Americans. We feel that Kuwait has unleashed an economic war on Iraq. It wants to weaken us and settle the border dispute in its favor with the help of Americans. This meeting is to decide the quantum of compensation that should be paid by Kuwait and the contribution by the oil rich Arab nations towards our debt. We do not want charity from anybody. We demand that Kuwait should pay 25 billion dollars as compensation and the meeting should decide the quantum of contribution by the oil rich Arab nations" Iraqi delegate made a forceful speech.

"We do not accept that we have stolen oil from Iraq and we are producing oil strictly as per OPEC quota. It is an unsubstantiated claim. We agree with the chair. Kuwait is ready to write off ten billion dollar debt. It is not a small amount for a small country like Kuwait. We are always ready to help the people of Iraq in any other way as in the past" Kuwaiti delegate made the statement.

"It is a shame that thieves want to help our people. Iraq is very ancient nation having thousands of years of history. We are not a created nation by the courtesy of British. We demand and take the money. We are not begging anybody" Iraqi delegates thundered.

"Iraq should not bully a small nation in to submission. It is not fair. I hope no country supports Iraq" Kuwaiti delegate pleaded.

"If we are a bully we would not have attended this meeting. Either you accept our demand or face the consequences" Iraqi diplomat threatened.

"We are not afraid of Iraq. We are ready to face the consequences" Kuwaiti delegate raised his voice.

"I know the dog will run towards his master for protection. But his master can't help this time" Iraqi declared

"We may be dogs but you are a pig" Kuwaiti traded his abuse.

Iraqi delegate got up and walked away in anger saying,

"You will regret for this. We will teach you a lesson"

Kuwaiti delegate got wild and spat on the table in disgust. Spitting is considered as the worst form of insult in the Arab culture. This act had its telling effect in the small hours of August 2nd 1990. Kuwait was invaded by Iraq at 02hours early morning

*   *   *

Saddam kept ready his tanks and artilleries in Basra. As soon he heard the failure of Jeddah meeting he ordered his troops to move with tanks, artilleries and helicopters. As the troops received orders, the Egyptian intelligence agent who followed the troop movement in Iraq made a telephone call to Amir of Kuwait at 12 midnight August first.

"Iraqi army is expected to cross in to your territory within an hour. It will be at your gates in two hours. There is no use fighting them. Better make your escape to Saudi. Nobody can come to your rescue. American were not prepared for this eventuality" saying this he put down the receiver.

Since saber rattling was going on between Kuwait and Iraq, Amir of Kuwait was prepared for this eventuality. He kept every thing ready in forty suitcases of various sizes. He ordered the members of the Royal family to assemble near the garage. He asked the servants to load the suitcases in twenty-two cars parked. He knew that that were twenty-three royal family members who can drive the car. Within twenty minutes from the telephone call twenty-two cars left the palace with more than forty suitcases. These suitcases contained floppies having information about the citizens, Swiss bank account details, investment papers, shares, gold, diamond and real estate papers. To put in a nutshell the entire wealth of Kuwait sans oil were loaded in those cars. All the cars traveled at a speed not less than 180kmph. Amir's Armour plated car was the first one to reach the western border post with Saudi. The security people were taken by the surprise when they saw the entire Royal family heading towards Saudi. Amir uttered only few words to the security. "I will come back to rescue the nation. Inshah Allah!" Amir spoke to the security. He speeded away in the darkness. But the darkness that engulfed Kuwait could not be wished away so easily.

As the Egyptian intelligent agent predicted one hundred thousand Iraqi solders with 700 tanks crossed in to Kuwaiti territory. Kuwait air force and army put up some resistance that delayed the movement of troops in to Kuwait by couple of hours. A dozen Iraqi helicopters whose pilots could not see the high-tension overhead lines in the night got entangled and got damaged. The Kuwait Air Force claimed that they have shot the helicopters. In fact the Kuwait air force planes took off and headed towards Saudi with VIPs instead of fighting the Iraqi invaders. The army reached the Dasman palace after the Royal family crossed in to Saudi. Amir's younger brother Fahd, who was left out for an unknown reason, tried to put up a fight with the army. He was shot dead in no time. He was the only Royal casualty. His body was thrown under the tank and the body got mutilated. A dead body of even an enemy has to be given due respect under the Islamic tradition. But his mutilated dead body was displayed as warning. When the commander came to know of the escape of the Royal family he was furious. He ordered the helicopter gunship to reach the border post. It was the first blunder they have committed and it was not the last. They did not expect the escape of Royal family. Had they sealed the border before moving their army the history of Kuwait would have changed forever? Within an hour helicopter gunship reached the airport and Radio station and took control over them. All the communication links of Kuwait with the outside world were cut. In fact the news about the invasion was the last broadcast by Radio Kuwait. The escaped people from Kuwait through deserts provided further details. The embassies of the western countries were ransacked. Some of the embassy staff were taken as hostages. Those who have escaped were given shelter in Kuwaiti homes. The tanks and the army moved in the motorways and expressways and other roads were blocked with barricade. They wanted to take over and secure the refineries and the power stations before capturing the government offices. The refineries were the moneymaking assets and power stations, which produce water and power without which life cannot exist in Kuwait.

When Kuwaitis heard that Iraqi army had invaded Kuwait, they loaded their four-wheel drive multi-utility vehicles with all the valuables they had and started their journey towards Mecca, Madina, Jubail and Dammam. It was not Haj this time. But it was a run for their life. Iraqi army did not prevent the escaping Kuwaitis. Iraqis was interested only in capturing the wealth of Kuwait. They were not interested in ruling over Kuwaitis. They knew very well that they were liabilities. They were happy that no expatriate population other than American, British and European tried to escape. But the army prevented the fleeing Americans, British and other European citizens. Some of them made good their escape through deserts.

The army took over the refineries and power stations in the first phase. Most of the expatriate population reported for duty in the refinery and power station as usual. They were either not aware of the invasion or they felt safer to be inside the refinery or power plants. They were asked by the army to do their duty as usual. The army assured that no harm would visit them as long as they did their duty and not indulge in any other activity. Palestinians were really happy. They hoped that they might get citizenship under Saddam's regime. But Indians were confused lot. Iraqi army treated them with great respect. They were confused and waited for the guidance from the Indian Government. Even the Government of India was confused. They condemned the invasion, as a violation of sovereignty of a member nation of U.N. GOI could not go beyond this. They knew that one hundred and eighty thousand Indians were trapped. They could not afford to make a wrong move which would jeopardize the security of the Indians in Kuwait.

Within four hours of occupation of Kuwait, U.N. Security council assembled in the New York and passed the resolution 660. It condemned the aggression and demanded the withdrawal of Iraqi troops from Kuwait. The secretary General of UNO Parease Decoreah was mild in his condemnation. He called for the immediate cessation of hostilities and the dispute between Kuwait and Iraq resolved amicably. President George W Bush and Prime Minister Margaret Thatcher called the invasion as naked act of aggression by Iraq. Countries like France, Germany, China, Russia, India and Pakistan expressed similar sentiments but mild in content. They appealed to Iraq to respect the sovereignty of Kuwait and resolve the dispute peacefully. No country hinted about army intervention to oust Iraqi army from Kuwait. Israel was the only country, which realized the danger in allowing Saddam to have a free run over Kuwait. It suggested a strong action to contain Saddam. Arab league kept its mouth shut for a whole day and passed a resolution on 3rd August. The resolution condemned the invasion. It appealed to the outside powers not to intervene as the dispute was to be settled by the league. By that time the international community was up against Saddam.

Saddam felt the heat and tried to appease the world opinion by his statements. He first tried to fool the world by saying that Iraq moved its troop in support of the uprising against the Kuwaiti Royal family. When the world did not buy the story, he said that his army went in to liberate Kuwaitis from the clutches of the Monarchy. He assured that he would soon establish a Kuwaiti rule by conducting election and within few weeks his troops would be withdrawn. He appointed Alaa Hussain Ali as the provincial governor of Kuwait He made all these statements to buy time to complete the invasion. Meanwhile the western media were disseminating horror stories from Kuwait. Most of the horror stories were motivated.

The escaped Amir met the president George W Bush and wept.

"Take our entire wealth and return our motherland. Our country will ever be grateful to America" Amir Sheik Jaber Al Sabah virtually wept at the feet of the president. Bush assured him that he would do everything possible to liberate Kuwait.

Amir on his part did not keep quiet. He paid ten million dollars to an agency to unleash the propaganda war against Saddam Hussain. This agency was responsible for the horror stories whether they were true or false which came from Kuwait. There were stories that Kuwaiti and Philippine women were raped and the babies were pulled out from hospitals and killed. It was not that all the stories were false. But most of them were inspired. It was very difficult to check the veracity of the stories at that time.

Only the four regiments of the Republican guard were professionally trained solders but the rest of the army was not properly trained army. These republican guards might have been informed of the true intension of Saddam. But the rest of the invading army was ignorant of the intensions of Saddam Hussain. They knew only one thing ie how to hold a gun. They were inducted in to the army to provide them with some employment. They were not informed about the purpose of invasion. They were ignorant of their duties as invaders. The republican guards were given the duty of protecting the vital installations, government offices, palaces, airport, Radio and T.V.Stations. The undisciplined army was given the task of controlling traffic, overcoming Kuwaiti resistance and maintaining the law and order in the city. The biggest problem faced by the Iraqi army was food and accommodation. They did not arrange for any supply line before the invasion. Probably they thought there was enough food in the Kuwaiti Super markets for the army to buy and eat. First the solders tried to buy food by paying in Iraqi Dinar. But the people refused to accept it. Some preferred to give the food free. Some resisted. The hungry solders started arson and looting. The anti social elements among the expatriate population joined the army in looting and arson. There were groups who stole air conditioners, T.V. sets, gold, electronic goods from the shops and unoccupied home and sold them to Iraqi solders in exchange for Iraqi Dinars. These goods and the spare parts stolen from the refinery and power stations were shifted in trailers to Iraq. Due to the economic problems caused by the war Iraqis were starved of these goods. There was ready market for these goods in Iraq. The army shifted all the artifacts in the Kuwait Museum to Iraq. The situation prevailed in the first few days of occupation were free for all situation. The solders laid their hands on the foodstuff wherever they were available. They occupied all the vacant public buildings and the private buildings whose residents fled. Normally in any invasion there is bound to be some resistance, beating and killings. In Kuwait occupation too this happened. The solders did beat people who resisted them. Some times they were shot. But it was not a wide spread phenomenon. These things happened without any order from the commanders. When the commanders received complaints they did take prompt action to prevent such incidents. The behavior of Iraqi solders was not as bad as it was made out in the western media. The author had some first hand knowledge and he talked to many Indians and Pakistanis. Their opinion about the behavior of Iraqi solders was that they were not arrogant. They did not indulge in wanton acts of arson and looting. They did out of necessity and greed. The real culprits were some greedy expatriate population who exploited the situation for their benefit.

On 6th of August the Security Council assembled again and passed the resolution 661. It imposed economic sanctions on Iraq and placed an embargo on oil supply from Iraq. On 8th August Saddam declared Kuwait as nineteenth province of Iraq and appointed the infamous "Chemical Ali" as the Governor of Kuwait. On 9th August Security Council declared the annexation of Kuwait as null and void. Saddam was happy that Americans did not threaten Iraq by moving its air craft carrier. He got emboldened and moved more than 5000 tanks and half million troops in to Kuwait as preparation for the invasion of Saudi Arabia. Saddam's move shocked the Americans.

6

OPERATION DESERT SHIELD

It was always the policy of the American government right from President Carter to protect Saudi Arabia, which has the largest oil reserve and the largest oil exporter. America was always committed to protect its interest and the interest of the industrialized countries. President Bush understood that Saddam would not be satisfied with Kuwait. He swiftly decided to protect Saudi Arabia from Iraqi aggression. He announced "Operation Desert shield" on 7th August. At that point of time his priority was to stop Saddam from marching further in to Saudi Arabia. He couldn't declare his intension to liberate Kuwait, as he didn't have the United Nations mandate for doing so. President formed a formidable coalition of 34 countries who were ready to contribute financially and militarily. Russia, China and India refused to join this coalition. Japan, Germany, Saudi Arabia and Kuwait were the largest financial contributors. Everybody knew who got the financial benefits from Operation Desert Shield and Operation Desert Storm.

Within a week the expatriate population understood that their ordeal would not end soon. They were in for a long, miserable and unforgettable summer in Kuwait. The actions of Saddam and America made it clear that they were heading for a worst showdown in the history. The expatriate population had nightmares thinking about living in a war torn country Kuwait, which depended on imported food and goods for its survival. Everybody wanted to get out of Kuwait at the earliest. But unfortunately Iraq did not permit them to escape to neighboring country Saudi Arabia as it had its plan to attack Saudi through its southern border Wafrah. Moreover Saddam wanted to use the expatriate population as human shield against the attack from America.

India's top priority was to evacuate one hundred and eighty thousand Indians trapped in Kuwait. They didn't want to rub on the wrong side of

Saddam. Foreign minister I.K.Gujral met Saddam Hussein in a cordial atmosphere and convinced him to permit the evacuation of Indians. He reluctantly agreed as he was in need of the services of the Indians to run Kuwaiti economy. But he agreed for the evacuation only through Amman. India started its evacuation from 13th August and completed the same in the middle of October. It operated its Air India carriers, Indian Air Force planes and carriers loaned from other Airlines from Amman to evacuate Indians. It operated maximum 16 fights in a day. The total number of flights was 488 and the number of Indian evacuated stood at 1,61,000. Few thousand people were evacuated by two ships.Only about 20,000 preferred to stay in Kuwait. Out of these twenty thousand people, ten thousand were Bohra Muslims who made Kuwait as their home and they didn't have any place in India to go. Some had assets in Kuwait to protect. Some wanted to take risk and protect their government jobs. Those who stayed had some economic interest in their mind. It was biggest evacuation operation in aviation history of the world. Indians traveled all the way from Kuwait to Amman by buses and cars. Terrible summer was as cruel as Saddam. The Indian organizations in the gulf countries helped them to mitigate their suffering by providing them with food and water. Authorities in Amman extended their helping hand in the orderly evacuation of the Indians.

During the first week of occupation there was enough food in the super markets. The American super market Safe Way in Fuhaheel was ransacked and looted by the army. The food stock in super markets started dwindling as there was no replenishment. The bakery had enough stock of wheat flour to produce bread. People started living on bread alone. The families normally stocked food supplies, which might last for few months. They too felt the pinch, as they were obliged to help their friends in need. The traffic in Kuwait city came down drastically since the Kuwaitis were either fled or gone underground. The petrol consumption came down drastically. The refineries were working normally. Petrol and diesel were available in all the petrol stations. All the private companies were closed since their owners fled away. Iraqi Regime demonetized Kuwaiti Dinar and the banks were closed. The army looted the cash in the banks. Those who worked in the refinery and power stations were given salary in Iraqi Dinar. They could fetch nothing with this currency. Those who had Kuwaiti Dinar preferred to carry it with them to India. They believed that it would regain its value once Kuwait was liberated. They didn't want to exchange them for Iraqi Dinar.

Santhi continued to work in the refinery for a new Iraqi boss. Her ex-boss fled away to Saudi Arabia. As the important documents and the keys were with her she was asked to report for duty whatever may be circumstances. She was given a special pass, which earned her special respect from the Iraqi army. She didn't have any problem in commuting between her home and work place. Mansoor's company was closed. He remained at home looking after the child. When Santhi returned from duty she went around the city to collect enough bread. She could travel to any place with the help of her special pass. She distributed the bread to the needy people every day. Iraqi solders saw people coming to Santhi's home to collect bread every day. They too started coming and begged for bread. One day one solder knocked the door. Mansoor opened the door and said,

"Sorry! We do not have any bread to give. Check for yourselves" saying this he allowed the solder to enter in to his house. He came inside and sat in a sofa set.

"We heard about the generosity of your wife. I am really hungry. Please give me some thing to eat" the solder begged him. Santhi was in the kitchen preparing the night dinner for them. She heard the solder. She brought ten chappathies and enough vegetables to go with the chappathies. The solder started eating the chappathies and relished the same.

"I have never eaten such a delicious food in my life. Thank you very much. I know that I have eaten the food meant for both of you. I cannot forget your hospitality. As a token of gratitude I want to give this gift" saying this he removed a Rolex watch from his wrist and handed over to Mansoor. He refused to accept.

"I fed you not because I was afraid of you. I never accepted any money for feeding people in need. There is a saying in India that God visit us in the guise of the guest. When we serve the guest we serve the god. Thank you for giving an opportunity to serve you" Santhi explained in chaste Arabic. The solder was wonder struck at listening to her Arabic and her generosity. He felt a bit ashamed and couldn't talk further. He left the place leaving the watch on the tea table. Mansoor wanted to call him to give back the watch. But Santhi prevented him and said,

"He wanted to say that generosity is not our monopoly and he too can show his generosity. Iraqis are proud people. Let him have the satisfaction" thus Santhi concluded. Mansoor was surprised at her way of

50

treating people. Sometimes he wondered whether he really deserved to be her husband.

The exodus of Indians and Pakistinis from Kuwait started as a trickle and then it became an avalanche. Pakistanis too joined the Indians in leaving Kuwait. But Pakistanis once reached Basra took a different route. They turned towards Iran and traveled through Iran to reach Pakistan. Those who had their own car were allowed to travel with their cars. Those who had money bought cars at a very cheap rate or stole them from the Kuwaiti's house with the help of the maidservants and drivers. Iran too helped the Pakistanis to the extent possible. There were accidents, which killed some Pakistanis on their way home. There were four casualties among Indians in a bus accident on the way to Baghdad. It was irony that those people who wanted to escape from Saddam Hussein, could not escape from the destiny. There were Pakistanis who considered the invasion as an opportunity and decided to stay. The Palestinians were the happiest lot. PLO Chairman, Yasser Arafat extended his support to Saddam Hussein. They expected that Saddam might solve their problems.

The result of the invasion of Kuwait had devastating effect on the world economy. The crude oil price swelled like a heated balloon. Impending war and the uncertainty associated with the war threatened the economy of the whole world in to recession. Surprisingly the gold price did not increase alarmingly. The reason was not far to seek. The biggest consumers for gold were Indians, Pakistanis and GCC citizens. Since they were the affected people the demand for gold did not increase dramatically.

The invasion of Kuwait came shortly after the end of cold war between America and Russia. This proved to be a godsend opportunity to the Americans to show the world that who the real boss in this world. The defense industry in U.S.A. worked over time to cash-in the opportunity. Margaret Thatcher outsmarted everybody and proved that nobody could match her loyalty towards America. Other European countries had no option but to toe the American line in full. A series of UN resolutions were passed without any difficulty. U.S.A drafted all of them with the help of Great Briton.

America started to build up ground troops, warships, fighter planes, transport aircrafts and armored carriers in an unprecedented scale. As per the western media information Iraq had deployed 1.2 million ground troops, 6650 tanks, 5100 armored vehicles, 3850 artillery guns, 750 fighter planes and 200 other anti-aircraft missiles, auk-auk guns and the scud missiles fixed and mobile. As per the western media, the Iraqi forces looked formidable. Besides these forces the western media made a big noise about the Iraq possession of chemical weapons. Saddam Hussein might have laughed at the exaggerated report about his strength in the western media. America assembled half a million ground troops, six air craft carriers and seventeen heavy, six light, nine marine brigade of the US army. In addition to these 2480 fixed wing aircrafts were stationed in the airfields near Dahran and Dammam. It took about three months for America to assemble these forces. Most of armaments were air lifted and the US army occupied all the available accommodation in the eastern province of Saudi Arabia. The Islamic fundamentalist raised their voice against the stationing of the infidels in their holy land. As the world opinion was against them they were silenced after a while.

During these three months India completed its evacuation successfully. Countries like Pakistan, Sri Lanka, Philippines, and Bangladesh etc successfully evacuated their nationalities by various means. Kuwaitis who chose to remain formed the Kuwaiti resistance movements. The roof top demonstrations by the abaya-covered ladies were given wide publicity in the western media. Kuwaitis who had some weapons adopted a hit and run tactics. They did not engage the army in any shoot out operation. All told the Kuwaiti resistance proved a minor irritant to the army. Palestinians gave full support to the occupation army. By this action they lost the good will enjoyed by them in the Arab world. Kuwait accused them as traitors.

There were peace initiatives mooted out by Russia and France. Saddam Hussein by linking his withdrawal from Kuwait to the withdrawal of Israel from West Bank and Syria from Lebanon, killed them. America was confident of its victory. There was no necessity for them to compromise with Saddam. American Generals roared like lions in the desert as they knew that they were fighting war at somebody's expense and they were sure to win with least number of casualties. Western media were jubilant about the impending war, which was expected to provide them with enough hot and thrilling news every day. They were sure that they would have the privilege of access to the war theater. Rarely any media was prepared to give the Iraqi side of the story.

*　　*　　*

Santhi and Mansoor were in a fix whether to leave Kuwait or not. They were not sure of their future during and after the war. They faced the risk of facing bombardment by the American coalition forces or Saddam Hussein may set fire to the entire Kuwait before the defeat. Anything could happen. Santhi couldn't think of going back to India since she didn't have anybody in India to depend on. More over her husband being a Pakistani might face problems in India. She ruled out the possibility of going back to India. The other alternative was to go to Pakistan. She was confident that her in-laws in Pakistan would accept her. But the problem was that her marriage was not registered with Pakistan embassy. Therefore she can't enter Pakistan as the wife of Mr.Mansoor. Pakistan embassy was closed in Kuwait. Pakistan embassy at Baghdad looked after the affairs of Pakistanis living in Kuwait. They have to register their marriage with Pakistan embassy if they want to go to Pakistan as husband and wife. She approached her boss for help for going to Baghdad. Initially he was reluctant to give permission. She revealed to him about her pregnancy and said,

"You know the condition in Kuwait Chief! Iraq is under sanction. War may break out any time. I need medical help before, during and after delivery. It may not be possible to get the same in Kuwait. Please let me go to Pakistan. I need your help for the safe journey to Baghdad. I request this help from you on humanitarian grounds. Please consider me as your daughter and render this help" She begged him with tears. Her boss was moved and he promised to help her to reach Baghdad safely.

Within days they started their journey in a car to Baghdad. They were dropped at Pakistan Embassy in Baghdad. They explained the ambassador their plight. They requested him to register their marriage and grant her Pakistani visa. He was ready to give Pakistani Visa and but refused to register their marriage on technical ground.

"Look Madam! Registration was refused in Kuwait. I do not know on what ground it was refused. Pakistan does not recognize the annexation of Kuwait. Therefore marriage performed in Kuwait can't be registered in Iraq. Better reach Pakistan and sort out your problems there." He explained his problem.

"This is a war situation. Normal rules do not apply. Please register our marriage. We are married and have a boy. Now I am pregnant. I do not know what problems I may have to face in Pakistan if I do not possess the status of wife. I may be even stoned to death for having illegal relationship with my husband. Please do something about this" She pleaded with the diplomat.

"I will refer the matter to Islamabad. Please wait for their orders. This is the best I can do" he concluded.

They left and stayed in a hotel. It was very expensive. They couldn't stay for a longer time since they had limited cash. She regretted for her decision not wear too much gold. It would have helped to face the crisis.

The reporters of the television channels and Radio channels mostly occupied the hotels in Baghdad. Jack William, the war correspondent for BBC television channel too stayed in the same hotel where Santhi and Mansoor stayed. He saw the couple with one-year old kid in the restaurant. He wondered why this couple is staying in this hotel. He wanted to know the story and approached Santhi,

"Madam! I am Jack Williams, war correspondent from BBC. I hope you speak English. May I ask why you are here?" He politely asked her.

He started the video camera and started shooting while Santhi talked.

"As you might have guessed I am an Indian. I am married to a Pakistani. I still remain as Hindu. I refused to get converted in to Islam. My husband too did not like my conversion. I got married two years ago. Pakistan embassy took objection to my religion and refused to register my marriage. We registered our marriage with Indian Embassy without any problem. Now I have one-year-old boy and at present pregnant. We have decided to leave Kuwait and go to Pakistan. We approached the Pakistan embassy in Baghdad to get our marriage registered to facilitate my entry in to Pakistan as the legally wedded wife of my husband. The ambassador was ready to issue me a visa but refused to register our marriage on technical grounds. I am very much reluctant to enter in to Pakistan without the status of legally married wife. We have limited amount of cash and cannot afford to stay in the hotel for a long period. I do not know when the Pakistan embassy would accept my request. I appeal to the prime minister of Pakistan to intervene in this matter and solve my problem quickly" she used the opportunity to appeal to the prime minister.

"Why don't you proceed to India first and then go to Pakistan?" the correspondent asked.

"We have a saying in India. For Sita, Ayodhya is where Ram lives. I am fighting for my right to enter Pakistan as legally wedded wife. I will not give up" She replied.

"In that case why don't you get converted in to Islam to solve the problem?" the correspondent provoked her.

"I would rather die than converting in to Islam for selfish reasons. Conversions should never be done without the change of one's faith" she asserted.

He switched off the video camera and turned to Santhi and assured her,

"I will do my best to solve your problem"

Next day in the war correspondents program Jack Williams appeared,

"I am Jack Williams from Baghdad reporting. The effect of the invasion of Kuwait is devastating. It caused untold sufferings to the individuals and families. Here is a heart-rending story of an Indian woman by name Santhi, married to a Pakistani. She narrates her story" as he said the video clipping appeared and Santhi started talking. Secretary to Prime minister Nawaz Sheriff saw this BBC program. He immediately rushed to the Prime minister's chamber. He was immersed in the files.

"Sir! There is an appeal to you from an Indian woman from Baghdad. She is married to a Pakistani. They want to get their marriage registered in our embassy in Baghdad" secretary informed him.

"We do not know the story. Let us wait for the report from Baghdad" P.M. replied. At that moment the telephone rang.

"Sir! President Bush is on the line. He wants to talk to you" his personal secretary informed.

He lifted the receiver.

"Bush speaking from white House. We are facing one of the greatest human tragedies in the history. You people are more interested in your religion and rules. Why don't you people think that you are human being first? We are fighting a war with Saddam Hussain. You are not fighting a war with India. Listen! I want you to accept her request and pass your orders to the embassy in Iraq immediately" he put down the phone. In the next one hour he received phone calls from Margaret Thatcher, U.N.Secretary General, Indian Foreign minister I.K.Gujral and the French president. He was stunned to receive so many calls on this matter. He called his secretary and ordered him to send the message to Baghdad immediately. Next day Santhi got her marriage registered and received her Pakistani visa for five years. They thanked Jack Williams for his timely help. They returned to Kuwait immediately.

They disposed all their belongings and one of their cars to an Iraqi with the help of her boss and received payment in U.S.Dollars. They packed all the expensive things in their car and started their journey towards Pakistan via Iran by road. The journey was tedious. They drove the car alternatively. They stopped on their way to take food and to get milk for their baby. Many Iranians refused to take money from them. One day Santhi vomited and got sick. They visited a hospital where she was treated. The doctor advised her to take rest for few days. But Santhi was confident that she could endure the journey. She collected enough medicines and thanked the doctor for her free treatment.

They reached the Pakistan border after five days. Their passports were checked at the border post. His car papers too were checked. Every thing was in order. But the officer-in-charge was delaying the stamping.

"Is there anything wrong officer?" Mansoor enquired.

"Everything is O.K. The religion of your wife is not mentioned in your wife's passport. It is mandatory in Pakistan to reveal the religion in the passport" the officer raised his doubt and continued "I may have to refer this matter to my higher authorities before stamping. Please wait" saying this he put the papers in his drawer.

Santhi was worried. But Mansoor being a Pakistani understood the problem.

"Please give our passports back. I have one more paper to attach" he asked the officer. The officer gave back the passports.

Mansoor took out a currency note. The number 20 was printed on the note and George Washington smiled. He kept the currency in his passport and returned the passports. The officer opened the passport and he too smiled.

:"You see! I always love Indians, Hindi movies and Amitab Bachan. Wish you a happy holiday in Pakistan" said the officer and returned the passports stamped.

While returning to the car Santhi raised a doubt,

"I was really worried. How on earth do you know he expects money?"

"You were born and brought up in Kuwait. Had you born and brought up in India you too would have understood" he joked. The baby too smiled innocently.

*   *   *

Mansoor made a telephone call to his family immediately after leaving the check post. His family was very happy when they received the news of their arrival. The whole village was waiting to receive them with lot of enthusiasm. It took two days for them to reach their village Sultanpur. It was situated about 100 kilometers from Rawalpindi. Sultanpur was a medium sized village with about 500 houses. The village depended on agriculture for its survival. There was very little industry around the village and the commercial activities were limited to provisional stores, hairdressing saloons, agriculture input shops and textile shops. Lahore was the nearest city to the village. The village did not have any bank. There was a madrasa to teach the children the Holy Quran. The children had to travel ten kilometers to attend a high school. So the literacy rate of the villagers was very poor especially among the females.

They reached the village at 6 o' clock in the evening. They were dead tired after their long journey. They were given buttermilk to drink. It was really soothing. Mansoor asked his brother to unload the luggage. He hugged everybody as per his family custom. But Santhi felt little shy to hug the ladies who were eager to do so. She greeted them saying "Namasthey" with her folded hands. The ladies have seen too many Hindi movies. They were familiar with the Indian way of greeting. They too said "namasthey" and held her hands affectionately. Santhi's mother-in-law took control of the situation and said,

"They are dead tired after seven days of journey in a car. Please leave them alone. Let them take rest for at least twenty-four hours. I want all of you to get lost immediately" saying this, she took Santhi inside the house. Before entering the house, she took the blessings from the parents of Mansoor by touching their feet. They were immensely pleased at the reverence shown by their daughter-in-law. As soon as she entered the house her mother-in-law took charge of the baby and asked,

"Beti! What do you want to eat?" being a woman she wanted to know the liking of a pregnant lady.

"I want some cooked Basmati rice and curd or butter milk, a banana and kheer (sweet pudding) if possible" Santhi expressed her preference.

Her mother-in-law ordered her younger son to fetch the best available export quality Basmati rice. Within half an hour Santhi had what she wanted. Mansoor ate the food that was available in the house. They went to bed at about 8 o'clock and did not get up till eight in the morning.

Santhi got up at eight. Mansoor was sleeping and her mother-in-law was feeding the baby. Santhi felt much better after the long night sleep.

The younger sister of her husband came with a cup of steaming tea. Santhi refused and said,

"I do not drink anything before brushing and bathing. Let me have my cold shower and come"

Within half an hour she came back from the bathroom fully dressed in a sari. She saw Mansoor sipping the tea.

"I am sorry Santhi. I couldn't refuse like you and it is a habit in our family to take a cup of tea as soon as we get up"

"Remember! It takes time and effort to develop a good habit. But bad habit is picked up in no time" she commented.

"Sure! I will remember that from tomorrow. Let me indulge for a day" he said apologetically.

"It is good that you have trained him well" her mother-in-law proudly said.

"Amma! (mother) Please permit me to do some cooking for the breakfast" she asked permission to enter the kitchen.

"As you wish beti!" she consented.

At about ten o' clock everybody had their breakfast and sat for chitchat. Ladies from nearby houses peeped in and joined the group. One of the young girls looked at Santhi and admired her beauty,

"I thought that south Indians are dark-skinned. You look like Hema Malini (famous Hindi cine-actress)"

Santhi felt shy and smiled.

"Now you look like Sri Devi" another young girl commented. These young girls knew India only through the prism of Hindi Movies.

"Do you know that the actresses you have mentioned are south Indians?"

"I really don't know" the girl admitted her ignorance with her eyes widely opened in excitement and she continued,

"Do you dance like Hema Malini?"

"I do. But I do not know whether my body will permit me to dance after the delivery" she replied.

"We want to see your dance bobby!(brother's wife)" the young girl expressed her wish.

"Inshah Allah! Mumkin khabi!" Santhi replied. Everybody laughed.

"Is it true that you earn three times that of Mansoor" neighborly old lady poked.

"It is because I work for a public sector undertaking and he works in a private company. I got this job on humanitarian grounds after my brother's death. Otherwise it is very difficult to get a job in KNPC. Even the Kuwaiti girls want to grab the job from me" Santhi clarified her position.

"Do you wear this bindhi (a red mark on the forehead) all the time" one of the married woman asked for clarification.

"Yes! It is the symbol of married woman in India. It gives a red alert notice to the males who look at her. After my bath the first thing I do is wear the bindhi. I would never like to show my face without bindhi" she clarified. The ladies were fully satisfied with the clarification. Earlier they thought that bindhi is something to do with Hindu religion. Many ladies wanted to wear bindhi. It added beauty to the face besides its significance.

"What type of dress you wear?" an educated lady wanted to know.

"Nighty is my casual dress in my home. I wear Salwar-kammeez in my work place during summer and pant-coat during winter. I wear silk saris when I attend functions with my husband. It is elegant and beautiful. I have brought some. I will show them some other day" she explained. All the ladies wanted to see the saris immediately. They couldn't resist their temptation. Santhi went inside and brought some to show to the women. For another one hour the ladies discussed about the saris and completely forgot Santhi. She had a respite from the valley of questions from the woman.

7

Operation Desert Storm

It was one of the rare occasions when the entire international community was united in condemning Iraqi invasion of Kuwait. On 29th November 1990 UN Security council passed a resolution unanimously. The resolution gave an ultimatum to Saddam Hussain to withdraw his troupes from Kuwait before 15th January 1991. It authorized US led coalition to adopt all means to liberate Kuwait if Iraq fails to withdraw by 15th January. Russia and France made an attempt to persuade Saddam to withdraw. Saddam was adamant and couldn't understand that his fate was sealed and so was US. It was so sure of the victory that it did not want Saddam to withdraw. Therefore war became inevitable. But the international community was apprehensive about the consequences of the war. Saddam threatened that he would scorch Kuwait in to a graveyard if he were attacked. As per the western media Iraq started threatening by spilling the crude oil in to the sea thereby causing the environmental damage. After the war the truth came out. It was the smart bombs that caused the crude spillage in to the sea.

The coalition led by US had 34 nations. They contributed finance, troupes, aircrafts, fighter planes, war ships and tanks. Notable among the nations who contributed were;

Troupes
USA (5,00,00), Saudi Arabia (50,000), U.K (43,000), Egypt (30,200), France (16,000), Pakistan (10,000), UAE (N A)
Tanks
USA (2000), Egypt (350),Saudi Arabia (280) U.K (160), France (40)
Naval ships
USA (110), U.K(1)

Air crafts

USA(1800), U.K(184), Saudi Arabia (245)

Helicopters

USA(1700)

Against this formidable show of strength of the coalition Iraq displayed

Troupes (3,36,000), battle tanks (3475), armoured vehicles (3080), armoured carriers (2475) and unspecified number of scud missiles.

Japan and Germany did not contribute troupes or weapons. But they made substantial financial contribution. Their contributions were next only to Saudi Arabia and Kuwait. Saudi Arabia opened up their ports, land, cities and all the facilities for stationing coalition forces. India did not contribute any troupe but it did provide refueling facilities for the aircrafts. Religious organizations in Pakistan did make noises against their government extending support to the coalition against Saddam Hussain. He described the ensuing gulf war as the "mother of all battles". He believed that he could give a tough fight against US led coalition. By calling it as Jihad against infidels led by Americans, he sought the support of the Islamic world especially the Arab countries. He hoped against hope that US public would not accept heavy American casualities and the war might end without him loosing power in Baghdad. He thought that he could hold against the coalition forces as long as possible and he could always withdraw from Kuwait at his will. Probably his victory against Iran made him over-confident about his ability to wage war.

The coalition forces utilized the period between 29th November and 15th January 1991 for building up troupes, positioning warship and installing Patriot missile defense system in Saudi Arabia and Israel. USA expected Iraq to fire its scud missiles at cities in Saudi (Dahran, Dammaam, Alkhobar, Jubail) and Telaviv. Therefore patriot missile systems were installed at these places. 15TH January was the dead line not only for Saddam but also for the coalition forces to complete its preparation for the so-called "mother of all battles". Western media made mountain out of molehill about the Iraq's ability to employ chemical and biological weapons against the coalition forces and the civilians. Therefore USA made enormous preparations to protect the troupes against chemical attack. The vulnerable civilians were provided with gas masks with elaborate instructions how to use them. All the media persons positioned themselves at the vantage points in Baghdad, Dahran,

Telaviv and Amman. They were all ready to provide the action live what was happening at the theater of war to every drawing room in the world. CNN was given the privilege to air the picture live from war zones by the coalition forces. CNN became a household name even before the start of the war.

On 15th January the whole world waited eagerly to know the reaction from Saddam Hussain. Nothing happened. Probably Saddam was waiting for an extension of the deadline. Usually this happens at the time of crisis. Some thing may happen at the last minute and the situation gets diffused at the interference of some power. It was different story this time. Even if Iraq announced withdrawal of its troupes, the coalition would have attacked saying that Saddam couldn't be trusted to keep his words. The whole attention of the world turned towards the coalition forces on 16th January. The military experts started discussing about various strategies to be adopted to get Saddam out of Kuwait without much damage to the oil installations in Kuwait. The major worry was what Saddam could do to the oil fields, refineries and power stations in Kuwait.

USA airlifted its troupes and stationed them in Saudi cities and moved its warships fitted with tomahawk missiles in to the Arabian gulf. Libya and Syria, the traditional supporters of Saddam let him down. At the time of Gulf war Saddam had only one supporter namely PLO. Countries like France, Russia, China, and India wanted the coalition to liberate Kuwait but at the same time they wanted to let Saddam to rule Iraq. They felt that only Saddam could keep Iraq united and without him it might get disintegrated in to three parts. But USA had other ideas.

8

LIBERATION OF KUWAIT

USA with its coalition partners started its offence with arial attack from Jubail city. Its main targets were refineries and power stations. The Iraqi army was spread all over Kuwait. Coalition forces could not attack the army without killing the civilian population. Another target was to prevent the Iraqi army retreating back in to Iraq. USA wanted to trap Iraqi Army before starting land offence. USA wanted to prevent the sale of oil from its ports Mina Al Ahmadi, Shuwaik and Mina Abdulla. While attacking oil tankers, oil pumps were hit by guided smart bombs. This hit damaged the oil pipe line and the oil started spilling in to sea. Immediately, western media started the propaganda war that Saddam Hussain started an environmental war. Iraqi Army did not cause the oil spill. The smart bombs caused the oil spill.

On 20th January the land offensive was started from Saudi border Wafra. Initially there was heavy fighting and the Iraqi Army marched in to Saudi Arabia. Saddam threatened that Iraq would take over the eastern province of Saudi Arabia. USA was allergic about American casuality. It wanted to win the war with least casuality among American marines. It wanted to divert the Iraqi Army by attacking from the sea.

The Iraqi Army was deployed along the border between Saudi and Kuwait. They dug bunkers and stayed there to fight against invading coalition forces through deserts. The Kuwaiti resistance was feeble and showed its presence by demonstrating on roof tops. The borders were sealed and the food supply was cut off. All the escape routes were sealed. Saddam wanted to withdraw in to Iraq. But USA was determined to eliminate the Iraqi Army. The Republican Gaurds, the professional solders guarded all the vital installations like Airport, palaces, government offices etc. They had enough stock of food. They could fight and inflict damages to the coalition forces. To demoralize the Iraqi Army especially the republican guards, USA resorted to carpet bombing. In a fortnight the coalition forces dropped thousands of tons explosives valued for more than 50 billion dollars. The armaments industry sent their entire inventory to the war front. They found it a great opportunity to sell all the outdated explosives to the coalition forces. The coalition forces could have captured the Iraqi Army without the large scale bombing that damaged the Kuwait's infrastructure. (Later Kuwait spent about 10 billion dollars to repair the damages caused by the bombing. All the contracts were awarded to USA companies. But these USA companies subcontracted all the jobs to Japanese, Korean, German and Indian companies and made 20% profit without doing any work to restore Kuwait economy. Kuwait was forced to buy one million cars from USA. Even though the coalition forces fought and liberated Kuwait, all the benefit went to USA. Germany and Japan paid 10 billion dollars each towards the war expenses. Total expenditure incurred in 40 days war was 100 billion dollars)

Saddam Hussain threatened that he would destroy all the oil wells and refineries if his army was forced to retreat. The retreating Iraqi Army wired all the oil wells and vital equipments in the refineries with bombs. The final assault by the coalition forces were made from Saudi deserts and sea route. Along the Saudi border the coalition forces marched with tanks and artilleries. Many Iraqi solders surrendered to the coalition forces without any fight. About 50,000 solders surrendered. It was big problem for the coalition forces to hand cuff them and transport them to Jubail city. Coalition forces especially the American solders did not want to take the trouble of arresting the Iraqis, feeding and transporting them. Therefore the coalition forces buried the Iraqi solders live in side their bunkers by running bull dozers over the bunkers. Later the media in USA revealed that about 50,000 Iraqi solders were buried alive. The sins committed by these solders were that they obeyed their superior's orders as true solders. All the Geneva conventions were broken by the coalition forces. The western media were completely biased against Saddam. This was the main reason why Al-Jazira was created in Qatar as an independent Arabic channel.

The coalition forces lead by Saudi commander entered Kuwait through Wafra border.

The retreating Iraqi army set fire to the oil wells and some important installation in refineries and power stations. The retreating Iraqi solders were massacred by the American force waiting at Basra border. Few lakhs of fleeing Iraqi solders were massacred by the American army.

While the coalition force entered Kuwait, they saw oil wells burning. At that time more than 100 wells were burning. The smoke emanating from these fires covered the sky above Kuwait. The fire could be viewed from a distance 100 kms. Fighting Saddam was no doubt challenging. But the military power of the coalition forces and money power of Arabic countries made it easy. But Agni (fire) was not Saddam. It showed its unprecedented fury. The heat of the fire could be felt even a kilometer from the fire. Nobody could go near the fire. It was a great technical challenge faced by USA. An open contract was given to USA for dousing the burning oil wells. With all technical expertise USA could not douse the fire. The Europe had better fire fighting expertise. The Polish team devised an ingenious method to douse the fire. There were 5000 hp sea water pumps available in the power stations. They used these pumps to pump sea water through one meter diameter pipes. At the end of the pipe a nozzle was fixed to create a water umbrella of a diameter of 20 meters. With this umbrella as cover a Poklin could move very near to the burning well. When the Poklin reached very near to the well its arm carried a big cup and covered the burning well. That was how burning well was doused. During the first few days they could douse one well a day. As they developed the expertise they could douse three wells a day. The last well was doused by Kuwaiti crown Prince.

Kuwait was liberated on 26th February 1991. All the Kuwaitis who fled to Saudi returned to their country. Kuwait felt indebted to USA especially George Bush for giving back their country. The economy of Kuwait was shattered and the ego of the arrogant Kuwaitis got a beating when they learnt that all their wealth could not protect them. Kuwait has become a slave to USA. George Bush decided not to attack Saddam and let him to rule Iraq. It was a clever decision. As long as Saddam remained as ruler of Iraq, Saudi Arabia and Kuwait have to depend on USA for protection. Therefore American Companies were assured of lucrative countracts from these two oil rich countries. George Bush Junior reaped the dividend of his father's victory and won the presidential election.

9

LIFE IN PAKISTAN (1991)

Santhi and Mansoor got settled comfortably in the village. Santhi was not allowed to do any domestic work by her mother-in-law. Santhi found it difficult to pass the time usefully. There was no T.V in the village. The only thing that connected her to the outside world was Radio. She used BBC world service to get unbiased and latest news about GULF WAR-1. She was eager to get back to work in Kuwait. At the time of liberation of Kuwait, anti-India sentiment prevailed among the Kuwaitis who felt that India did not take part in Gulf war. Santhi was not sure whether she would be called back by KNPC because she cooperated with Iraqi Army commander as the chief of KNPC. Her in-laws wanted their bahu to live with them for few more years.

Santhi delivered another boy in the local hospital. Her in-laws were very happy to have two grand sons. The second son was named as Rahim Ali Khan. Santhi continued to live as a Hindu woman. She never had any problem from the village people. The baby was taken care of by her mother-in-law well. All that she did was to feed the baby. Santhi did yoga and exercise to get back her original body shape. The neighbors and friends insisted Santhi to practice Bharatha Natyam. Mansoor too encouraged her to practice Bharatha Natyam. They were eager to see her dance. She reluctantly agreed. She knew that she lived in Pakistan where mullahs rule the roost. A fatwa may be issued any time by some fanatic Qazi against her dance. She wanted to avoid any confrontation with them. But the fate had its own way of doing things.

One day Santhi was invited to speak in a meeting organized by Human Rights Activist Asma Jahangir. Santhi spoke about the necessity of the woman's education. She spoke in chaste Punjabi which she learnt in Kuwait. When she rose to speak there was big ovation from the woman.

"I have noticed that only 5% of the woman folk in Punjab province are educated. This is very low compared to that of India. In India women and men are equal in education. In fact pass percentage India for girls is more than that of boys. Why I mention this is that politicians in Pakistan always compare with India. I ask the politicians to increase the literacy of woman and see what they can do for Pakistan. In my opinion, woman are more hard working and less corrupt. I have no faith in any of the present day politician in Pakistan. I have great faith in woman of Pakistan that they can compete with not only their counter part in India but also with any country in the world. If half the population in Pakistan is kept out of employment and most men want to get out of the country how is it possible for Pakistan to progress. Pakistan depends heavily on American aid for its survival. It is a shame. Pakistan with its natural resources and hard working population should be able to survive without any aid from anybody. The military in Pakistan claims to be the savior of the country. But it spends 26% of the nation's budget. Pakistan with its large size of army, corrupt bureaucracy and selfish politicians cannot survive without aid from somebody. Women are kept illiterate deliberately to satisfy the religious fanatics. I appeal to woman to go to school and get educated. Do not expect that some leader would come and save you from slavery. You have to take your rights. That is possible only if you are educated and do not depend on men for your survival.

I am sure that I have taken a great risk in delivering this speech. I am sure that god by any name would save me from the religious fanatics. I thank one and all for giving me this opportunity to express my view".

As she concluded there was big applause from the audience.

The local woman leader got up and thanked Santhi for her bold speech. She continued

"Santhi is a very good dancer. She is as beautiful as Sridevi and she can dance better than Hema malini. We are proud to say that she is our bahu. We wish that she should give her performance as early as possible"

Santhi got up and said

"After the delivery I did yoga and exercise to make my body fit. I did not practice dancing. I have to practice for three months to give a dance performance. Please bear with me and wait for my announcement"

The crowd was happy that she accepted and they were ready to wait to watch the dance program

Santhi practiced a dance for a song which she wrote.

Dunia jaane aurath ka thakkath kya
Shor machau hum kisi se kum nahi hai
Rasoye hum nai chodenge lekin gulami be nai karenge
Bacha palne wala hath vathan ko be palsakthe hai
Hamara pyar se sub ko jeethenga
Hum ye saabith karenga chudi pehne vale hath computer be chalyaha
Roti subji hum kammayange kissise beek nai mangenge.
School banayenge hospital banayenge
Padne vaasthe vilayath nai jaayenge
Ilaj karnekeliye India nai jayenge.
Ye hamara wathan hai ham nai thodenge vada.
Vathan ko banayenge aisa muluk duniya thekthe rehjayange.
English meaning of this Urdu song
The world will soon know what the woman power is
Shout and proclaim that we are not inferior to anybody
We will neither abandon kitchen nor accept slavery
The hands that take care of children can take care of this nation too
We will win over everybody with our love
The hands that wear bangles can use the computers too
We will earn our bread but will never be a slave
We will make schools and hospitals
We will not go to foreign country for study
We will not go to India for treatments
This is our nation and we will keep our promise
We will make our contry to become the envy of our neighbors.

Santhi came to the stage to start her performance. Suddenly there appeared hundred men with weapons and shouted "We will not allow this dance. This dance is Hinduism performed by an Indian. Allah ho akbar!"

Santhi took the mike in her hand started her speech.

"This dance is an art to entertain people. The rules of this dance were codified by Bharath Muni. The cosmic dance was performed by Lord Shiva. That is the only connection this dance has with religion. By performing this I am not propagating any religion. I married a Muslim. We live happily. We have shown to the world a Muslim and Hindu can live under the same roof happily. Many Muslim countries live as enemies. Recent example is that Iraq, a Muslim country invaded another

Muslim country Kuwait and vandalized the country by setting fire to the oil wells. That is why I am here. History has proved again and again religion can never be binding force between nations. If it were a binding force we should have only one Muslim country. Inside Pakistan we have divisions. We have shias, Sunnies, ahmadias boras, Sufis etc. Here I am the standing example. People in this village love me as their bahu. They do not care whether I am a Hindu or Muslim. I really hesitated to give this performance. But love shown by these people made me to agree to give this dance program. Please allow me to fullfil my promise to these people"

Santhi with folded hands begged them to allow the performance. But the religious fanatics did not relent

"This is Pakistan. We will not allow an Indian woman to give a pagan dance which is against our religion. Go away otherwise we will kill you." They shouted and started moving menacingly towards the stage. The village people were ready to fight with them. They too started shouting

"She is our daughter-in-law. We are ready to give our lives to protect her"

It was an explosive situation.

Santhi took control of the situation

"I am ready to take the challenge. I do not need anybody to protect me. I can protect myself. If there is man in this crowd please come forward and fight with me solo. Before the start of the fight I inform you that I will kill the man whoever comes forward to fight with me. Therefore he should sign on a paper that if he is killed I should not be held responsible and nobody should complain to the police that I killed the man."

She informed the crowd. The crowd became silent. One man came forward and signed the paper. He approached Santhi casually thinking that she was after all a woman. Santhi took a karate posture immediately and attacked him. She pierced his neck with her two fingers. The man got paralyzed and fell down. It took hardly a minute for Santhi to do this. She thundered to the crowd

"Is there any other man to challenge me?"

There was silence. On seeing the results no body dared to challenge Santhi.

She calmed down and said.

"I could have killed him. I took pity on his family and let him live. He will be alright after few days"

The villagers got relieved and looked at Santhi with awe.

The dance program was started. Santhi danced for one hour. The crowd watched her dance spell bound. This dance program changed her life. She became a heroin in Pakistan

The next day all the news papers published the news about Santhi. News paper gave a headline as follows

"An Indian woman takes mullahs head on"

Pakistan Times gave a headline like this

"Tigress takes lions in their den."

Santhi became a celebrity overnight in Pakistan. The newspapers visited Sultanpur and took interviews of Santhi and Mansoor. Story about their life in Kuwait, their fight to get their marriage registered and their flight from Kuwait during invasion were published in half dozen newspapers.

She was invited by many women's organization to give speech. Some invited her to give dance program.

Santhi declined all the invitation.

She gave a statement

"I am a house wife. I am not interested in politics. I delivered a boy recently. I have to nurse him. My village people love me as their daughter-in-law. I do not want them to get trouble from religious leaders. I have not come to Pakistan to create problems for my in-laws and their relatives. I will soon return to Kuwait and live my life happily with my husband and children. My husband wants to have a daughter like me. I have to fulfill his wish. I thank all the organization who invited me. I deeply regret to decline all the invitations."

This statement calmed down the religious fanatics. But the women's organizations were very much disappointed with her statement. They were happy that a messiah has come to save the women of Pakistan. But their happiness was short lived. After few months people of Pakistan forgot Santhi.

10

LIFE IN KUWAIT 1992

After liberation Kuwait started restoring their country. Indian companies were not awarded any contract. Kuwaitis were disappointed with India's policy. India took pains to explain that their first priority was to take care of their citizen. That was the reason why India could not take a hard line position against Iraq. India had good friendly relation with Iraq. Moreover India is a democratic country. It has to respect the sentiments of the people especially Indian Muslims. Indian Muslims regarded Saddam Hussain as their hero who fought against America. Kuwaitis slowly understood and appreciated India's position. Moreover Kuwait could not afford to live without the services of the skilled labor from India. During the reconstruction Indian labor played a significant role in restoring Kuwait's economy. KNPC Chief always had a soft corner for Santhi. Due to the prevailing anti-Indian sentiment he could not recall Santhi. He had to manage with a Kuwaiti secretary. She was efficient. But she always used to come late and her frequent absenteeism annoyed the chief. He tolerated her for some months. Being a Kuwaiti it was difficult for KNPC to send her away without a strong reason. Late coming and absenteeism were normal for a Kuwaiti. Luckily the Kuwaiti secretary got a better job from another public sector. She resigned the job. KNPC Chief happily relieved her from post. Immediately Santhi was recalled to join duty in January 1992.

Mansoor and Santhi felt relieved and happy to leave Pakistan. But the parents and the villagers felt very sad. Everybody from the village came one after another and talked to Mansoor and Santhi. They expressed their sorrow and some people cried. Santhi felt emotional to know how she made such an impression in such a short time. She consoled them and promised that she would visit the village every year without fail.

On 29th January both took a flight from Karachi to Kuwait. Santhi joined duty on 1st of February 1992. Every body in KNPC welcomed her. Every body praised Santhi for exhibiting such courage against Mullahs. Every body wanted to know how she could immobilize a man within a minute.

"It is very simple. I have learnt the art of Varma from a Guru who came to Kuwait from India. This art should not be misused. So the experts in this art never use it for selfish reason or for money. They teach this art to people whom they think worthy and needy. I used a technic of Varma to paralyse the man. I did not disclose this secret to any body in Pakistan. I was afraid that pressure may be brought on me to learn the art. That is why I kept it a secret" she concluded

Santhi was given the flat where she lived before invasion. Mansoor remained in the house to take care of the children. He did not feel bad about this arrangement. In fact he enjoyed parenting the children. Santhi used to leave the home early in the morning at 6.30 am. She returned from the office at 3.30 pm. Thursdays and Fridays were holidays. On these two days Mansoor used to take rest and visited his friends. Thus their life sailed smoothly. She became eligible to get one month holiday in January. They planned to visit Pakistan in January 1993. KNPC paid all salary arrears and gratuity till invasion. Santhi received substantial amount. She saved some amount from her salary. Both put together she had decent amount. Both discussed about how to spend the money usefully.

Santhi suggested

"I want to spend this money to provide education to the women in Sultanpur village. Let us start a school in our village. School should have both English and Punjabi medium education. I hope my father-in-law would give the necessary land for starting the school"

Mansoor replied

"I thought of opening a hospital for the poor. Any way starting a school is not a bad idea. Education is more important than medical facilities"

Santhi suggested

"We will start a hospital in 1994 with the help of some kind hearted doctors. Let us search and find some doctors during our visit. Mansoor couldn't agree more with her.

They booked their too and fro air tickets to Karachi in Pakistan Air lines.

*   *   *

11

LIFE IN PAKISTAN 1993

Mansoor formed a trust to run the School. The trust was named as "Mohamed Ali Jinnah Educational Trust" A committee was formed with some educated people. A correspondent was appointed to run the school. The school admitted only girls. A building was constructed with the donation from Santhi. The committee decided to collect only 100 rupees per month as fee from the students. The fees collected were enough to pay the salaries to the teachers. To meet other expenses the committee decided to collect donation from the villagers. There was heated discussion about the uniform for the girls. Nobody disagreed with Salwar Kammeez. There was difference in opinion among the members whether wearing of hissab to be made compulsory or not. Some wanted to make it compulsory. But Mansoor was particular in avoiding hissab.

He expressed his opinion

"The children do not know what the religion is. Only when they grow they learn about religion. During their study let us not burden them with the study of Koran at the tender age. First let them learn languages, science, mathematics, history geography and other social sciences till they become majors. They may be taught religion when they are in a position to understand the religion. I am against children reciting Holy Koran and brain washing them without understanding the meaning."

There was stiff resistance from some members to his suggestion. Some elders came out with a compromise formula. Wearing hissab was made optional. If any girl wanted to wear a hissab she should not be prevented from doing so.

Mansoor agreed with the compromise formula.

Santhi and Mansoor left Pakistan in February 1993. The school was inaugurated in June 1993 by Asma Jahangir. Mansoor was presnt for inaugural function but Santhi could not make it. She could not get leave. In the inaugural address Asma Jahangir said

"I miss Santhi very much in this function. It is she who planted the seed and provided the manure. The committee is watering the plant. All the credit goes to Santhi. Without her inspiration the school would not have come up. Every girl looks at Santhi as her role model. It is the irony that a savior has to come from India whom we consider as our enemy. We forget that more Muslims live in India than in Pakistan. Muslims live in India more peacefully than here. We have not fulfilled the dream of our Qaide Azam Mohamed Ali Jinnah. He believed that a separate nation for Muslims would provide a better economic opportunity to progress faster than India. Actually India marched ahead in every field except in Cricket. The very purpose of the partition was defeated by the corrupt politicians and the military. I don't have any faith with our men folk to rescue our nation from bankruptcy. Only when these young girls grow and vote we may get some good politician. I pray Allah that this school should grow and provide such leadership"

Mansoor gave vote of thanks and the inaugural function was news worthy.

*   *   *

On 27th January Benazir Ali Butto became the Prime minister of Pakistan. Santhi felt happy that a lady became the P.M of Pakistan. She wanted to visit Pakistan in February with her Husband. They found that school started by them was not doing well due to paucity of funds. She decided to do something to get funds for the school. They already decided to open a hospital. One of the Sheiks in Kuwait promised to donate funds for a maternity hospital in Sultanpur. She decided to invite Benazir Ali Botto for inaugurating the hospital. Santhi took two months leave. She worked hard along with her husband to finalize the hospital project. They entrusted the work to a contractor. January 2005 was fixed as the inauguration date. Santhi assured that fund would not be constraint to complete the project in time.

Both went back to Kuwait. They constantly monitored the project by phone call and email. They arranged to send money in time so that the project was not stopped for want of money. It was a race against time to complete the building, fixing all the medical equipments in place. Getting gynecological doctors to man (woman?) the hospital was a stupendous task. They had to persuade some gynecologist working in Kuwait to work in Sultanpur.

They too felt that if an Indian was doing such a service to woman of Pakistan, woman of Pakistan also should do something to match her. Sulatanpur Hospital could get some good gynecologists. The Hospital was named as "Benazir Ali Butto Maternity Hospital". The hospital had 100 beds with all the sophisticated equipments. The naming of hospital attracted the attention of the people all over Pakistan. She became the talking point in the media. Soon most people in Pakistan came to know who Santhi was and why she married a Muslim. The woman of Pakistan had a great admiration for her. On seeing the popularity of Santhi some media person commented that she may be next P.M.

Benazir made her inaugural speech

"I became the prime minister because of my father. People of Pakistan had a great respect to my father. He was brutally executed by the military Junta. Due to the sympathy created by the untimely death of my father I became what I am today. I have not achieved on my own merit. But look at Santhi. She has all the handicaps. She is an Indian. She is a Hindu. She has nobody to support except her husband. Yet she achieved something that no woman in Pakistan ever dreamt. What made her to achieve this?. It is her education and her values. She does not believe in anything that divides one human-being from another. Caste, religion, race, language and nationality divide the human-beings in the name of patriotism. Santhi has done so much to the woman of Pakistan I dare to say that Santhi is the god-sent bahu to teach a lession to religious fanatics.

Now she is our unofficial ambassador of Pakistan to Kuwait. I request her to start more such projects to help the woman of Pakistan. I will always support her in all her social work. So far I have not heard of her speech. I understand that she speaks good Punjabi. I request her to speak."

Santhi stood up and started her speech.

"I thank Madam Benazir for her praise. I do not know whether I deserve the praise. I will try my best to fulfill her expectation. I never imagined in my life that I would ever marry a Muslim and live in Pakistan that too as a celebrity. It is the will of the God. India and Pakistan became two nations only 48 years ago. They lived as one nation for thousands of years. I consider this separation is temporary. 48 years is a small period in the history of human race. There were so many nations in Europe fighting with each other for thousands of years. Yet they could form an European Union within few decades. South Asian nations were culturally and historically bound with each other. I will not be out of my mind if I say that one day a South Asian Union would be formed and it would be one of the super powers in the world.

I would like to place a request to Madam Benazir. We are running a school exclusively to cater to the needs of girl children. We charge a nominal fee. The fees are hardly enough to pay the salary of the teachers. We manage the school with donations. The committee in charge of the school is not able to get enough donations due to the internal bickering. We find it difficult to add new classes. I request our Madam Benazir to extend her helping hand to run the school successfully" she used the occasion to get the aid from the government to the school.

The Prime Minister got up and made the announcement.

"I accept her request. I order that the government would pay the salaries of the teachers. In addition to this a grant in aid of Rs one million would be paid to meet other expenses.

I hope that Santhi would be satisfied. I wish that this school would become a college and a University in my life time. In other words I wish to live till this school becomes a University".

The crowd became jubilant when they heard the announcement. They had all praises for Santhi who was the architect of the school and Hospital. Everybody praised Mansoor to get such a wife. Mansoor and Santhi became hero and heroin of Sultanpur

12

LIFE IN PAKISTAN 1996-1999

Benazir Butto mismanaged the economy of Pakistan. She had confrontation with army, the president Leghari and the judiciary. There was rampant corruption in Pakistan. Benazir was accused of spending the government money lavishly. She was accused of siphoning the funds and buying properties in UK. Her husband Zardhari was nicknamed as "Mr.Ten percent" by the media and public. Pakistan faced bankruptcy. It approached IMF and UAE government for aid and loan. UAE declined the request. IMF agreed to provide loan with stringent conditions which the Benazir government could not implement. Benazir's differences with army, Judiciary and the president grew by the day. Her government was dismissed on 5th November 1996. She appealed to the Supreme Court. But the Apex Court upheld the dismissal. An interim government was formed with Malik Meeraj Khalid as the Prime Minister. The cabinet was loaded with the friends of the President Leghari. The interim government tried its best to set right Pakistan's economy. However it could not do anything substantial during the short period of 3 months.

The election was held on February 17th 1997. The turn out touched an all time low of 27%. PML (n) won a two third majority in the National Assembly and simple majority in three provinces (except in Baluchistan). Nawaz Sheriff had a very good opportunity to set right the economy of Pakistan. But he too failed. He did not attack the root cause of the problem. Pakistan spent 26% of its budget on its army and 46% to repay the debts. He decided to cut the army to size. He appointed Purvez Mushraf as the Army Chief. He expected Mushraf to tow his line. But his expectation failed. Mushraf consolidated his position in the army and started acting on his own without consulting the prime Minister.

The Kargil war was masterminded by General Javed Hussain in 1998. The intrusion began on 18-12-98. During the winter months India and Pakistan had an understanding to withdraw their forces from their positions in Kargil district to escape from severe winter conditions. India withdrew its troupes in the winter months of 1998-99. But Pakistan decided to use the opportunity to intrude in to Kargil district with their chosen paramilitary forces assisted by the army. Pakistan expected India not to detect the intrusion before June 99. By that time Pakistan would have occupied substantial area and captured the strategic positions inside Indian Territory. Then Pakistan would be in a position to dictate terms with India to solve Kashmir problem. Pakistan expected India not to attack in to Pakistan's territory due to its nuclear deterrence. But things did not work in the way Pakistan expected.

In the early May 1999 a shepherd detected the movements of Pakistani solders and reported the same to Indian Army. Immediately Indian Army took action. It used high tech high altitude warfare without crossing LOC. Pakistan did not expect India to use its air force on the intruders. India code named its operation as "Operation Vijay"

The conflict ended in July 1999 when Indian army captured substantial portion of the occupied area. Due to the international pressure especially from America on Nawaz Sherif Pakistan withdrew from the rest of the area occupied by the intruders. Pakistan accepted a casuality figure of 270 solders. But the estimate by the retired army personnel was more than 1000. Nawaz Sherif was kept in dark about the Kargil operation till May 1999. He was informed about the operation during an army brief. He was shocked to know that he was not informed of the operation and all the intrusions happened without his knowledge.

He felt humiliated when America forced him to withdraw. He got wild and sacked Mushraf from the post of Army Chief. At that time Mushraf was in Sri Lanka. As soon as he returned he declared an emergency and arrested Nawaz Sherif in October 1999. Saudi Arabia intervened and gave asylum to Nawaz Sherif in Saudi Arabia. Musraf let Nawaz Sherif to leave with the understanding that he would not come back to Pakistan.

President Mushraf initially denied any involvement of army in Kargil operation. Later it was revealed that Mushraf himself crossed LOC and spent a week inside Indian Territory to do reconnaissance operation before Kargil intrusion during the winter months of 1998-99. It was his personal project. When Kargil operation became a great set back he wanted to use proxies to take revenge upon India. He hit the idea of hijacking an Indian Airlines passenger plane. He wanted to use the passengers as hostages to get back some top militants who were in Indian Jail. He wanted to humiliate India and at the same time help the militant organization get back their leaders from Indian jails.

He did not involve himself personally in this operation. He learnt this lession from Kargil conflict. He entrusted this job to the Army and ISI.

Mehraj-ud-din alias Javed alias Daand, the longest surviving militant was used by the Army and ISI to organize the hijacking in coordination with United Jihad Council headed by Syed Salah-ud-din. Dawood brothers used havala money to finance the project.

Five Pakistanis with fake passports (arranged by ISI) boarded Indian Airlines Flight IC-814 from Katmandu. Necessary weapons were supplied by Pakistan Embassy in Kathmandu. The hijacked plane with 176 passengers landed in Amritsar, Lahore, Dubai and Kandahar. The plane was kept landed for 7 days during the negotiations. Pakistan stood firmly stuck with its lie that it has nothing to do with hijacking and it was done by the jihad elements based Jammu Kashmir.

Taliban in Afganistan facilitated the negotiation between the Indian government and hijackers. After seven days of negotiation Indian government agreed to hand over three militants namely Moulan Massod Azhar (Chief of JEM), Omar Sheik and Mustaq Latram in exchange for the passengers. It was alleged that some undisclosed amount of Money also was paid to hijackers.

The hijackers got down from the hijacked plane and crossed in to Pakistan. Initially Pakistan denied their presence in Pakistan. Later it was found that they lived in Pakistan carrying their Anti-India propaganda. India felt humiliated and Mushraf felt it as his personal victory.

13

PAKISTAN POLITICS 1999-2009

Pakistan was put under Martial law in October 1999. Mushraf allowed Tarar to continue as the president. He designated himself as the Chief Executive Officer of Pakistan. He continued to hold the post of Chief of the Army. Nawaz Sherif was arrested and tried in the military court. He was charged with sedition. When he was about to be sentenced to death by the Terrorism court, Saudi Arabia and USA intervened and compelled Mushraf to strike a deal with Nawaz Sherif. As per the deal signed by Mushraf with Nawaz Sherif, he would be exiled to Saudi Arabia and never come back to Pakistan.

In 2001 USA declared a war on terror after September 11ᵗʰ 2001 attack on twin towers. Mushraf was forced by circumstances to be a partner in war against terror. But at the same time he could not alienate the religious parties if he was to continue his regime. Therefore in public he was conducting a war on terror to support USA. But in private he supported all the militant organizations. He wanted to use the militants to wage a proxy war against India

On December 13, 2001 five LeT militants entered Indian Parliament through gate no 12 and started firing. Security personnel prevented them from entering in to parliament. During the gun fight twelve people, including the five men who attacked the Indian Parliament, were killed. India claimed that the attacks were carried out by two Pakistan based Terrorist groups fighting against Indian rule in Kashmir. India charged that LeT and JeM are backed by Pakistan's ISI. Pakistan denied the charge. In the Western media, coverage of the standoff between the tradional rivals focused on the possibility of a nuclear war between the two countries and the implications of the potential conflict on the United States-led War on Terrorism in Afghanistan. Tensions de-escalated following international diplomatic mediation which resulted in the October 2002 withdrawal of Indian and Pakistani troops from the International Border.

Aziz completed his term as P.M in 2007. In 2005 Iftihar Mohamed Choudhary was appointed as Chief Justice of Supreme Court by Mushraf. But he proved to be independent Judge who refused to tow the line of the dictator. Mushraf felt uncomfortable with Choudhary and asked him to resign. "It is an illegal action" declared Choudhary and refused to resign. Mushraf suspended Choudhary which ignited a countrywide agitation against Musharaf. Chief Justice decided to challenge his suspension in the Supreme Court and thus on 20th July, 2007, won the case and was restored back to his position. This never went down well with the General Mushraf who imposed emergency in the country, suspended the constitution, suspended all the judges and put them in house arrest with their families. Even then the judges gave an order declaring the emergency null and void. The news of his suspension sparked greater unrest. Civil opinion, distressful economical situation and the authoritarian actions decided the departure of Musharraf as chief of army staff in 2007, and made him resign in 2009. After the new government came, the then Prime Minister Yousaf Raza Gillani, released all the judges. However he did not restore the judges their position.

On 15 November Geo News reported that Chaudhry had ordered the Islamabad Inspector General of Police to take action against his and his family's house arrest and their possible relocation to Quetta. According to the channel, Chaudhry held the interior secretary, the commissioner, the deputy commissioner and the assistant commissioner responsible for his house arrest. He said he was still the Chief Justice of Pakistan and the official residence was his by right.

Just after general elections in February, on 24 March 2008, on his first day of premiership the Pakistani PM Yousaf Raza Gillani ordered Chaudhry's release from house arrest.

In October 2008, Chaudhry visited the Supreme Court building.

The Lawyers' Movement announced a "long march" from 12-16 March 2009 for the restoration of the judges, especially Chief Justice Iftikhar. The government of Pakistan refused to reinstate the judges and declared section 144 in effect in three of the four provinces of Pakistan thereby forbidding any form of gatherings of the "long march". Arrangements were made to block all roads and other means of transport to prevent the lawyers from reaching the federal capital, Islamabad. Workers of the main political parties in opposition and the lawyer's movement as well as other known persons from the civil society were arrested. Despite these efforts, the movement continued and was able to break through the blockade in Lahore en route to Islamabad in the night between 15 and 16 March 2009. A few hours later, on the morning of 16 March 2009, the prime minister of Pakistan restored Chaudhary Iftikahar as chief justice of Pakistan through an executive order after which the opposition agreed to stop the "long march".

With Aziz constitutionally completing his term and the suspension of the Chief Justice in 2007, Musharraf dramatically fell from the presidency in 2008 after voluntarily resigning due to fear of impeachment by the elected opposition parties. Musharraf went in to a self-imposed exile in London, but has vowed to return for the next election. In his absence in Pakistan, the country's courts issued arrest warrants for him and Aziz for alleged involvement in the assassination of Benazir Bhutto and Akbar Bugti.

Between 2006 and 2008 ISI Chief and Let planned the 26/11 Mumbai attack operation which killed 168 people mostly American and Israelis. In Pakistan ISI was under the director control of President. Without the knowledge and approval of Mushraf, ISI could not have carried out a mission with international ramification. From the confessions made by David Headley during the Chicago trial it was proved beyond doubt ISI was the master mind behind 26/11 Mumbai attack. LeT selected 10 militants and trained them to carry out the mission. They used David Headley to get information about the targets. He visited Mumbai five times during 2006 and 2008. He was a double agent. Even though Mushraf was not in power when the attack took place, he could not escape from the responsibility for Mumbai attack. All the planning and arrangements were done during his periods of Presidency.

14

ASSASSINATION OF BENAZIR BHUTTO

The **assassination of Benazir Bhutto** occurred on 27 December 2007 in Rawalpindi, Pakistan Bhutto, twice Prime Minister of Pakistan (1988-1990; 1993-1996) and then-leader of the opposition Pakistan Peoples Party, had been campaigning ahead of elections scheduled for January 2008 Shots were fired at her after a political rally at Liaquat National Bagh, and a suicide bomb was detonated immediately following the shooting. She was declared dead at 18:16 local time (13:16 UTC), at Rawalpindi General Hospital. Twenty-four other people were killed by the bombing. Bhutto had previously survived a similar attempt on her life that killed at least 139 people, after her return from exile two months earlier.

Though early reports indicated that she had been hit by sharpnel or the gunshots, the Pakistani Interior Ministry initially stated that Bhutto died of a skull fracture sustained when the force of the explosion caused her head to strike the sunroof of the vehicle. Bhutto's aides rejected this version, and argued instead that she suffered two gunshots before the bomb detonation. The Interior Ministry subsequently backtracked from its previous claim. However, a follow-up investigation by Scotland Yard found that while gunshots were fired, they were not the cause of death, agreeing with the Interior Ministry's original assessment that the explosion forced her head into the roof of the vehicle.

PPP, suggested that the killer opened fire as Bhutto left the rally and the bullet hit her in the neck and chest before he detonated the explosives he was wearing. Javed Cheema, an interior ministry spokesman, stated that her injuries were caused either by her having been shot or from pellets packed into the detonated bomb that acted as pressed skull fractures, oval in overall shape, on the right side of Bhutto's head. He apparently saw no other injuries and downplayed the possibility of bullet wounds, although he had previously spoken of them. One anonymous doctor said that Pakistani authorities took Bhutto's medical records immediately after her death and they told doctors to stop talking.

According to Washington post, the crime scene was cleared before any forensic examination could be completed and no formal autopsy was performed before burial. Despite the ambiguity surrounding her death, Bhutto's husband Mr Asif Zardari did not allow a formal autopsy to be conducted citing his fears regarding the procedure being carried out in Pakistan. Due to which, even today the true cause of her death remains uncertain.

Elections and electoral fraud report

Pakistan's election commission met on 31 December 2007 to decide whether or not to delay the January 2008 elections. Two days before the meeting they hinted at the need for postponement since the election process was severely affected. A senior election commission official subsequently announced that the election would be delayed to the later part of February.

Senator Latif Khosa, one of Bhutto's top aides, reported that Benazir was planning to divulge evidence of fraud in the upcoming election following the event where the assassination took place. The pair co-wrote a 160-page dossier on the subject, with Bhutto outlining tactics she alleged would be put into play, including intimidation, excluding voters and fake ballots being planted in boxes. The report was titled "Yet another stain on the face of democracy" In a statement he made on 1st January 2008, Khosa said:

"The state agencies are manipulating the electoral process. There is rigging by ISI, Election Commission and the previous government."

Khosa said that they had planned to give the dossier to two American law-makers on the evening of her assassination and release it publicly soon after that. One of them claimed in the dossier that US financial aid had been secretly misappropriated for electoral fraud and another said that the ISI had a 'mega-computer' which could hack into any other computer and was connected to the Election Commission's system. A spokesman for President Musharraf called the claims "ridiculous".

In the run up to the election, the 'sympathy vote' was considered crucial for the Pakistan Peoples Party, which was expected to win the National Assembly. The election results yielded a majority for the Pakistan

Peoples Party in the National Assembly, and in the Provincial Assembly of Sindh.

Economy

Following a three-day shut-down, the benchmark index, the KSE100 index, of the Karachi Stock Exchange fell 4.7%. The Pakistani rupee fell to its lowest level against the U.S. dollar since October 2001 The stock exchange has a history of recovering after political unrest. The Pakistan Railways suffered losses of PKR 12.3 billion as a direct result of riots following the assassination. 63 railway stations, 149 bogies, and 29 locomotives were damaged within two days of Bhutto's death. In the first four days after the assassination, Karachi suffered losses of US$1 billion. By the fifth day, the cost of country wide violence amounted to 8% of the GDP

Responsibility

On 27 December 2007, al-Qaeda commander Mustafa Abu al-Yazid claimed responsibility for the assassination, telling several news outlets that "We terminated the most precious American asset which vowed to defeat the Mujahideen". In his statement to the media, he further claimed that al-Qaeda second-in-command Ayman al-Zawahiri ordered the killing in October 2007. Asia Times Online also reported that it had received a claim of responsibility from al-Yazid by telephone. U.S. intelligence officials have said that they couldn't confirm this claim of responsibility. Nonetheless, U.S. analysts have said that al-Qaeda was a likely or even prime suspect. For its part, the Pakistani Interior Ministry (of the previous Musharraf administration) stated that it had proof that al-Qaeda was behind the assassination, stating that the suicide bomber belonged to Lashkar-e-Jhangvi an al Qaeda-linked Sunni Muslim militant group, which was blamed for hundreds of killings. The Interior Ministry also claimed to have intercepted a statement by militant leader Baitullah Mehsud said to be linked to al-Qaeda, in which he congratulated his followers for carrying out the assassination. On 29th December a Mehsud spokesman told the Associated Press that Mehsud was not involved in the assassination: "I strongly deny it. Tribal people have their own customs. We don't strike women. It is a conspiracy by government, military and intelligence agencies." The Pakistan Peoples Party also called the government's blame of Mehsud a diversion: "The story blaming al-Qaida or Baitullah Mehsud appears to be a planted story for diverting the attention," said Farhatullah Babar, a spokesman for Bhutto's party. On 18th January 2008, CIA Director Michael Hayden claimed that Mehsud and his network were responsible.

Bhutto, in a letter to Musharraf written on 16th October 2007, named four persons involved in an alleged plot to kill her. Intelligence Bureau (IB) Chief Ijaz Shah, former chief minister of Punjab Chaudhry Pervaiz Elahi, former chief minister of Sindh Arbad Ghulam Rahim, and the former ISI chief, Hamid Gul posed a threat to her life. British newspaper The Times suggested that elements within the Pakistani Inter-Services Intelligence with close ties to Islamists might have been behind the killing, though it asserts that Musharraf would have been unlikely to have ordered the assassination. October 2007 emails from Bhutto saying she would blame Musharraf for her death if she were killed, because the Musharraf government was not providing adequate security, were also published after Bhutto's death. Soon after the killing, many of Bhutto's supporters believed that the Musharraf government was involved in the assassination. On 30 December Scotland Yard on Sunday quoted MI5 sources saying that factions of Pakistan's Inter-Services Intelligence may be responsible for the assassination. Bhutto anticipated that three senior allies of President Musharraf were out to kill her in a secret email to Foreign Secretary David Miliband written weeks before her death.

United Nations inquiry

A formal investigation by the United Nations commenced on 1st July 2009. The report concluded that the security measures provided to Bhutto by the government were "fatally insufficient and ineffective". Furthermore, the report states that the treatment of the crime scene after her death "goes beyond mere incompetence". The report stated that "police actions and omissions, including the hosing down of the crime scene and failure to collect and preserve evidence, inflicted irreparable damage to the investigation."

Pakistani government

According to state television, Musharraf held an emergency cabinet meeting after he received word of the blast. He then addressed the nation, saying that "We shall not rest till we tackle this problem and eliminate all the terrorists. This is the only way the nation will be able to move forward; otherwise this will be the biggest obstacle to our advancement." In a televised address, President Musharraf publicly condemned the killing of Bhutto, proclaiming a three-day mourning period with all national flags at half mast. Mahmud Ali Durrani, the Pakistani ambassador to the United States, called Bhutto's death "a national tragedy" and stated that "we have lost one of our important, very important and, I would stress, liberal leader".

D-Company

D-Company is a term coined by the media for the organized criminal group controlled by wanted terrorist and crime boss Dawood Ibrahim. D-Company is directly linked to a range of organized criminal and terrorist activities in Pakistan, India, and the United Arab Emirates. Several members of the group are on the terrorist and/or wanted persons list produced by Interpol

Dawood Ibrahim established a booming criminal syndicate in the 1980s. Ibrahim was designated by the U.S. Department of Treasury as a Specially Designated Global Terrorist (SDGT) in late 2003, following the release of information that Ibrahim allowed al Qaeda to use his smuggling routes to escape fom Afghanistan, and for his support of LeT. Three years later, President George W. Bush designated Ibrahim and D-Company as a significant Foreign Narcotics Trafficker under the Foreign Narcotics Kingpin Designation Act. While it is unlikely that D-Company will ever formally assimilate into either the al Qaeda or LeT structure, the organized criminal group's connection to these terrorist groups continues to present a significant threat to peace and stability in South Asia. Not only is Dawood Ibrahim capable of smuggling terrorists, weapons, and logistical supplies across borders, but D-Company has the ability to control criminal enterprise across a region which would greatly increase al Qaeda and LeT's potential for growth and violence.

Funding

D-Company generates billions of dollars in revenue from legitimate business activities such as real estate and bank overhaul transactions, as well as illegal criminal enterprises around the world, especially in India,

Pakistan, and the U.A.E. Other prominent members of the gang include Chota Shakeel, Tiger Memon and Abu Salem, now in the custody of the Indian police. It is closely linked to a range of organized criminal and terrorist activities in South Asia, the Persian Gulf, Africa and South East Asia.The organization has a history of rivalry with the Mumbai police and other underworld dons such as Chhota Rajan, Ejaz Lakdawala who was arrested in Canada in 2004 and Arun Gawli

History

The D-Company is the largest underground business in South Asia. Its operations include arms trafficking, contract killing, counterfeiting, drug trafficking, extortion, and terrorism, being responsible for 1993 bombings in Mumbai which killed 257 people. It was alleged that D-Company planned further terrorist attacks in Gujarat following the communal riots of 2002.

In 2011, Indian intelligence agencies managed to link D-Company with the 2 G Spectrum scam, through DB Realty and DB Etisalat (formerly Swan Telecom) promoted by Shahid Balwa. Later in March security at CBI headquarters in Delhi was tightened after it had been suggested that D-Company might launch an attack in an attempt to destroy documents relating to the ongoing probe of the 2G spectrum scam.

Dawood is one of the twenty terrorist wanted in India. The list was provided by India. But Pakistan refuses to accept the presence of Dawood in Pakistan. He was one of the biggest irritants in improving relations between Pakistan and India. The whole world knows he lives in Pakistan like a king. His political and money power are so enormous nobody in Pakistan can dare to touch him.

Lashkar-e-Taiba literally *Army of the Good*, translated as *Army of the Righteous*, or *Army of the Pure*) is one of the largest and most active terrorist Islamist organizations in South Asia, operating mainly from Pakistan.

It was founded in 1990 by Hafiz Muhammad Saeed, Abdullah Yusuf Azzam and Zafar Iqbal in Afghanistan With its headquarters based in Muridke, near Lahore in Punjab province of Pakistan, the group operates several training camps in Pakistan-administered Kashmir

Lashkar-e-Taiba has attacked civilian and military targets in India, most notably the 2001 Indian Parliament attack and the 2008 Mumbai attacks. Its stated objective is to introduce an Islamic state in South Asia and to "liberate" Muslims residing in Indian Kashmir. The organization is banned as a terrorist organization by India, Pakistan, the United States, the United Kingdom, the European Union and Australia. Some experts such as former French investigating magistrate Jean-Louis Bruguière and New America Foundation president Steve Coll believe that Pakistan's main intelligence agency, the Inter-Services Intelligence (ISI), continues to give LeT intelligence help.

Jaish-e-Mohammed

JeM is a major terrorist organization based in Kashmir. Its primary motive is to separate Kashmir from India and it carried out many attacks primarily in Indian administered Kashmir. It was banned in Pakistan since 2002 under the pressure from India and USA. Yet it continues to operate in Pakistan with all the facilities.

According to B. Raman, Jaish-e-Mohammed is viewed as the "deadliest" and "the principal terrorist organization in Jammu and Kashmir" The group is regarded as a terrorist organization by several countries, including India, United States and United Kingdom.

15

GULF WAR II

In 2000 Parvesh Mushraf has declared himself as Chief executive of Pakistan. Tarar continued as president. Pakistanis felt a sigh of relief. They were so much fed up with corrupt elected governments given by Benazir and Nawaz Sheriff that they came to the conclusion that only Military can ensure stability and unity of Pakistan. Mushraf expected that expatriate Pakistanis would pour money in to Pakistan and the economy may be rescued. But it did not happen. Therefore he had to depend on US Aid for the survival of Pakistan. But religious fanatics ensured that Pakistan did not tow the line of USA. Mushraf sucessfully played the double game. He promised everything asked by USA. But when he came back to Pakistan he always danced to the tune of Religious organization and Jihadis. He did a balancing act between USA and religious organizations till 11th September 2001.

11th September changed the history of the world. President George Bush Jr declared a war on terror. Mushraf took this an opportunity and joined the war on terror. But he did not do enough to fight the war on terror. America accused Pakistan of training and helping Taliban and other militants in the name of fighting against India. Mushraf wanted to have a friendly government in Afghanistan. He felt that the understanding with Al Quida and Taliban would help to achieve his goal.

In the meanwhile USA faced fiscal deficit problem. Bush Jr did not want to take harsh measures required to contain the fiscal deficit which ran in to trillions of dollars. He wanted to win his presidential election in 2004. To ensure his re-election he continued his emphasize on war on terrorism. He wanted to create jobs by encouraging armament industries, oil companies and construction companies. Gulf war I gave a very good boost to the American economy. George Bush Jr wanted to repeat the performance of his father and get re-elected in 2004.

Bush accused Saddam Hussein of possessing Weapons of Mass Destruction. (Later it was found to be false). Further he accused Saddam of supporting militants with his oil wealth. Bush was supported by Britain but Germany and France refused to support him. Russia and China opposed him. Yet he prepared for the invasion. The whole world was against him. However the majority of Americans supported him. They were brain-washed by misinformation unleashed by American Administration. On 15th January 2003 a month before invasion there were 3000 protests (36 million people) all over the world. In Rome a record number of 3 million people took part to demonstrate against war in Iraq.

America with the support of his allies invaded Iraq on 19th march 2003. Troupes from Poland, Australia and Great Britain took part in the operation. America expected Kuwait and Saudi to give financial support to the war. However people in the streets of Kuwait and Saudi were against Iraq war. Saudi did not give any help to America. Kuwait refused to provide financial support. It provided only water, fuel and infrastructure support. Kuwait provided base in Doha east to the American military. American troupes launched a conventional war to invade Iraq. March is normally a cool month in Kuwait. But in the year 2003 Kuwait was unusually hot and there was unprecedented sand storm during the invasion. Probably even the god did not like the invasion. American troupes had a tough time in combating heat rather than enemy. (The author was working in Doha East and personally witnessed all the actions in the war) The war ended on 1st of May 2003. The objectives of the war set by president were three fold.

1. To remove Bath party and Saddam Hussien from power
2. To find out WMD and destroy them.
3. To establish democracy in Iraq

But the real motive behind the war was

1. To prove to the world that USA is the only Super power. It can do whatever it wants to do
2. To help the companies he expected to suppor him in his re-election compagn in 2004

3. To divert the attention of American public from the economic crisis faced by America by creating a fear psychosis about international terror directed against USA.

After the gulf war II only one of the officially stated objectives was realized. Saddam Hussein was captured live. Bath party was removed from power. But America could not find any WMD. USA occupied Baghdad (Cenral proince), UK occupied Basra (Southern province), Kurdish rebel occupied northern province. USA could not establish any democracy in Iraq. A civil war broke out and thousands of people were killed. Iraq became a country of chaos. USA could not achieve the objectives as stated by Bush. It was one of the greatest misadventure committed by USA after Vietnam War

If Bush had achieved his objectives he could have won the election without any problem. But 2004 presidential election was one of the closely fought elections. Bush Jr got 50,000 popular votes less than John Kerry. There were large scale irregularities in the election process. In Florida 36,000 people belonging to minority group (who usually vote for Democratic Party) were left out from the Electoral College. Many minority people were prevented from voting due to security check. Bush won the Florida. This gave the edge over Kerry in the number of Electoral Colleges won. Thus bush won the presidential election by fraud. This was described by many commentators as "STOLEN VICTORY"

16

LIFE IN KUWAIT 1993-2003

When Santhi and Mansoor returned to Kuwait Ram was 2 years old and Rahim was one year old. Mansoor decided to stay in the house to take care of the children. Ram was admitted in an Indian School. He chose English as the first language, Urdu as second language and Arabic as third language. Next year Rahim followed suit. When both the children went to school Mansoor got bored inside the house. Both husband and wife discussed the problem.

Santhi started the conversation

"You may find it difficult to kill the time when the children are in the school"

"Yes what to do. I have to accept" replied Mansoor.

"Look! I have an idea. I will get you a job in a private company. I will appoint a servant maid to take care of the children in my absence. She can help me in cooking, washing and cleaning" Santhi made a sensible suggestion.

Mansoor did not agree with the suggestion.

"I do not mind you employing a servant maid to help you. I cannot allow the servant maid to take care of our children. Either you will take care of the children or I will do it. I cannot compromise on this issue" Mansoor was firm in his decision.

"I have another idea. I will buy a Toyota pick up. You can drive the pick up and run it on rent when the children are in the school. I will arrange for a work visa through some sponsors by paying some money" Santhi suggested.

Mansoor agreed to the suggestion. Soon he started driving a pick up for rent. He could make some money because he had lot of Indian and Pakistani friends who always called him whenever they needed a pick up. He saved this money in a separate account. He had the bitter experience during gulf war I. He believed that anything could happen in Gulf countries. Expatriate should be ready to face any unexpected event.

*   *   *

In 2000 when Mushraf took over as president, his government stopped the government support to the school run by Mohamed Ali Jinnah educational trust. The trust made an appeal to the public to increase the donations. Very few people responded to the appeal. They requested Santhi and Mansoor to provide some financial relief. They did provide financial assistance. But it was not enough to tide over the situation. The committee requested Mansoor to visit Pakistan and sort out the problem with the government. It was March 2003. Companies in Kuwait took Gulf War II as an opportunity and made good profit by supplying goods needed by the American Army. Drivers took great risk to deliver goods in side Iraq during the invasion and made a fortune out of this opportunity.

Mansoor and Santhi discussed the problem

"I suggest that you go to Sultanpur and do something to save the school. If you appeal probably more people may come forward to donate. You may try with the government to restore the support" Santhi suggested.

"I am ready to risk my life to save our school. I will make some trips in to Iraq. I may get good amount that can save our school" Mansoor replied. Santhi did not agree with his idea.

"You may risk you life. But it is a foolish thing to do so. It is better for you to go to Sultanpur and do whatever possible to save the school" Santhi concluded

Mansoor reached Sultanpur in June 2003

Mansoor met the elders and discussed ways and means to save the school. All the people were of the opinion that he should approach the Government to restore the financial aid.

He met some senior officers in the education department. Every body advised him that only President Mushraf could help him. He used his influence as an expatriate from Kuwait. He was surprised when he got the appointment with President Mushraf.

When Mansoor entered the president's cabin, he felt a bit nervous. But he managed to present his case

'Mushraf Saab salaam alaikum!. My name is Mansoor Ali Khan. I come from Sultanpur. I am working as driver in Kuwait. We run a school for girls in our village. During last 11years government provided financial support to the school. Now it was stopped by your government. If we increase the fees many parents may stop their girls coming to school. It may be a great set back to the women's education in our country. Please restore the aid"

Mansoor requested politely.

Musraf ordered for cup of tea for Mansoor. He started his talk

"When you asked for appointment I enquired and got full information about you from our intelligence agencies. You are married to an Indian Hindu woman. She is working as the secretary to the Managing Director of KNPC. She saved you from terrorist attack in Kuwait. She challenged the Mullahs successfully and got a wide publicity in the media. She is a well known person among the women of Pakistan. If she visits Pakistan and ask for donation I am sure she will get enough money to run the school for another 10 years. If your wife can help you why do you expect me to help" Mushraf was in mood to drag Santhi in to this problem.

"I do not want her to come to Pakistan and get in to trouble with militants. More over it is not her problem. It is my problem. I have to sort it out" replied Mansoor.

"So your wife remains as an Indian. She is the enemy of Pakistan" said Mushraf.

"She is neither an Indian nor a Pakistani. She is a human-being living in Kuwait. I have many Indian friends. As far as I know they are not enemies of Pakistan. If some body does not agree with you it does not mean that he is your enemy. Any way we are moving away from the subject. Let us discuss about the school. Please tell me whether you can help or not" Mansoor demanded a reply from the president.

"Sure I can. But you have to do me a favor. You have to visit India with your wife. I want some information which is not sensitive but it will be useful to further the peace process with India. I have written the information I need in a piece of paper. You may go through the paper and give your reply" Mushraf gave a piece of paper.

Mansoor read and replied

"So you want me to spy for Pakistan in India. I will not do this whatever may be circumstances. I may be a Muslim and Pakistani. But I am a good human-being and behave like one. In the name of Patriotism you should not expect me to do some thing which is against my nature. I am sorry. I will go back. I may beg in the streets of Kuwait to save my school" having said this he left the cabin. There was no reaction from the president.

In those days anything said and done by Mushraf was news. Some reporters who waited outside met Mansoor.

One of reporter asked

"What was your mission? Did you succeed?"

"No! I didn't"

"Why?" reporter asked

"I wanted a favor from the president and he is ready to oblige if I agree to spy in India" Mansoor spilled out the beans to the media.

The media got in to act. Some reporters visited Sultanpur and got the whole story about the school and Santhi. The hungry media flashed the story in the headlines. President was shocked to read the news. He wanted to control the damage caused by the news He immediately called for a news conference and explained

"I never asked Mansoor to spy in India. I turned down his request for help and it made him angry and uttered this baseless allegation. I wanted his help to understand India. He mistook it as spying. Any way I will meet him and clear his misunderstanding" Mushraf made his damage control statement.

Next day day he invited Mansoor and told him

"I thought that whatever we have talked was confidential. I never expected you to reveal the conversation to the media. Any way! Forget what happened. I agree to restore the financial support to the school. Go back to Kuwait peacefully. You have accomplished your mission. By the by I expect you to withdraw your allegation against me in the media" Mushraf made it clear that his offer was conditional.

Mansoor consulted Santhi. She told him to accept the offer. She said

"We should not forget our mission. Sometimes we have to compromise with truth to achieve something good for the society" she consoled him

17

LIFE IN PAKISTAN 2002 TO 2008

Mansoor returned to Kuwait in 2003. USA and UK occupied Iraq. A civil war broke out in Iraq. The militant group supported by Iraq fought against coalition forces. There was conflict between Shias and Sunnies. There was conflict between Kurdish war groups and the interim government. There was chaos inside Iraq. Nobody felt safe inside Iraq. Bomb blast and killing were everyday affair.

A total 4446 U S solders were killed between 2003 and 2012. As per WIKI LEAKS total death in the civil war in Iraq was 109302 As per Lancet survey there was 601027 violent deaths. There was no accurate figure on the number of injured in the conflict. It could be anywhere between half million to one million. Billions of dollars were spent on this war. Yet nothing was achieved by USA except hanging of Saddam Hussein. In the history no country ever spent so much money and killed so many millions for the sake of one person. The irony was that it was committed by the super power which has the responsibility to protect weak countries against their strong enemies.

Kuwaitis were happy that Saddam was removed. But they were not happy about the price paid in terms of civilian and military casualities. In private conversation they criticized America. But in the public no body dared to oppose USA since Kuwait depended on USA for their security.

Mansoor was aware of this predicament. But Santhi was bold enough to express her opinion against Arab countries. One day three friends visited her boss. As usual the conversation turned towards politics.

"American economy would get a big hit due to Iraqi invasion. It was forced to foot the bill on behalf of coalition forces. We expected Kuwait and Saudi Arabia to be pleased with our job and open their purse. No such thing happened. Bush was personally rewarded by Kuwait but nothing to our country" said the American friend.

"U K supported America when Germany, France, Russia, Japan, China and India did not support. We proved to be the special ally of America. Yet Kuwait is not ready to give any special treatment to UK." British friend.expressed his disappointment.

"Don't forget we have parliament and laws which the King and the Prime minister cannot overrule. Kuwait has done whatever it could do. USA never asked us before invading Iraq. Invasion was the decision of USA. Kuwait was only informed of the decision. We knew the true motive of Bush behind his decision to invade Iraq. Kuwait could not be blamed if America got in to trouble in Iraq" Kuwaiti friend defended his country's policy.

At that moment Santhi entered in to the Cabin with tea, coffee and Biscuits. As usual The British took black coffee, the American took Indian Tea and the Kuwaiti took Turkish coffee.

"Let us have some Indian wisdom in addition to the coffee and biscuit from Santhi. I know she is bold and out spoken" the boss invited Santhi to join the conversation.

"Kuwait business benefited financially from Iraqi invasion. It was a boon for its traders who sold goods at a good profit to Americans. But Kuwait suffered politically. Kuwait created a permanent enemy in Iraq. Kuwait may feel safe under the protection of USA. But every thing has a price tag attached to it. I do not know how long USA would protect Kuwait. We have a saying in India that we cannot choose our parents and neighbors and they cannot be wished away. In my opinion Kuwait should help Iraq to restore its economy and pave the way for a true democracy in Iraq. Only friendship with Iraq would help Kuwait in the long run" Santhi concluded.

"Once again she proved that she is a wise Indian. I accept that she argued for Iraq convincingly. I am sure she would prove to be a great politician if She enters politics" the boss praised Santhi.

*   *   *

Santhi did not enter in to politics. But the fate dragged Mansoor in to politics. When Santhi returned from her office she saw Mansoor telling stories to their Children.

"What are the stories you tell our children?. I brought the story book Pancha thantra. You can read the stories from this book and tell them. They are interesting and educative" Santhi said and placed the story book on the table and went inside to prepare some coffee and snacks for the children.

She came back with coffee and two plates of samosa for the children. The conversation was resumed by Mansoor.

"I will read this book later. I am worried that our nation is going to dogs. Look at the political parties in Pakistan. The leader of PPP, Benazir is in exile in Dubai and another leader of PML(N) Nawaz Sheriff is in exile in Saudi Arabia. Now Zardari was released from jail. He joined his wife and children in Dubai. President Mushraf, the dictator is accepted by the world including India as the legitimate ruler of Pakistan. Probably the world has come to the conclusion that Pakistan can never get truly elected democratic government. Pakistan is destined to be ruled only by Generals either in uniform or in civilian dress. I am not able to digest this. I pray Allah to change this situation" Mansoor lamented.

"God helps only those who help themselves. Things do not change by silent prayers. Change takes place by words or deeds. If you want a change you have to speak the right words at the right place at the right time or you may have to jump in to action." Santhi said philosophically.

"I want my country to be ruled by democratically elected government. I don't mind whether it is PPP or NML (N) or Tahrek-e-Insaf (party of Imran Khan) or MQM. I know that all the politicians are corrupt. But a corrupt democratic government is any day better than dictatorship. Even a benevolent dictatorship would turn in to corrupt one over a period of time. During a civil war a military government may be required to bring orderliness to the nation. Once the order is restored the country should be ruled by a democratic government. If the democratic government is proved to be corrupt then it is the fault of the people who elected government. Any way people may learn to elect a good government after some trial and error" Mansoor spoke his mind.

"The people of Pakistan were helpless because the elections conducted in the past were neither fair nor free. They were always rigged to suit the army. Pakistanis almost reconciled that they have to live with the military governments or military supported governments" Santhi explained.

"Do you have any idea what trigger would force Mushraf to order a free election in Pakistan?" asked Mansoor.

"Either the Judiciary in Pakistan should revolt against Mushraf or all the major political parties should join together and oppose Mushraf" suggested Santhi in her wisdom.

"Do you think that judiciary would ever revolt?"

"May be if they are personally threatened" predicted Santhi

"Do you think that major political parties in Pakistan would ever join together to fight Mushraf?"

"They have already done and formed Alliance for Restoring Democracy in January 2003. Both Benazir and Nawaz Sheriff are living a bomb throw away from you. Why don't you meet them and discuss the subject?" Santhi jokingly asked.

"Why not! What do I loose? Nothing! Let me pull the mountain with my hair. If the mountain moves, it is a credit to me. Otherwise I may loose my hair. I may get back my hair within few months. O K! Let me try my luck" inspired by the joke Mansoor spoke enthusiastically.

Nextday he went to Pakistan Embassy and got the residential addresses of Benazir Butto and Nawaz Sheriff. He decided to go to Dubai first to meet Benazir. When he applied for visa he used his trust name to get a visa. He got appointments from both of them through email. Both of them were ready to meet anybody from Pakistan. Both of them were missing Pakistan. They would love to talk to somebody from Pakistan.

Benazir lived in her family home in Dubai with her children and mother. When Mansoor reached Dubai Zardhari too joined the family. When Mansoor met Benazir, her husband and mother too joined the conversation.

"Welcome Mansoor Bhai! I heard about your wife from the media and Asma Jahangir. I remember I have done some favor to your trust. I hope that you will not ask anymore favor from me because I am not in power." jokingly Benazir began conversation.

"Now I have an opportunity to thank you for your help. Do you know that the grant was cancelled by Musharaf. I had to fight all the way through media to get back the grant from the government" Mansoor briefed the news.

"Thank Allah! You were lucky to live in Kuwait. Otherwise he would have found out some excuse to put you jail" Zardhari intervened and commented about Mushraf.

"I have come on a mission as per my wife's advice to meet you. I am an ordinary citizen of Pakistan. I do not know whether I have the credentials to make such a proposal to restore democracy" Mansoor hesitatingly opened the topic.

"I am already aware of Alliance for restoration of democracy in Pakistan. I am ready to join hands even with devils for that purpose." Benazir spoke without any hesitation.

"PPP and PML(N) are the two major political parties in Pakistan. Each should not consider the other as rival. Once both of you have good understand and join other smaller parties can not dictate the agenda." Mansoor submitted his proposal and waited for a response from Benazir.

"If this idea came from your wife it must be good. I accept it. But I do not know how to implement the same. Do you have any idea?" Benazir asked

"Of course I have done my home work. I have an appointment with Nawaz Sherif during this week" Mansoor clarified.

"What are you waiting for? Jump in to the plane. I think Sheriff is living in Riyadh. Convey my regards to Sheriff Bhai" she bid farewell to Mansoor.

It was not an easy task for Mansoor to meet Nawaz Sheriff. Saudi security was very tight. Saudi intelligence agencies asked many questions about his motives. He did not want divulge his proposal. He was not sure whether Saudi would go against Musharaf. Saudi Arabia is not famous for its democratic credentials. However they were sympathetic about his request to collect funds for his trust. So they allowed him to meet Mian Shahib Nawab Sheriff at his residence.

Nawab Sherif lived with his family of eighteen in a house provided by the Saudi Government. When Mansoor met Sherif, he was alone and no body was with him. It appeared to Mansoor that Sherif was not keeping good health. May be he was mentally depressed.

"Salaam Alaikum Mansoor Bhai. I am happy to see some body from Pakistan. How is the situation in Pakistan. It appears that Cow boy Mush is getting entrenched in his Chair. I do not think Mush will ever order an election in Pakistan. If he does it may be rigged" Nawaz spoke in a distressed tone.

"There is always light at the end of the tunnel. Every thing has an end. So is the dictatorship in Pakistan. I have a good message for you. I met Benazir only few days ago. She agreed to cooperate with you to fight the general election. If you ok my proposal I will proceed in this matter. Probably I may have to take some help from US embassy. They may not directly help me. I have some friends in US embassy. They may guide me in this matter. I am new in this business of Backroom diplomacy" Mansoor presented his proposal.

"I do not know how to thank you. Insah Allah! He will help you to succeed in your mission. I think it is better to have a written agreement between us" Nawaz assured his cooperation for the mission. Mansoor felt satisfied and left Riyadh on the same day.

Mansoor waited for an opportunity to meet a proper person in PPP who commands respect from all political parties in Pakistan. He found that senior vice Chairman of PPP MAKHDOOM AMIN FAHIM to be the correct person to bring Benazir and Nawaz together against Mushraf. He met him at his Karachi residence and explained his proposal

He welcomed his initiative and said

"Pres. Mushraf is playing his innings successfully because the opposition bowlers are weak. Before we stage our struggle we should wait for the adversary to commit a mistake. We should take advantage of his mistake and strike him with our full force. Both Benazir and Sherif are sitting outside the country. They cannot mobilize the people. The people should rise spontaneously and revolt against Mushraf. At that time if we strike we may succeed. Keep the dialogue going between two. At the right time we will arrange the meeting between the two leaders."

Alliance for Restoration of Democracy

ARD was formed in January 2003. The important components of this alliance were PPP, PML(N), PML(Q) and Pakistan Democratic Party. There were 11 smaller parties representing ethnic groups joined ARD at a later date.

The first leader of the ARD was Nawabzada Nasrullah Khan, who was also the leader of the Pakistan Democratic Party (PDP). Following Khan's death in September 2003, a new position of president was established to "balance the two major components of the alliance, the PPP and the PML-N". Accordingly, on 8th October 2003, Javed Hashmi, acting leader of the PML-N was elected as president of the ARD, while Makhdoom Amin Fahim of the PPP was elected chairman of the ARD. In March 2005, Fahim was reported to be the chairman of the ARD and in January 2005, Hashmi continued to be the leader of the ARD.

The aims of the ARD include the following:

(1) To restore democracy.
(2) To restore the 1973 constitution.
(3) To remove the Legal Framework Order
(4) To remove President Musharraf from the military if he is going to continue in the role of President

A golden opportunity knocked at the door of ARD, when Mushraf dismissed the Supreme court Chief Justice Iftikhar Mohamed Choudhry on March 9th 2007. He was replaced by Acting Chief Justice Javed Iqbal. This triggered a countrywide protest by the lawyers. The lawyers were supported by the opposition parties.

In July 2007 Mushraf government demolished Lal Masjid on the pretext that it was illegal construction. If the government applies this rule almost half the buildings especially the mosques were to be demolished. The real reason was Musraf depended on the religious parties for his survival. Emboldened religious organizations started running a parallel government within Pakistan. Musharaf felt that the dog reared for biting the enemy started biting the master. He said enough is enough and took action against Lal Masjid to show the religious organizations their place in the country. By his action against Lal Masjid, Mushraf lost the support of Religious parties. Economy of Pakistan was not doing well. So he could not get support from the public.

To control the agitations President Musharaf declared emergency on 3-11-2007 and later it was lifted on 15-12-2007. During the emergency period he gave up the post of Army Chief on 28-11-2007 and declared his intensions to contest the election. But things became too hot for Mushraf. USA sensing the mood of the public and political parties, forced Mushraf to lift the emergency and conduct the poll at the earliest. Accordingly the general election scheduled in January 2008 was postponed to 15-2-2008.

18

GENERAL ELECTION 2008

On 3 November 2007, President and Chief of Army Staff Pervez Musharraf enacted a state of emergency. Election was initially postponed indefinitely. However, it was later stated it would be held as planned. On 8 November 2007, Musharraf announced that the election would be held by 15 February 2008. Following the assassination of Benazir Bhutto, the Election Commission announced, after a meeting in Islamabad, that a 8th January vote was no longer possible and the election would take place on 18 February.

A **general election** was held in Pakistan on 18 February 2008, after being postponed from 8 January 2008. The original date was intended to elect members of the National Assembly of Pakistan, the lower house of the Majlis-e-Shoora. Pakistan's two main opposition parties, the Pakistan Peoples Party (PPP) and the Pakistan Muslim League (N) (PML (N)) won the majority of seats in the election. The PPP and PML(N) formed the new coalition government with Yosuf Raza Gilani as Prime Minister of Pakistan.

Following the election, Musharraf acknowledged that the process had been free and fair. He conceded the defeat of the PML (Q) (the party which supported Mushraf) and pledged to work with the new Parliament. The voter turnout for the election was 35,170,435 people (44%). Bye elections for 28 seats (23 provincial and 5 national) have been delayed number of times. They were held on 26 June 2008.

PPP got 120 seats in the national assembly and PML(n) got 90. Total number of seats was 337. PPP won majority in Sind province, PML(N) in Punjab province, NAP in North West Frontier and PML (Q) in Baluchistan

Yousuf raza Gilani (of PPP) was elected as Prime minister.

Pakistani presidential election, 2008

On 28th August the Election Commission of Pakistan announced that five people had been validly nominated as candid for the post of President:

o   Asif Ali Zardari, PPP
o   Saeeduzzaman Siddiqui, supported by the PML-N
o   Mushahid Hussain, PML-Q
o   Faryal Talpur, covering candidate for Zardari
o   Roedad Khan covering candidate for Siddiqui

On 30 August, Talpur and Roedad withdrew their candidacies.

Zardhari got 481 electoral vote against 153 votes received by his nearest rival Siddiqui supported by PML(N). Zardhari was declared elected by the election Commission. He was supported by the following parties

1.PPP 2. Jamiat Ulema-e-Islam 3 Awami National Party 4.MQM .5 All Party Minority Alliance

By the end of August 2008 Zardhari was sworn in as the 11th President of Pakistan by Mushraf.

19

LIFE IN PAKISTAN 2008-2013

When Mushraf declared emergency on 3-11-2007 Mansoor felt that time has come for him to jump in to action to save the country from the Dictator. He sought the advice from his wife. She said

"I appreciate your patriotism. Now our sons Ram and Rahim are 18 and 17 years old. They can take care of themselves. In fact at this age boys prefer to be away from their father. I don't think they will miss you if you go to Pakistan to enter politics. You should promise that you will visit us whenever we need you"

"I promise! I am only a phone call away from you. But you should also make a promise. I want your advice and if necessary your presence in Pakistan. I am better known as husband of Santhi. Your presence may help me to attract the media." Mansoor requested.

"Sure! I will. You have to give me at least a week's notice to arrange for air tickets"

"In that case you have to buy a season ticket between Kuwait and Karachi" Mansoor joked.

"Don't make me a VIP. I know what happened to Benazir. I want to live for another 10 years and see our sons get married" worried Santhi replied.

Mansoor left Kuwait in the month of Novemeber 2007 to join main stream Pakistan politics. Before going to Sultanpur he met Makhdoom Amin Fahim, the current Chairman of PPP in Karachi. The reason why Mansoor chose to take advice from Fahim was that he was the only decent politician he knew.

Known as a humble politician, Makhdoom entered in the political arena in 1970 when he was elected as Member National Assembly from southern district of Thatta in Sindh province. Since then, he has contested eight elections from elections held in 1977, 1988, 1990, 1993, 1997, 2002, 2008, remaining undefeated and creating a national record. Makhdoom Amin Fahim, however, boycotted the non-party elections of 1985 held by General Muhammad Zia-ul-Haq-led military regime in line with the decision of his party. In 1993 he contested as MPA and MNA, and was the only Parliamentarian in Pakistan to win both seats unopposed. After that he gave up the MPA seat to his younger brother and he won unopposed.

Makhdoom was offered the post of Prime Minister in 2002 by then President Gen. Pervez Musharraf, keeping in mind his party's leader Benazir Bhutto's refusal to appoint Mr. Amin Fahim's son Makhdoom Jameel Zaman as the Chief Minister of Sindh. He was offered the post of Prime Minister twice before in 1988-1990 and 1993. He remained loyal to his party and did not accept offers from then Prime Minister Nawaz Sharif and the military dictators. Makhdoom Amin Fahim was the senior vice-chairman of PPP, and was the Parliamentary Leader, (President) of the same party in the National Assembly. He was twice the Federal Minister during the tenure of Benazir Bhutto. He was Communications Minister from December 1988 to August 1990, Railways Minister from December 1988 to March 1989. In the next tenure, he was the Minister for Housing and Works from January 1994 to November 1996.

*   *   *

Due to the inflow of funds from gulf countries the school and hospital started by Mansoor made him a VIP in and around his village. He would be welcome to join any party he liked. PML(N) was more popular in Punjab province than PPP. That was the reason why PPP was interested in roping in Mansoor in to the party. Fahim advised Mansoor to join PPP and he assured him a proper position at the district level after General election. Mansoor joind PPP at the time the agitation by the lawyers against Mushraf was in full swing.

Mansoor was offered a ticket in the Punjab provincial election by PPP. However he declined the offer. He knew that PPP would not come to power in Punjab. He was sure of his victory in Punjab provincial Assembly.But he did not want to sit in the opposition. He felt that he would better spend his time in social work and help the people. But he predicted a landslide victory for PPP in the National Assembly due to sympathy wave created by the assassination of Benazir Butto.

During the campaign in the general election in 2008 he worked hard for all the PPP Candidates. Every body acknowledged that but for his work PPP could not have won so many seats (more than expected) in Punjab. Every body expected that he would be rewarded in some form or other at the National level. But Mansoor wanted Makhdoom Amin Fahim to become the Prime Minister of Pakistan. He was known supporter of Makhdoom He felt that he was the only honest politician in Pakistan and he deserved the post. He lobbied with all PPP members of National Assembly to get Fahim elected as P.M.

There was overwhelming support among the members of the National Assembly to elect Makhdoom Amin Fahim as the Prime Minister. But the Cochairman Zardari wanted a loyal and amenable leader as the Prime minister. Zardhari was afraid of the court cases pending against him. If Fahim were appointed as Prime Minister, being an honest politician he would not hesitate to allow the law to take its own course. His decency and honesty stopped Fahim from the post of Prime Minister.

On 22 March 2008, after weeks of consideration, the elite members of the Central Executive Committee presided by Asif Ali Zardhari accepted the nomination of Gillani over populist Ameen Faheem for the post of prime minister. Meanwhile, the Pakistan Peoples Party completed consultations and negotiations with the other parties to form a coalition alliance and the alliance endorsed the nomination of Gilani. On 22nd March at 9:38 PM Islamabad, Gillani was officially announced by the Peoples Party as its candidate for the premiership of the country. Many analysts said that they would not be surprised if Zardari succeeded Gillani after a few months. But Zardhari confirmed that he was not interested in the job of prime minister and that Gillani would serve until 2013 as P.M. Speculation that Zardhari might be gunning for the premiership grew stronger when he picked the less popular Gillani over Ameen Faheem, a much powerful member of the central executive committee.

On 24th March 2008, Gillani was elected as Prime Minister by Parliament, defeating his rival, Chaudhry Pervaiz Elahi of the PML-Q, by a score of 264 to 42. He was sworn in by Musharraf on the next day. On 29th March, he won a unanimous vote of confidence in Parliament. He became the 16th Prime minister of Pakistan

Profile of Yousaf Raza Gillani

Yousuf Raza Gilani was born in Karachi (9th June 1952).Gillani's political career started in the military government of President General Zia-ul-Haq in 1978, after he joined as a member of the Central Working Committee (CWC) of the Pakistan Muslim League (PML), alongside industrialist Nawaz Sharif. He soon left the PML, because of political differences with the PML's leadership. He was chosen by General Zia-ul-Haq as a nominee for public servant work in Multan. In 1983, Gillani became chairman of the Multan union council.

He first ran in non-partisan and technocratic 1985 general elections and was elected as the Member of the National Assembly (MNA) from Lodhran, but was later affiliated with the Pakistan Peoples Party after developing serious political differences with the Pakistan Muslim League (PML), led by conservative leader Fida Khan. The constituency seat was held by Saddique Baloch. Gillani fell out with Prime Minister Mohammad Junejo and was sidelined from the Pakistan Muslim League (PML) by the senior leadership. Later, he was ousted by Prime Minister Junejo and was replaced by other members. According to Gillani's personal account, he went to Karachi to meet with Benazir Bhutto during the 1980s and presented his political experience, wanting to join Peoples Party. After securing a party ticket and successfully running in the 1988 general elections, Gillani joined the first government of Prime Minister Benazir Bhutto and became minister of the Ministry of Tourism (MoT) in March 1989 until January 1990. Later he became minister of Ministry of Housing. Since then, he had been a senior member of parliament for the Multan District. After his party securing the plurality in the 1993 general elections, Gillani was elevated as the 15th Speaker of the National Assembly by the-Prime minister Benazir Bhutto, a post he held until 16 February 1997.

On 11th February 2001, Gillani was imprisoned in the infamous Adiala Jail by a military court instituted under President Pervez Musharraf on accusations and charges of corruption, and released on 7 October 2006.

After 2008 general elections he became the first prime minister from the Saraiki-speaking belt (Multan) and also held the distinction (thus far, the only prime minister to have achieve this milestone) for successfully presenting five consecutive federal budgets. As Prime minister, Gillani announced the formation of the Truth and Reconciliation Commission, rehabilitation of the troubled and war-torn tribal belt, and promised to reduce the federal budget deficit as well as announcing his ambition to improve the system of education. This was followed by announcing the new agriculture land and economic policy that lifted the ban on labour and students' unions. Also, his cabinet worked on a new energy and nuclear policy to tackle the energy crisis in the country. But his policies, without meaningful economic reforms, led to a high rise in inflation and sharp decline in economic performance, a period referred to as "Era of Stagflation"

In 2011, the relations with United States suffered a major set back and resentment when the United States unilaterally conducted a secret offence in Abbottabad, which resulted in successful execution of Osama Bin Laden. Immediately after learning the news, Gillani and President Zardari chaired a high level meeting with the senior military leadership in Islamabad. Gillani reportedly announced that: "We will not allow our soil to be used against any other country for terrorism and therefore, I think it's a great victory, it's a success and I congratulate the success of this operation." Later Gilani blamed the world for their failure to capture bin Laden. The relationship between Pakistan and the United States fell to a new low following the Salala Incident, with his government and the elite military establishment reassessing their diplomatic, political, military and intelligence relationship with the United States.

A consistently strong U.S. ally Gillani was ranked as 38th most powerful person in the world by *Forbes*. After years of confronting and resisting the Supreme Court of Pakistan rulings to reinstate the corruption cases against Benazir and Asif Zardari, he was convicted by the supreme court of violating the article 63(1)(g) of the constitution of Pakistan, on 26 April 2012. The verdict was rendered by the Supreme Court when it found him the guilty of contempt of court for refusing to reopen corruption cases against president Asif Ali Zardhari, but it gave him only a symbolic sentence "till the rising of the court", a sentence lasting 30 seconds. Finally, on 19th June 2012, he was disqualified and ousted by the Supreme Court from holding the prime minister office, with the Chief Justice Iftikhar Chaudhry clarifying that: "Gillani had ceased to be the prime minister and is disqualified from membership of parliament on 26 April 2012, the date of his conviction". Thus Gillani's political carrier came to an end in an unceremonious way.

Pakistan"s Relationship with India during Gillani's Period

Mushraf played a double game. He wanted to show to the people of Pakistan that he was doing all that was possible to improve the relation with India. But in private he supported the militant groups through ISI. India wanted Pakistan to deport 20 criminals (including Dawood Ibrahim, Chota Shakeel) wanted in India in many criminal cases. But Pakistan refused to cooperate with India to extradite them. Pakistan maintained that they were not in Pakistan soil.

Gillani followed the same policy. When Mumbai attack took place, India and USA provided solid evidence to show that it was planned by ISI and executed by Laskar-e-Toiba. But he did not own the responsibility. He tried to defend the position of his country and made only some vague promise that his country would bring the culprits to justice if sufficient evidence was provided against the perpetrators of the crime. The accused roamed freely in Pakistan and they were allowed to make inflammatory speech against India. Pakistan tried unsuccessfully to disown Kasab who was caught and sentenced to death by Indian Court. In February 2013 he was executed by India.

Relationship withAfghanistan

Since assuming office of the premier, Gillani was planning to visit neighboring Afghanistan but some unresolved issues like absence of a joint platform to discuss bilateral issues, border conflicts, and different views on the war on terror prevented the trip. Gillani visited Afghanistan with Chief of Army Staff General Ashfaq Pervez Kayani and ISI Director-General Lieutenant-General Ahmed Shuja Pasha. After successful dialogue, it was mutually decided to form a Reconciliation Committee headed by foreign ministers of both the countries.

On 22 December 2011, Gillani told the audience at the National Gallery that conspirators were plotting to bring down his government.

Economic Policy of Pakistan under Gillani

After 2008, the value of US Dollar increased as compared to Pakistani Rupee, indicating the country's return to "Era of Stagflation" (a virtual period faced by Pakistan in 1990s).

In his first days of government, Gillani attempted to continue the Privatization programme of Shaukat Aziz, but the programme was abruptly terminated after the global recession took a sharp rise, and a severe financial crisis hit the country's economy. Gillani accepted the resignation of two Finance ministers and surprisingly appointed the former minister of privatization and investment in the government of Shaukat Aziz, Dr. Abdul Hafeez Shaikh as a new Finance Minister. Attempts to discontinue the nationalisation programme by Gillani's government was abandoned and instead replaced it with a new system based on state capitalism. The state-owned corporations were set off to privatization menu and his government approved a new menu of privatization based on public private partnership (PPP) with transfer of management control and 26% shares of 21 state owned enterprises (SOEs). No timetable was given. Instead his government announced that the privatization process would be completed when international market revived. During his first year of government, Gillani's government obtained unprecedented loans from International Monetary Fund which increased the level of poverty in the country.

20

MANSOOR'S POLITICAL CARRIER

M ansoor's political carrier started in 2007 just before the general election. His contribution to the success of PPP candidates in Punjab province was not recognized by top leadership in PPP due to internal politics. More over his lobbying with MNA members to support Fahim for Prime Ministership annoyed Zardhari and he was not interested to give him any responsibility to Mansoor in the party as expected. After the election of Prime Minister, disappointed Mansoor met Amin Fahim at his residence. He was welcome by Fahim. Both discussed about the future.

"Mubarak! Gillani offered you the post of Commerce Minister. Are you going to accept the post" enquired Mansoor.

"I am a disciplined solder of PPP. Therefore I have to accept. More over I was not after any particular post. In the past I have twice declined the post of Prime Minister. To serve the people of Pakistan one need not necessarily be the Prime Minister. As far as I am concerned I can serve them even as an ordinary citizen of this country. We should never seek any post. They should come to us. Only then we can feel that we are recognized. It is easy to preach. I know your pain that your good work is not recognized. This is normal in politics. Do not loose hope. A time will come and your good work would be recognized." consoled Fahim

"Bilaval is too young to be the leader of a political party. I am not happy to serve Asif Ali Zardhari. He is known as Mr. Ten percent. When people criticize him I am not able to defend my leader. I move with people at the grass root level. In these circumstances I can not work for my party whole heartedly. Please advise me what I should do?" Mansoor requested.

"I understand your dilemma. You have three options before you. You can join a political party which you think is good enough for you. You can start your own party. You may renounce politics and continue your social work. Choice is yours. Any way, consult your wife before taking any decision. She is wiser than me" advised Fahim.

"Of course I will not take any decision without consulting Santhi. I will book air ticket for Santhi immediately" said Mansoor and took leave.

Santhi reached Sultanpur within few days. They discussed about their future. Mansoor explained what Fahim has advised.

"What he said is correct. I do not know why Fahim, a man of principles agreed to work under Gillani who is well known for his corruption. He should have come out of PPP and started a new party and I am sure that his image would have gone up. By accepting the post of Commerce Minister he degraded himself and lost an opportunity to play an important role in the Pakistan politics. What is your opinion about Imran Khan?" Santhi suddenly switched the topic

"Imran Khan has many faces. He is farmer Cricketer, commentator, writer, columnist, philanthropist, educationist, social activist and the last but not the least an unsuccessful politician. On the negative side he has a play boy image. He calls himself a liberal which means anti-religious in Pakistan.As far as his religious belief is concerned he is a confused man. As a cricketer he is a legend in Pakistan. He was very successful as a cricket commentator, writer, educationist and columnist. But as politician so far he has not made a big impact in Pakistan politics" Mansoor gave a brief profile of Imran Khan.

"You have some influence only in Punjab province and nothing in other provinces. Therefore starting a party on your own will not work out. You have to join some political party. You joined PPP because of Benazir and Fahim. Now your equation with Bilaval and zardhari is not good. Therefore you have to quit. Next option is PML(n). Its leader is corrupt and he has soft corner for fundamentalist forces. PML(N) is rulled out. PML(Q) is supporter of Mushraf. MQM and ANP are only a regional parties. The only National party worth joining is PTI (The party of Imran Khan). Therefore I advise you to join PTI and grow with Imran. The age is an advantage for Imran. He is not accused of any corruption. He is not a fundamentalist. He favors a peaceful settlement of Kashmir issue with India. I do not find any reason why he should not be future P.M of Pakistan when younger generation joins the voter list. As per his wife's advice Mansoor joined PTI. He was appointed as district president in the Punjab province.

In 1996, Khan founded his political party, Pakistan Tehreek-e-Insaf (PTI), which emphasized on anti-corruption policies. The newly formed party was unable to win a seat during the 1997 Pakistani general election. Khan supported General Pervez Musharraf's military coup in 1999, believing Musharraf would end corruption and clear out the political mafias. According to Khan, he was Musharraf's choice of prime minister in 2002 but he turned down the offer. The 2002 Pakistani general election were held in October across 272 constituencies. Khan anticipated a good show in the elections and was prepared to form a coalition government if his party did not get a majority. He was elected from the NA-71 constituency of Mianwali and being the only party member to have secured a seat, PTI won only 0.8% of the popular vote. Khan was sworn in as an MP on 16 November 2002. He remained part of the Standing Committees on Kashmir and Public accounts and expressed legislative interest in Foreign Affairs, Education and Justice.

On 6 May 2005, Khan became one of the first Muslim figures to criticize the alleged desecration of the Qur'an in a U.S. military prison at the Guantánamo Bay Naval Base in Cuba. Khan held a press conference and demanded that Gen. Pervez Musharraf secure an apology from the American president George W. Bush for the incident. In June 2007, the federal Parliamentary Affairs Minister Dr. Sher Afgan Khan Niazi and the Muttahida Qaumi Movement (MQM) party filed separate ineligibility references against Khan, asking for his disqualification as member of the National Assembly on grounds of immorality. Both references, filed on the basis of articles 62 and 63 of the Constitution of Pakistan, were rejected on 5th September 2005.

On 2nd October 2007, as part of the All Parties Democratic Movement, Imran Khan joined 85 other MPs to resign from Parliament in protest to the presidential election scheduled on 6th October 2007, in which General Musharraf was contesting without resigning as army chief. On 3rd November 2007, Khan was put under house arrest at his father's home hours after president Musharraf declared a state of emergency in Pakistan. Khan had demanded the death penalty for Musharraf after the imposition of emergency rule, which he equated to "committing treason". The next day, on 4th November, Khan escaped and went into hiding. He eventually came out of hiding on 14th Novemebr to join a student protest at the University of the Punjab. At the rally, Khan was captured by students from the Jamaat-i-Islami political party, who claimed that Khan was an uninvited nuisance at the rally, and they handed him over to the police, who charged him under the Anti-terrorism act for allegedly inciting people to pick up arms, calling for civil disobedience, and for spreading hatred.

On 30th October 2011, Khan changed the political picture of the country by addressing more than 100,000 supporters in Lahore, challenging the policies of the current government, calling this new change a "tsunami" against the ruling parties, followed by another successful public gathering of 250,000 supporters in Karachi on 25 December 2011. Since then Imran Khan has become a real threat for the current ruling parties and future political prospect in Pakistan. According to International Republican Institute (IRI)'s survey, Imran Khan's Pakistan Tehreek-e-Insaf (PTI) tops the list of popular parties in Pakistan both at the national as well as provincial level, leaving Pakistan Muslim League-Nawaz(PML-N) and Pakistan People's Party(PPP) behind. On 30 June 2012, It was because of the principled stance of Pakistan Tehreek-e-Insaf (PTI) chief Imran Khan on the critical issues faced by the country that a survey conducted by an international research organisation has found him the most popular leader of the country, the party said in a statement on Friday. According to a survey conducted by the Pew Research Centre under its Global Attitudes project, the PTI chief had 70 percent approval ratings, moving up the list by 18 percentage points over the past two years. In 2010, his ratings stood at 52 percent.

On 6 October 2012, Khan led a vehicle caravan of protesters from Islamabad to the village of Kotai in Pakistan's South Waziristan region. The purpose of this demonstration was to protest U.S. drone missile strikes against Islamic militants in Pakistan's tribal regions. Khan was joined by a number of Americans, including members of Code Pink, a U.S. based anti-drone activist group. Some observers suggested that part of Khan's motivation for the public rally was to build support for his PTI party ahead of national elections in 2013.

Khan's proclaimed political platform and declarations include Islamic values, to which he rededicated himself in the 1990s; liberal economics, with the promise of deregulating the economy and creating a welfare state; decreased bureaucracy and the implementation of anti-corruption laws, to create and ensure a clean government; the establishment of an independent judiciary; overhaul of the country's police system; and an anti-militant vision for a democratic Pakistan.

Khan told Britain's *Daily Telegraph* "I want Pakistan to be a welfare state and a genuine democracy with a rule of law and an independent judiciary." Other ideas he has presented include a requirement of all students to spend a year after graduation teaching in the countryside and cutting down the over-staffed bureaucracy in order to send them to teach too. "We need decentralization, empowering people at the grass roots," he has said. Recently, he was threatened of death by the Pakistani Taliban (PTT) if he went ahead with his march to their tribal stronghold along the Afghan border because he called himself a liberal. After the 2008 general elections, political columnist Azam Khalil addressed Khan as one of the "utter failures in Pakistani politics".

Pakistan Military was eager to see that the incumbent Prime Minister should not weaken the military. Imran stated in his interview that he is against the Drone attack inside Pakistan that killed many civilians. He wanted a stronger Pakistan Army fight the militants on its own without the help of USA. This statement made Imran Khan as the darling of Military.

Forty percent of the population is below 25. This younger generation is not interested in Religion. They are crazy about cricket. For these young people Imran is a hero and savior. In the coming general election in May 2013 these people are expected to vote for PTI.on a large scale. That is why Imran Khan predicts a landslide victory for his party in the national and provincial election.2013

Only PML(N), PPP and PTI are nationalist parties. The public image of Zardhari, Nawaz Sheriff have a taken beating during the last five years. Nawaz Sheriff's rating in Punjab has increased marginally. But his rating in other provinces has gone down dramatically canceling any advantage he may derive in Punjab. The popular rating for PPP has gone down in all the provinces. In 2008 PPP won on sympathy vote after assassination of Benazir. In 2013 it may loose that advantage. Instead PPP may loose further ground due to the mishandling of Judiciary and the pending criminal cases against Zardhari and Gillani. Deterioting economy may add to the woes of PPP. More over Pakistan never returned the ruling party to power due to incumbency factor.

Imran Khan was sure of his victory in Sind, Khyber Phaktoon and Balochistan. But he knew that PML(N) was strong in Punjab. He was sure that he can swing the votes in Multan (He is a Pustun from Multan). He wanted a strong man to support him in Punjab. He selected Mansoor as his strong man in Punjab. He was made in charge of Punjab province. Media speculated he would be made a minister if Imran Khan formed the next Government in Islamabad.

21

GENERAL ELECTION MAY 2013

The 2013 election in Pakistan was around the corner, and this was the time when all the political parties start their struggles to gain popular support. However, the voting behavior of the people depends on various factors.

Firstly, party affiliation holds a significant number of people to vote for the party they had been affiliated with, no matter what the circumstances are and how successful was the party in governance or opposition. Secondly, the leadership of a party also plays a crucial role in shaping voting behavior. The charisma of the leader is a compelling factor that leads the public to vote for his party and bring him in power. Zulfiqar Ali Bhutto gained popular support not because of the manifesto of his party, but it was his charismatic personality and powerful communication and oratory skills that brought People's Party in power in the 1970 general elections.

Thirdly, the candidates chosen from different electorates and their agendas to overcome the issues of their respective community are also liable to shape the voting behavior. Most of the time people don't consider the manifesto of the political party important, because for them their prime issues hold greater importance. During the election speeches and public rallies, the major portion of a candidate's speech was focused on what his agenda was for his community, and the candidates promise for the development of their constituencies.

Finally, people have strong attachment with their ethnicities, and they tend to vote for the candidates belonging to their ethnic group in their electorates. ANP has always enjoyed winning a few seats from Karachi because of the Pathan minority residing in Karachi who tend to affiliate themselves with the Pathan nationalism.

Given these three variant factors of voting behavior, predicting results of the 2013 elections was not an easy task. Chairman Pakistan Tehreek e Insaf Mr Imran Khan was very hopeful that his party would sweep the upcoming elections. No doubt he has a charismatic personality and the way he has led the political campaign across the country to gain public support was commendable. But that alone was not the deciding factor. Despite the fact that seeing his successful political gatherings, many renowned politicians have joined his party which has boosted PTI's position, a lot needs to be done. There is no specific voting bank of PTI. Throughout the electoral history, the two major ruling parties PPP and PML-N have enjoyed popular support in their electorates. Punjab has always remained a voting hub for PML-N and rural Sindh for PPP. Similarly MQM has always enjoyed power monopoly over Karachi and Hyderabad, the Muhajir majority regions. The electoral history clearly indicates that interior Sindh and rural Punjab has always served as a hub for PPP, Urban Sindh for MQM and Urban Punjab for PML-N. Khyber Pakhtunkhwa and Baluchistan had shown varied support. In 2008 elections, MQM won 51 out of 166 seats in the Sind assembly and 25 seats in the National assembly. Out of the 25 seats, 18 parliamentarians were elected from Urban Sindh. The statistics reveal no different results in the previous elections either. In 2002, MQM won 17 seats in the parliament, 13 from Urban Sindh.

Considering these statistics, predicting that PTI would clean sweep the 2013 election is an overstretched perception. To win a considerable number of seats, Baluchistan and Hazara Division can serve as potential electoral hubs, as these regions have always shown varied results. PTI's support in Punjab has increased drastically over the past few months to make the environment competitive. It is yet to challenge the monopoly of PML-(N) in Punjab and that of PPP in interior Sindh. For PTI to win a clear majority, first, they need to focus on the neutral electoral zones which have shown varied results. Second, they need to come up with some thought provocative policies for overcoming the prevalent issues, and third, they need to create a strong electoral base.

Imran Khan was confident of his victory. So he decided to go alone without any coalition arrangement. Only in Punjab he was not sure of his victory. He expected that ANP and MQM would retain their seats. He hoped that all the youngsters who joined electoral list would vote for him. PPP lost popularity even in Sind province which was its strong hold in all the elections. PTI expected PPP supporters in Sind and Punjab would vote for him in large numbers. Imran attracted more crowd as the election date approached. Military was ready to support him if he won the election. He wanted the educated electorate, woman and the young come out in large numbers and vote for him. Imran felt that a higher turn out will benefit him to sweep the election. He wanted the turn out to be more than 60%. Only when the turn out is more than 60%, Pakistan would get truly a representative government.

He promised the following to the people of Pakistan in his manifesto

1. He would give top priority to education and increase the allocation four fold. Importance would be given women's education.
2. He would make the military strong and strengthen the fire power of military so that it would be in a position to fight the Taliban without any help from USA.
3. He would encourage FDI from overseas Pakistanis by offering suitable incentives
4. He would copy the Bihar model for economic development.
5. He would prevail over Obama to stop the Drone attacks and start the dialogue process with tribal people in Waziristan and FATA area.
6. He would route out corruption in Pakistan within 3 months
7. He will cut down all unnecessary expenditure in the government. He expects to cut 10% every year by reducing the government staff either by voluntary retirement or by abolishing posts.
8. He will see that all the rich people pay their taxes. Strict action will be taken against tax evaders.
9. He will give free education and health care to the people who live below poverty line.
10. He will take serious steps to improve the relations with the neighbors especially India and Afghanistan.
11. He will establish an Islamic Wefare state in a New Pakistan

PTI released its manifesto with these Eleven Point program. People from all walks of life appreciated the manifesto especially the poor and the young. More and more people started joining PTI as the election date approached. Opinion polls predicted a close neck to neck fight between PTI and PML(N). Some even predicted that PTI would be the single largest party slightly short of majority. Many predicted there would be coalition government headed by Imran Khan or Nawaz Sherrif after the election.

All the political pundits predicted victory for PML (N) in National assembly and Punjab provincial assembly based on the past data. But they added that PTI could be the dark horse.

The eyes of the whole world were focused on Pakistan Election. One thing was comman among all the nations concerned. They all wanted the Zardhari Government to go and a truly democratic government established. Every country especially India, USA, UK and Afghanistan wanted to see that Military and ISI influence was reduced after the election. They expected the new government to focus on development of Pakistan. They did not want Pakistan to behave as if it is the representative of Muslims in Asia.

Imran addressed more meetings in Punjab province than other provinces. Mansoor arranged a very big rally in his native place Sultanpur. He presided over the rally and at the end of rally there was a public meeting addressed by Imran Khan. In the meeting Imran spoke

"My dear brothers and sisters! This is a day of reckoning in the history of Pakistan. After the election I am sure that our party will form the government at national level and in all the four provinces. Pakistan will get a truly representative government at the national level after this election. I am sure that we will sweep all the provincial elections except Punjab where there is close fight between our party and PML(N). After seeing massive rally organized by Mansoor Bhai, I am convinced that we will sweep the Punjab province too. I appreciate the social service rendered by Mansoor in Sultanpur in providing free education and health facilities to the poor. What Mansoor has done for this area I want to do to the whole country? This is possible only when the same party rules at the National level and at the province. I request the people of Punjab to vote for PTI and see a new Pakistan emerging as a strong and respectable nation. I do not want to explain my policies in detail. Our manifesto is already released. I do not promise that I can eliminate corruption overnight. But I can reduce it to an acceptable level within three months. Without the change of mind of the public and the government officials this is not possible. I have a great faith in youth and the women in changing the mind of the elders. Therefore I appeal to the youth and women not only to vote PTI to power but also to change the mindset of the elders to build a new Pakistan that is corruption-free and prosperous. I want to change the present image of Pakistan as intolerant and failed state. Only when Pakistan is strong in economy and in military we can sit across the negotiating table with India and discuss peace. When India feels that it will not gain anything by making peace with us then why should it agree to give concessions? A negotiation is always involves give and take. Sentiments and justice do not work in international peace negotiations. Only when we have something to offer to India we can expect something in return from India. When we solve our problem with India we can concentrate on the development of Pakistan. All these years, civilian and military governments used India-bogey to keep them in power. I will no longer do the same. I will try my best to promote peace with India and Afghanistan. In that process if I have to loose power I will be only a happy man to do so." Imran Kahan concluded his speech.

At night Mansoor has arranged for a dinner at his home. Imran readily agreed since he wanted to enjoy the hospitality of Santhi who made a special visit all the way from Kuwait to attend his meeting. After the dinner conversation started about poll prospects and strategy to be adopted to get majority in the national and provincial assemblies.

"We have run out of ideas to electrify the election campaign. May I borrow some ideas from the Indian Wisdom" Imran looked at Santhi and asked.

"Pakistan Taliban is the biggest threat to our compaign. They are indulging in violence against the so called secular parties. In their opinion our party is not secular. They see you as their ally to fight against USA. I think that it is not good for us. It is fine to oppose drone attack. But it is not wise to oppose USA blindly. All these years Pakistan survived with the aid from USA. We cannot throw the baby in to the water and ask him swim. We cannot afford to take the risk of antagonizing USA. Only when Pakistan become strong enough economically we can afford to take anti-USA stand. Even India is not able to antagonize USA. It would not be pleased if we are seen as pro-Taliban. I want to you remind you that the media has named you as Taliban Khan. More over you are treated by the Army as their "Blue boy". Generally people hate the Army for its role in the last 66 years. People dislike politicians who are afraid of Military. Nawaz Sherrif scores better in this count. He told the media in no uncertain terms that the Prime Minister is the boss and the

Army has to obey him. You could not dare to make such a statement. Your anti-american stand may fetch votes in KP and Balochistan. But in the urban areas of Pakistan it would not bring votes as you expect. You promised to establish an Islamic Welfare state in new Pakistan. In the past political parties and military dictators played this card of Islamisation and failed to get support from the people. Religious parties never got more than 5% of the votes. The people know that Islam is not in danger. They don't want to be deceived by those who use Islam for selfish reasons. You talk about welfare state. How can you make a welfare state out of a bankrupt country" Santhi expressed her view and paused for the reaction fro Imran Khan.

"I do know that the media has nicknamed me as Taliban Khan. There are four stake holders in Pakistan namely Army, Political parties, people and militant groups including PTT. The people have the power to make any political party as ruling party provided there is a free and fair election with a turn out of atleast of 60%. We never had a free and fair election in the past with an average turn out of 40%. That is why we never had true democractic government. In this election I want a truly elected democrated government. To ensure a free and fair election the Military should remain neutral. The potential for disturbing the poll process by the militant groups is enormous. That is the reason why I took a soft stand on them. It is a tactical decision. We do not have vote bank as such. We have to depend on youth, women and neutral votes. PPP has a traditional vote bank in Sind and PML(N) has a committed vote bank in Punjab. The only way we can get a majority in MNA is to get substantial support in KP and Balochistan. My anti-american stand is aimed at getting votes in KP and Bolchistan. I accept your view that we cannot afford to antagonize America. But once we come to power we can always make amendments to suit the situation. America knew that whatever I say is for the consumption of Pakistanis. This is politics."

"Yes! I truly admire your tactics to check-mate the military and militants. Nawaz Sherrif expressed his anti-military stand. Therefore the Army is in our favor. The militants think that we are not against them. They will allow us to conduct our poll campaign without any disturbance. All said and done I have reservation about our policy of appeasing the Taliban and military. We cannot change the vote bank of PPP and PML(N). We have to rely on the youth who never voted and the women who were prevented from voting in the past. We should aim at increasing the voter turn out. Anything above 50% would give us the advantage. We should increase the awareness among the people to come out and vote in large numbers. That should be our strategy. We should increase the entertainment value of our campaign. Song and dance would help us to attract more crowds. I would like you add some more spices in your speeches. I want you make the following announcements to attract youth and women

1. Make an announcement that all the college students in Pakistan would be provided with free laptops.
2. All the women would be provided with woman-oriented government free T.V.Channels
3. Every district will have a world class cricket stadium.
4. All the poor school children from villages would be given free cycle to travel to their schools.
5. All the poor students would be given free lunch.
6. Every poor women would get a gift voucher for Rs10,000 at the time of her marriage. She can buy whatever she wants. She can apply with the marriage certificate and income certificate issued by any competent authority.
7. The income tax limit will be raised by Rs50,000.

If you make this announcement I am sure nobody can beat PTI in this election" Santhi poured her wisdom.

"Madam! Stop! Stop! Tell me how I am going to fulfill my promises. Wherefrom I will get funds for implementing my promises" Imran sought clarification.

"Now you are learning the real politics. There is a saying that he is not a politician who says no and she is not a woman who says yes. Politicians are the experts who predict things and they are also experts in explaining why his prediction failed and he should put the blame on opposition parties, foreign hands and India. Promises made before election are like bubbles made out of air and soap solution. I do not say that you should cheat the people. Get in to the chair with your promises and if you find it difficult to implement a promise, find out a good reason to divert the attention of the people by creating a group which is opposed to the idea. The group you have created would fight the government to stop implementing your idea. You can blame this group and escape." Santhi explained her idea.

"It is truely Machiavellian. I do not know from where you have learnt this? Let me have the secret. I will use it" Imran asked seriously.

"It is not a secret. This techniques are available in "Artha Sastra written by Koudilya two thousand years ago" Santhi disclosed the secret.

"What a surprise some body has written a book on politics two thousand years ago! I couldn't believe it. It is similar to Machiavellian.' Imran exclaimed

'But it is better than Machiavellian. It is the oldest treatise written on politics even before Aristotle and Pythagoras. Next time when I meet I will bring the book" concluded Santhi.

"As a true party worker I will not question your strategy. I will work for success of our party.Thank you for your visit to our home. We will cherish the memory of this day. Thank you once again" Mansoor expressed his pleasure.

"Pleasure is mine" Imran thanked the couple and took leave.

Imran did not make any announcement as advised by Santhi during his election campaign

All told his speech at Sultanpur has made a very big impact on the electorate. As a result the Punjab Governor (belongs to PML-N) decided to issue free distribution of lap tops to the students. A survey has indicated that popular rating of Imran Khan has gone up by two percentages.

Media reports suggest that it is tough for Imran to get decent tally of seats in Punjab where 148 out of 272 MNAs were elected. He wanted to do something to turn the tide against Nawaz Sherif in Punjab. He had no doubt that he can attract the youth with his image and speech. But he was not sure of the same with the women because of his play boy image. He decided to bring Santhi to campaign for him. He felt that a lady campaigner can change the game. It is like introducing a fast bowler kept in reserve for a critical period. He requested Mansoor to bring Santhi to Punjab. A series of meetings were arranged in Punjab in various places. In a large gathering in Lahore Santhi spoke

"Pakistan's future will be decided by this election. The time has come for the people of Pakistan to decide whether they want the same old leaders to continue their rule or a new leader with a clean image to come to power. Our leader vows to route out corruption from our country. He wants Pakistan to live with honour. We the Pakistani people are proud and hard working people. It is a shame on the Pakistanis to beg USA for aid. Why do we need aid from anybody? We have enough natural resources to become a self sufficient Al our problems started because we wanted beat India in every field whether it is military or missile technology. Where was the necessity to compete with India? Why not we concentrate on development of Pakistan and increase the literacy rate?

Today India is not our problem. Kashmir is not our problem. It is India's problem to solve with the Kashmiri people. Nobody has appointed Pakistan as the representative of Muslims in Asia. 1971 defeat of Pakistan by India has proved beyond doubt that "two nation theory" was given a decent burial. Pakistan has to acknowledge this truth and accept that it is not the leader of Muslims in Asia. Once we accept this fact we will stop meddling in the affairs of other countries. The same thing applies to Afghanistan. Why Pakistan is worried about that country? It is our neighbor and a Muslim country. So is Iran. We are not trying to meddle with the affairs of Iran. Then why should we try to meddle with Afghanistan?. Whenever USA, the super power tried to meddle with the affairs of other countries it has landed in trouble. It was defeated in Vietnam, Iraq and African countries like Libya. Where, USA with large military and number one economy in the world could not succeed how Pakistan can succeed. When India tried to interfere in the civil war in Sri Lanka it had to make a hasty retreat to save their face. In the 21th century no country however big it may be, cannot interfere and influence other countries. In Pakistan religious outfits declare that they will raise the Islamic flag at the Red Fort, New Delhi. The people of Pakistan and the government listen, enjoy and ignore their speech. Thus the militants are encouraged and they do not want to abide by the rules of the government but they want to run their own government within government. Our party will change this situation and see that Pakistan will not interfere either directly or indirectly in the affairs of other countries. At the same time we will not allow any nation however big it may be to interfere in our affairs. This is a promise from our leader Imran Khan.

Now I turn to the status of Women in Pakistan. The literacy rate among the women in Pakistan is one of the lowest in the world. We cannot call ourselves a civilized nation if we keep our women folk illiterate. Our party will give top priority to women's education. We will see that all the girl children are enrolled in the schools within a year.

We need money to implement the promises. Our party will formulate attractive incentives to invite FDI from expatriate Pakistani living in Gulf countries, USA and Europe. We want to increase the standard of education in Pakistan. We will allow other countries including India to set up schools, colleges and Universities. We want to erase the present image of Pakistan as nation of drivers. We do not promise that we can carry out all these promises overnight. But our leader will take all necessary steps to take our country in this direction.

I once again request our women folks to come out in large numbers and vote for PTI. Now is the time for the women to take power in their hands and decide the future of our country.

I know that I have gone a little farther than our leader permitted. I request him and our party people to remember that I am not the party member. My party can always disown my speech if it proved to be inconvenient to them.

I give a slogan "Let Imran bat for you and get 1000 runs"

Thus she concluded her speech in chaste Punjabi.

The next day all the news papers carried the story and printed her speech. All the religious parties were up in arms against her. They shouted that she has insulted Pakistan by telling the truth. But by and large the neutral people appreciated her boldness in calling a spade a spade. So far no politician spoke so frankly about Pakistan. The reason as speculated by the media was that she has a country to live and being a PIO she can always go back to India and escape from the militants. In total she stirred a hornet's nest in Pakistan politics. She became the darling of the media. Whatever she said in different places was reported in full in all the news papers. She was invited to a T.V.show. But she declined the invitation because of her tight schedule. She promised that she would give an interview before leaving Pakistan. Before the election date she received a call from Kuwait to return immediately. Later she learnt that Nawaz Sherif has pressurized Kuwait government through Saudi Arabia to call her back. He jittered on seeing the news about Santhi in the media. Imran Khan and Santhi occupied the centre stage of Pakistani election campaign. As a damage control exercise she was made to go back to Kuwait.

Santhi called Imran by phone before leaving

"Sorry Boss I have to leave in the middle of the election compaign" she said

"Don't worry! You have done enough for me. It is too hot in Pakistan. You need some rest. The only way to take rest is to get away from Pakistan and relax in your air-conditioned home in Kuwait. Mansoor would continue your work equally well as he knows your mind. Keep in touch with us. We need your advice at any moment. I do not think that KNPC would switch of your cell phone" said Imran jokingly.

"I am sure that I will be present in your swearing in ceremony as P.M" Santhi said with confidence.

"I appreciate your optimism. Take care of your health in Kuwait. Good bye!" Imran expressed his concern for her health.

Next day she joined duty in KNPC. Her boss welcomed her

"Welcome to the Tsunami from Pakistan" the boss said jokingly.

"Please give me the keys. I want to complete my pending works immediately. By the by! May I know why did you call me urgently back to Kuwait? I am sure Kuwait will survive few more weeks without me" Santhi enquired.

"It is top secret matter. You are not an ordinary person any more. Soon you may become an international personality. You are more knowledgeable than me. Make a correct guess. I will give you a gift" the boss said.

"Nothing is secret in Pakistan. It is Nawaz Sherif who used his influence with Saudi and forced me to get out of Pakistan. I could have refused to come back. But my life may be put in danger. Anything can happen in Pakistan. I am too small a person. I do not want to embarass Kuwait either. It has given me a good husband and decent life. I have guessed it right. Please tell me what the gift is?" Santhi asked casually without taking the gift offer seriously.

"I know that you are not a person interested in material gift. I will give a special leave for 15 days. Please take rest in your home. Switch off your cell phone. I will not call you for 15 days. After 15 days I know you will compensate with your work. Don't worry. Things can wait for you. Wish you good rest. Now you can leave this place after giving me a cup of tea." said the boss and buried his face in to file.

Santhi reached home and made a good coffee for her before their children come back from the school. Ram and Rahim came back from school. They were so happy to see their mother back.

"I never expected you come back before the elections. Our father needs you more than us. We know you will go back as soon the election result is declared. Don't worry about us mom. We can take care of ourselves. Our maid cooks better than you. There is no problem with our food. I want to hear some stories from you mom" Ram said.

After dinner she told some stories which are relevant to the youngsters. They enjoyed the stories and went to bed early to show that they were good boys.

Santhi switched on the T.V to listen to the news. She switched to NDTV channel. Burqa Dutt was talking in T.V show. The show was about Pakistani election and its impact on Indian security. Santhi was curious to know what Indians think about Pakistani election.

Burqa was giving the introductory speech

"Our today's topic is Pakistan election and its effect on Indian security. Our panel members are Manish Tiwary, Sushma Swaraj and Lallu Prasad. The election result will be out on 12th May. Either Imran or Nawaz Sheriff is expected to win the election and form the government in the centre and in some provinces. We in India are very much interested to know what will happen to the peace process initiated by our Prime Minister. First let us hear from Manish Tiwary. He started his speech

"Rahul will be the P.M soon. I am sure Imran will win and he is very good friend of Rahul. Now the trend is that people are fed up with old faces like Advani, Modi and Mayawathi. People want young dynamic leaders. Therefore Imran Khan will win and he will improve the relation with India if Rahul becomes the P.M"

Sushma interfered and said

"Imran is not young. He is more than 60. How do you say the relation will improve? We have seen Pakistan for the last 66 years. Nothing is changed. We have seen military dictators and political leaders of all kind. As far as India is concerned Pakistan will never change its color whoever may be the leader. Nawaz Sheriff tried to improve the relation with India in 1999. But Mushraf spoiled it with his Kargil adventure. I hope if Nawaz wins he may pick up the thread from where he left. Modi will be the P.M. in 2014. If he becomes the P.M, Pakistan will think twice before sending some militants for bombing our cities."

Lallu spoke

"Both of you think that only your parties have the right to rule this country. I am sure a third front will be formed. I will be the P.M in 2014. When I visited Pakistan, people gave me rousing reception. Many people told me if I contest the election in Pakistan, I will become the P.M" Lallu said seriously.

"Probably they were so much fed up with Pakistani politicians they are ready to accept even Lallu Bhai as their P.M". Sushma passed a sarcastic comment. Lallu did not understand the sarcasm and laughed along with others.

"Lallu Bhai is the comedian, Rahul is the hero and Modi is the villain. Every body knows who will win at end" Manish commented

"In cenema either the hero or the villain dies. But the comedian never dies. So I will be the P.M in 2014" Lallu turned the table against Manish Tiwary

Santhi felt that the show turned out be more entertaining than educating, she wanted to change the channel and took the remote. At that moment Burqa made announcement

"Our special correspondent reports directly from Islamabad"

The correspondent spoke through telephone

"This is Ashok from Islamabad. Imran's chances of winning this election increases every day. The Star campaigner Santhi, an Indian women married to a Pakistani turned the tide in favour of Imran Khan. Sensing the danger Nawaz sheriff managed to send her back to Kuwait where she works. Imran is disappointed but her magic may lead him to victory."

Burqa Dutt made an announcement

"Soon our channel will contact Santhi and get her interview. You can expect Santhi to enter the drawing rooms of Pakistani homes through our channel. Wait for the announcement. Till then good bye to the audience"

Next morning telephone bell rang and Santhi took the receiver and said "Hello! I am Santhi from Kuwait. How can I help you?"

"Santhi! This is Burqa Dutt from NDTV Channel. Are you a regular viewer of our Channel? Do you know me" asked Burqa.

"I am a busy working woman. I do not have much time for T.V. Yesterday I happened to view your T.V comedy show." Santhi mocked at the program.

"Yesterday we did not broad cast any comedy program. Oh! Now I understand what you mean. Wherever Lallu is there there is no dearth of comedy. So is with Manish Tiwari. He is known for his uncharitable comments on personalities. Sushma is restrained but hits hard at the opponents. That is why we have chosen them as our panelist" explained Burqa.

"Your program was entertaining but not educating the viewers. I expected that your panel to make good analysis on the fortunes of the top three leaders in Pakiatan. I am disappointed. Sorry to say this" Santhi told Burqa frankly.

"You were in the battle scene. You know better than us. Why don't you educate us?. We are ready to invite you for T,V show" Burqa said.

"I am sorry. I cannot come to India. My boss ordered me to take rest. My presence in India will send a wrong signal. It will affect the poll prospects of our party" Santhi sensibly declined the request.

"Is it possible to get a live telephone interview tonight? I think you have a web camera attached to your T.V." requested Burqa.

"I have the facility. I talk with my husband frequently. That is why I have installed this facility. I accept your request with one condition. No personal question!. Only political! Please do not try to put words in my mouth. I know your tricks. I have faced media in Pakistan. Please do not try your smartness with me" she accepted with precaution.

"I accept your condition. I will see that you don't regret. Be ready for the interview at 10 p.m IST ie seven thirty Kuwait time" said Burqa and cut the line.

At 10 pm IST sharp Burqa called Santhi and informed "Swith on your T.V. You are live in our program. Please answer the questions"

'Shoot the questions Burqa! I am ready" Santhi replied.

"Do you think that your party will get absolute majority at the national and provincial governments?"

'Yes and no. At the national level our party may be the single largest party. We may miss one or two provinces. Even in those provinces our numbers will be substantial. No body can form the government without our support."

"How do you say so?"

"It is a simple logic. The influence of PML(N) is limited to Punjab. Our party has made a big break through by the efforts of my husband and Imran Khan. Military establishments are against PML(n). Punjab and Sind decide the prime minister. We are giving a tough fight in Punjab. Sind was the strong hold of PPP and MQM. MQM may retain its influence. But PPP is leaderless. Zardhari has very poor image as Mr.Ten percent through out Pakistan. Bilaval is not cooperating with his father. He is only ball picker in the contest. Therefore PPP may loose heavily in Sind. Loss of PPP will be gain for us. The youth which forms 20% of the electorate will vote for the first time. They will vote for us. In the democratic set up a 10% swing will result in landslide victory. In other provinces too PTI will capture substantial number of seats. PTI is the only party who has increased its membership manifold during the last one year. We are strong at least in three provinces namely Sind, Punjab and K P. At the same time we are not weak in the other provinces. Wheres PPP and PML(n) are strong only in one province but weak in other provinces. After the election PTI will be the only national party."

"Thank you for the analysis. How do you say that youth will vote for you?"

'Youth was watching cricket from their childhood. For them Imran Khan is a hero who made them proud in the field of cricket. They expect the same in the field of politics. More over all are fed up with old faces. They want to try a new leader. There is no body to compete with Imran Khan"

"What about Bilaval. Can he attract youth?"

Santhi replied with a smile.

"Bilaval is a cricket player in the school team. But Imran is renowned cricket captain in the national team. There is no comparison. It is like comparing Prianka with Indra Ganthi"

"How do you expect the neutral people to vote for your party?"

".These middle class intellectuals go by the image of the leader. Imran Khan, as an honest cricket player, as a social worker and as a philanthropist, has a very good image among the neutrals. More over he is one of the few politicians not tainted by corruption charges"

"Your speech at Lahore created many enemies for you in Pakistan. Do you feel threatened?"

"No! If my speech made one enemy I have gained 10 friends. No politician ever told the truth to the people of Pakistan. When Pakistan army surrendered to Indian Army with 93,000 solders in Dacca Yahya Khan described it as an understanding between the commanders on both sides. When Pakistan was forced to withdraw from Kargill, Mushraf called it a military victory for Pakistan. Lies! Lies! That was what all the leaders either military or civilian fed the people. The pity was that many people believed them. The same was true with our religious leaders. They want the people to accept whatever they say and any dissent is termed as blasphemy. They want to use this weapon and shut the mouth of the liberals. I have decided to call the bluff. I know that I am taking a personal risk. At the worst I may be killed by a bullet or a bomb. But I want the people of Pakistan to know the truth. Realization of truth will bring prosperity. Lies may give temporary comfort but in the long run it will bring disaster. I appeal to the people of Pakistan through your channel. Imran Khan is your savior. If you loose this opportunity you may not get the same again. Use this opportunity to save Pakistan and make yourself a proud people."

"What is your policy towards India? Why have you not made this as an issue in your speech?"

"In this election India and Kashmir are not the issues. All the major parties are in favor of improving relations with India. Only some religious parties raised issues about the hanging of Afsal Guru and Ajmal Kasab. But it did not get any response from the people. Even the religious parties could not make issue of India and Kashmir. In the previous elections all the political parties vied with one another in championing the cause of Kashmir. Now political parties realized that Kashmir issue would not bring votes"

"After the election if you are given a minister post will you accept?"

"You are asking a personal question. I decline to answer. You have broken my condition. Therefore I stop this interview" Santhi said and cut the line. It was an unexpected and dramatic end to the interview.

*   *   *

The general election date was announced on 25th March 2013. Election was held on 11th May 2013.

Pakistanis would elect 272 representatives to the National Assembly and 577 representatives to provincial assemblies in Sindh, Khyber Pakhtunkhwa, Punjab and Baloochestan. The political party that secures 172 seats in the National Assembly, either independently or in coalition with other parties would lead the next government.

The children from political dynasties, technocrats, current and former army generals entered the battle to shape the electoral outcome.

Pervesh Musraf returned to Pakistan by the end of March 2013, after getting the anticipatory bail from the High Court. In a press meeting he announced his intention to contest from Karachi for MNA. He expected a big applause from the audience. But what he received was shocking. He received a shoe missile and joined a shoe club of VIPs. He was undeterred by the shoe. He declared that Kargil adventure was military victory but the politicians converted it in to a political defeat. The people of Pakistan laughed at him and treated him as joker. An old case was opened against him. He was arrested and kept in house arrest.He was charged with sedition and waiting for trial. The Army was unhappy about the treatment meated out to Mushraf. Probably the Army felt that their supremacy is threatened. Kayani, the Army Chief issued a weiled threat to all political parties that nobody can separate Islam from Pakistan. This is an indirect warning to the political parties that army may intervene in the name of saving Islam. Otherwise the Army has no business to make such comment about the policy matters.

Three individuals have the edge to be the leaders of Pakistan's next government. They are Asif Ali Zardari, Nawaz Sharif and Imran Khan. Zardari and Sharif represent the old style politics whilst Imran Khan claims to present a new political movement in Pakistan. Zardari is the widower of a political dynasty and Sharif an industrialist from the Punjab. Khan is appealing to the 18 million young people, new voters who grew up watching him play cricket matches for the Pakistani national team. He appeals to women and youth by promising them that he will make a new Pakistan a secure place where no body can threaten them. Zardari has been in Pakistani politics since when he married Benazir Bhutto, the country's first female Prime Minister in 1988. He is originally of Balooch ethnic origin.

Zardari became president in 2008 following his wife's assassination and he shares the PPP chairmanship with his son Bilawal. Presidential term ends in September, four months after the national elections and it is expected that Zardari wanted to serve another term as President. The PPP's influence in the Senate, where it won a majority in the March 2012 elections, might help but it would not be easy for Zardari to win. An electoral college consisting of the Senate, provincial assemblies and the National Assembly actually elect the president. He faces opposition from military, judiciary and the groups supported by the Saudi regime.

Mian Muhammad Nawaz Sharif is the Leader of the Pakistan Muslim League (PML-N). Sharif is from Punjab and his family's real estate and agriculture holdings are valued at over 100 million dollars. Like Zardari, he had difficult ties with the military and judiciary, the institutions that aided his downfall in 1999. Sharif hoped to come back into the mainstream Pakistani politics. Under his leadership the PML-N opposition has criticized the current government's policies. Sharif had the Saudi backing but his party lacked the national base like PPP or PTI

One of the largest vote areas for PML-N is southern Punjab where the group like salafi, takfiri, Sepah-e-Sahaba Lashkar-e-Jhangvi, Jaish-e-Mohammad, and Lashkar-e-Taiba have strong support. Punjab elects 148 out of 272 National Assembly members. It was reported that in 2010, officials from PML-N visited the Sepah-e-Sahaba madrassas and met with its leader while campaigning in by-elections. This might suggest that a PML-N has nexus with extremist outfits. It may use it to get political advantage. If PML(N) comes to power it may compromise with extremists much against the wishes of Military establishments. Whatever the political mileage it may derive from this nexus it may not be enough to capture power at the national level. At the best it may capture power in Punjab by compromising with extremists.

Imran Khan was the chairman of his own political party, the Pakistan Tehreek-e-Insaf (PTI). He presented a new style of politics. Security establishments were not happy either with PPPor PML(N). So they were ready to support PTI which opposed drone attack. They felt that Imran may not weaken the Military which the other two were trying to do. Khan's party was targeting the educated middle class, women and young voters in Punjab. The PTI called for an end to VIP culture in Pakistan which was responsible for the widespread corruption in the country. Zardari, Sharif and Khan clearly were the front runners. On 11th May Pakistanis would decide who will be the next P.M.

Few days before the election date (11th May) Imran Khan met with an accident during his campaign. He suffered injuries in his head, spinal chord and neck. He was hospitalized for three weeks. He could not cast his own vote. There was a wave of sympany from the people of Pakistan. To cash on the sympathy he made an appeal to electorates from his bed through video conferencing. He said that he has done his best and now it was the turn of the people to create a new Pakistan by voting for his party. On 12th May he will come to know how his accident helped him

On 12th May, results started pouring in right from 10 O' clock in the night. Imran Khan was in the hospital bed. No media person was allowed to visit him. Only his close associates were allowed. Through out the night he did not sleep. The news about initial leads increased his hope. As the time passed he was disappointed. PML(N) established a clear lead. PTI and PPP were trailing behind. PML (N) was way ahead of these two parties. Imran was hoping to finish second in MNA and form a government in KP. In the early morning he slept with that hope. But his hope did not materialize. He finished third with 29 seats. The only consolation was his party was the single largest party in KP. His party was in a position to form the government in KP.

The results were given below

National Assembly	
PML (N)	128
PTI	29
PPP	32
MQM	18
JUIF	11
ANP	1
Independants	29
Others	32
Total elected seats	272

PML(N) emerged as the single largest party National Assembly with 128 seats. PPP emerged as the second largest party with 31 seats and PTI as the third largest party with 29 seats. APML (Mushraf's party) secured only one seat. The same was with ANP. MQM did farely well with 18 seats.In Punjab province PML(N) received two third majority and it was expected to form the government.

PPP and PML(N) had their vote bank, which PTI could not break. It did not have any vote bank in Pakistan. Whatever the votes it got were from the neutral people and the young. The government servants did not want Imran Khan to come to power. They had their vested interest in maintaining the status qua. They didn't want their privileges cut by the new government. They did as much damage as they could to spoil the chances of PTI. Nawaz sheriff was expected to form the government with out side support or with the support of independents who have 29 seats in National Assembly.There was no need for PML(N) to form coalition government. PML(N) did not have a majority in Senate. To get the majority, PML(N) wanted to form a coalition government at the centre and Punjab with JUI(F). There were some elements in PML(N) opposed this move.

MNA has 90 nominated MNA s. President nominates from each party in proportion to the elected strength in NA.

On 22nd Imran Khan was discharged from the hospital. In the first week of June working committee of PTI met to discuss the cause of poor performance by the party. Santhi was invited as the special invitee.

ImranKhan presided over the meeting. He spoke

"I thank every one of you for putting their best effort. But unfortunately the result is not up to our expectation. There was large scale rigging in some constituencies. It was not an excuse for our poor performance. We have gathered to find out the reason for our poor performance and to take necessary correction in our policy. Pakistan never returned the ruling party to power in the past. I expect the same in the future. In 2018 either PPP or PTI should come to power. PPP has its vote bank. But it is leaderless to encash the vote bank. Therefore we stand a better chance to come to power in 2018. Please believe me we will form the government in the centre and some provincial assemblies in 2018. We should start our work from tomorrow. Only then we can realize our dream of making a new Pakistan. I would like the members to give their views without any fear." Imran opened his speech.

One of the member got up and said

"We have accepted all corrupt people who wished to join us. We talked about eradicating corruption. But at the same time many corrupt people were given tickets because they were considered as winnable candidates. This dented our image as crusader against corruption"

Another member got up and said

"Our government servants, military, contractors and business community are comfortable with corruption and tax evasion. They want the status qua to continue. Only the common man is interested in routing out corruption. But this section is a divided one. They do not vote as a single block"

Third member got up and spoke

"We supported the military which many people didn't like. We hesitated to condemn Taliban. This is the main reason why people did not accept us as savior of Pakistan"

Imran Khan rose up and said

"I accept all your criticism. But nobody has given the guidance how we should carry our mission in the future. I hope that our special invitee would throw some light on future course of action":

Santhi rose and started her speech. There was big applause from the members. It surprised Imran. "Thank you for inviting me as a special invitee. I am not the member of the working committee. Yet I am bestowed with this honour. It shows how much respect our leader gives to the women folk. Right from the beginning we know that we depend on youth, women and neutral voters. Neutral voters did not support us. The reasons were given by the previous speakers. But we have not done any thing to attract the youth and women. We promised an Islamic Welfare state. The youth and women are against Islamisation of our country. They are the people affected by the Islamisation. Islamists do not want to give equal rights to women. Youth are fed up with religion. They are forced by their elders to follow the religious practices. How many youngsters are interested to grow a beard and do five times Namaz? How can you expect them to accept your call for establishing an Islamist Welfare State? Pakistan is bankrupt country. How can you convert it in to welfare state? The oil rich countries and developped countries find it difficult to maintain a welfare state. People of Pakistan did not believe that PTI would establish a welfare state. People are not seriously interested in Islamisation of our country any more. I say this with confidence from the fact that people are no more interested in Kasmir issue. This was accepted by Yasin Malik. He made an appeal to Pakistanis not to forget Kashmir. People are dead against Talibanisation of our country. This is for the criticism. I give my suggestion to the party about future course of action. It is for the party to accept or reject

1. We should insist on development rather than welfare.
2. Our first priority is to establish true democracy and rule of Law.
3. We should agree with Nawaz Sherrif to send back the Army to barracks from the public undertakings and other establishments. We should clip the wings of our Army not to interfere in the government policy matters. If Army is asked to fight against Taliban they should do so without any reservation. ISI must be brought under the full control of the Prime Minister.
4. In the peace time the army should be used for building the infrastructure of the country. Venezula has shown that army could be used to increase the standard of living of the people.
5. Any policy decision initiated by Nawaz Sherrif to bring in foreign investment should not be opposed in the name of self-respect.
6. We should oppose the drone attacks. But at the same Pakistan should extend its full cooperation in eliminating Taliban from Pakistan soil.
7. Top priority should be accorded for women's education and empowerment

8. We should remove all the corrupt people from our party and show to the people that we take the business of eliminating corruption seriously.

As Santhi spoke Imran Kahan was watching her speech with keen interest. He replied.

"What Santhi says is that PTI should take a new Avatar to create a new Pakistan. I have an open mind. I don't know how many of you agree with her. I want the members who support her to raise their hands"

. There were only few hands raised. One of the members got up said

"What she suggested is a drastic change in our policy. I do not know how this change would succeed. Our change in policy should be gradual after reading the pulse of the people. Otherwise we may loose the good will earned in this election"

Imran Khan in his concluding speech said

"We appreciate the suggestions given by Santhi. But we can't change our color over night. We have five more years for the election. We need not hurry up to make changes in our policy. As and when needed we will make changes to increase our support base. All of you should work hard among the people to instill confidence in our party. I am always open to suggestions. Please don't hesitate to come with suggestions" The meeting ended with vote of thanks from the chair.

22

FORMATION OF GOVERNMENT IN PAKISTAN 2013

PML(N) formed its governments at the centre, and in Punjab province. PTI formed a coalition government in KP with the help JI, QWP and independants. PMAP formed government in Balochistan with PML(N) as its coalition partner. PPP formed the government in Sind. Nawaz Sherrif received congratulations and cooperation from India, USA, Afghanistan, Britan and other countries. PML(N) and PTI agreed to cooperate with each other to establish true democracy in Pakistan. Nawaz Sherrif was sworn in as Prime Minister on 5th June. Along with him 10 other cabinet rank ministers were sworn in.

Sherrif took emergency action to set right the economy and to improve the power situation. He could attract foreign investment as the investor sentiment improved after the election. The whole world appreciated Pakistan for its smooth transistion of power from one civilian government to another. A turn out of more than 55% was considered as a tribute to the democracy.(Some questioned the figure as manipulated). It was a mile stone in the history of Pakistan.

Nawaz Sherrif was invited by Manmohan Sing to visit India on a mutually accepted date. Sherrif invited Sing to attend the swearing in ceremony. But Sing did not attend as he felt that it was premature to show such bonhomie with Pakistan. Sherrif hoped that he would pick up the thread from 1999. President Mushraf spoiled the peace initiative by his Kargill misadventure.

USA wanted Pakistan's help to eliminate or to negotiate with Taliban in Afghanistan. President Obama sent John Kerry to Islamabad for a discussion. John Kerry made his visit in the first week of July. He had a personal discussion with Nawaz Sherrif

"Welcome to Pakistan! Please convey my thanks for all the help so far extended by your administration. The only thing that irritates us is your drone attack on KPand Waziristan. We are ready to nuetralize Taliban by negotiatians or by some other means. Please give us a chance by halting the drone attack. It is a great insult on our sovereignty." Sherrif made his opening remarks.

"We are ready to stop the drone attack provided you promise to cut off your assistance to Taliban both in Pakistan and Afghanistan. Your military should cooperate with us in eleiminating Taliban." John Kerry replied.

"At present our Army headed by Kayani is in no mood to cooperate with us. He will retire in October. I will appoint my man as the Chief of the Army. You may have to wait till November for us to move in that direction. Till that time I hope that you will hold your drone attack" Sherrif made a request.

"I cannot promise. But I will convey your request to our President. Any way I am happy with the outcome of the meeting. I am in way back via New delhi" Kerry informed about his visit to India casually.

"May I know your subject of your discussion with Dr.Sing" Sherrif asked eagerly.

"Nothing special!. It is only a courtesy call. We may discuss about Afghanistan. India has some influence with Karzai government. We have decided to leave Afghanistan soon. We need some help from India." Kerry added some more information.

Nawaz Sherrif was pleased to get the news directly from John Kerry. He said

"Thanks for your information. We will meet in November or December." Sherrif concluded.

Nawaz Sherrif's top priority was to improve the power situation. He took action on war footing. He streamlined the operation of thermal power stations. He gave top priority for movement of coal. He sacked some influential heads of the power utility corporation. By these actions the power position improved to some extent but not to the extent he desired. As a short term solution he floated the idea of buying power from India. As a long term solution he decided to invite foreign investments in the power sector by offering liberal terms. Lot of companies from

Germany and France came forward to set up gas based power station. He took urgent steps to expedite the Iran-Pakistan gas pipeline project. This irked the Americans. Iran-Pak pipeline has progressed to a level that cannot be reversed. USA tolerated the irritance. Pakisatn had no other option. It went ahead with the project ignoring protest from USA.

Nawaz Sherrif did not take any drastic action to cut down the defence budget. But he did indicate about downsizing the military at an approprieate time (read after October). Before doing that he wanted to strengthen the peace process.with India. He planned for a troup reduction along the border with India. He knew that this was the only way to cut down the defence expenditure which was eating the lion's share of the budget. General Kayani, sensing the popular mood of the nation, kept a low profile. He waited till his peaceful retirement in October.

Nawaz Sherrif planned to visit India. All the militant groups exerted pressure on Sherrif to extract concession in Kashmir policy in exchange for MFN status for India. All the religious parties were against the visit. Imran too joined the chorus. Probably he did not want Sherrif to take the credit for making peace with India. But Sherrif took a strong decision to visit and improve the trade relationship with India. He knew very well that Kashmir problem could not be solved overnight. He wanted to take the first step of improving trade relationship by giving MFN status. In return he wanted trade concessions from India. He wanted to discuss all the problems including Kashmir issue. His intension was to see that any hiccup in the political issues should not become the stumbling block in trade negatiation. In short he did not want to come back with empty hand. Army was not happy about his visit. It encouraged the militant groups to increase the infilteration in to Kashmir Valley. It gave fire support to the infilterators. This resulted in sporadic cease—fire violations by the Army. It always put the blame on Indian Army. However the hot line between Sherrif and Dr.Sing helped to diffuse the crisis created by the militants and the Army. Nawaz Sherrif expected this situation. He made the ISI to report to him directly and got all the sensitive information immediately.

On July 27th Sherriff visited India. He had warm welcome. He was received by Dr.Sing at the airport. Later President of India hosted a dinner in the Honour of Sherrif. Sherrif was very much pleased. He visited Taj Mahal and Rajghat. The agenda of the meeting between Sherrif and Dr. Sing was fixed as follows

1. Discussion about granting MFN status to India
2. Reducing the negative list by both the sides
3. Free flow of magazines, films, books etc
4. Easing the visa regime
5. Reduction of troups in the border
6. Agreement on "No-first use of Nuclear weapons" treaty.
7. Some kind of settlement in Kashmir issue
8. Siachen issue
9. Free-trade agreement
10. .Opening the education sector to India.

There were long discussions between politicians and officials. Some of contentious issues were postponed for another meeting. There were agreements on most of issues related to trade and culture. Kashmir remained unsolved. Pakistan did not agree for "No-first use of Nuclear weapon". Sheriff pleaded that India being strong in the convential weapons, Pakistan cannot defend itself without the nuclear deterrant. He said if he agrees for the treaty the military may take over and he may not be able to go back as happened before. India understood his predictment and dropped the idea. However India agreed for troup reduction if the military was used to eliminate Taliban. On its part it demanded that infiltration stopped across the border. It did not want to commit any thing on the troup reduction. It was an oral understanding between Sherrif and Sing.

The visit ended on a happy note. Nobody expected that all the issues could be solved in a single visit. The progress made in this visit was substantial. However the opposition parties and miltants groups in Pakistan called the agreement as sell out to India. In India BJP called the agreement as appeasement and aimed at Laksabha election to get the minority votes. USA and the international community welcomed the accord between two nuclear powered neibhors as path-breaking.

In the first week of October Lt.General Rasheed was appointed as the Army Chief. It was believed that he was hand picked by Nawaz Sherrif. Sherrif had already brought ISI chief under his control. Now the Army chief too was brought under his control. Everybody expected that Nawaz Sherrif was in full control of the nation. But in Pakistan something always goes wrong. In a society ridden with fuedalism, terrorism, militancy, fanatism and corruption things cannot improve in months or years. Any time some danger may come from unexpected quarters.

Taliban was active and their hold on the civilians increased after PTI came to power in KP. There were frequent bomb blasts. PTI headed government hesitated to take on Taliban against the wishes of their coalition partners.

USA continued with their drone attack. It wanted to quit Afghanistan at the earliest but at the same time they wanted to tame the Taliban in Afghanistan and Pakistan before leaving. This was possible only with the help of Pakistan. John Kerry made a vist in November to discuss the subject of Taliban. He was welcome by Nawaz Sherif.

"Welcome to Pakistan. We are very much embarassed by your decision to continue drone attack in Waziristan and Fata ares. Unless the attack is stopped we will not be able to move against Taiban. I invite President Obama to Visit Pakistan and see the changes I have made" Sherrif opened the talk with his frank disapproval of American policy.

"Sentiments have no place in international politics. Taliban is hiding in Wazirisatn and Swat area and attacking the NATO troups. ISI has links with Taliban. This is unacceptable. Drone attack is the only tool we have to control them. Your military is not doing enough to contain them. We sympathize with you. But your army is not cooperating with us. I hope you understand us. We do not want to remain in Afghanistan for ever. But we cannot leave the job half done and get away to satisfy your government. The more you cooperate with us earlier we will leave Afghanistan" Kerry took pain to explain the American position.

"It is the question of our sovereignty and prestige of our nation. We swallowed our pride when you entered in to Abbotabad and killed Osama. Fault was ours. Therefore we had to swallow the bitter pill. Taliban is a threat to us too. But drone attacks kill more civilians than the Taliban. To kill one Taliban you are killing 50 civilians. It is not fair. We should explore other ways to control them without killing the civilians" Sherrif pleaded with Kerry. He shot a question

"So what do you want us to do?"

"Give us some time. Stop the drone attacks. We will negotiate with good Taliban"

"So you think you can prevail over them?"

"We hope so. We need three months time to enter in to meaningful negotiation with the moderate Taliban and we will try for a ceasefire to start with. Then we will give ultimatum to them to lay down their arms"

"In case they don't lay down the arms what will you do?" Kerry asked

"We will try to isolate the Taliban from the civilians and cut down the funds and arms supply. If we failed we will think about using our army to curb their activities"

"All the people have the same long beard and dress. How do you identify good Taliban?" asked Kerry.

"Our ISI will help us to identify good Taliban"

"How do ISI know who is good Taliban?

"ISI helped the Taliban and they gave the information about drone attacks. If ISI really wants to terminate Taliban it can" assured Sherrif.

"How are you going to control ISI? At present it is government within government and it is not accountable to anybody because all their actions are classified as secrets. Some time it happens with CIA too. They act without the consent of our president" asked Kerry.

"It is not difficult. Whoever controls the purse controls the army and ISI. Believe me we can?" explained Sherrif.

"Don't you think our drone attack will help you to control Taliban?" asked Kerry.

"No! Your drone attack increases the civilian support to the Taliban. Once the drone attack stops the civilians will not cooperate with Taliban. Then it will be easier for us to take military action against Taliban" Sherrif tried to convince Kerry.

"I see your point. I will convey your request to Obama and see whether he agrees with you. Let us hope for the best. I will take leave. Tomorrow I will be New Delhi on my way to Washington"

"May I know what is the subject of discussion with India?" asked Sherrif

"Nothing serious! It is a courtesy call. I may continue the discussion about Afghanistan. We need their help if we have to quit Afghanistan" Kerry said and took leave.

After few days the message came promptly from Obama.

"We are ready to stop the drone attack provided Pakistan controls Taliban. As long as the Taliban does not do any mischief in Afghanistan we will not press the button. We retain the right to retaliate without informing you"

It was considered a great success for Sherrif in Pakistan

The next day one of the reporter asked in a press meet

"Have you promised something to USA to stop the drone attack?"

"Yes! I did. USA has no faith in our army. I promised that the civilian government will control army and ISI" replied Imran

"Is it possible for you to control Military and ISI which was never done in Pakistan?"

"Why not! In all the countries in the world the civilian governments control military. Pakistan cannot be an exception."

When he was further questioned he gave a comprehensive statement.

"The PML(N) will install civilian supremacy over Pakistan's military. I would rather resign if the Army and the ISI did not function under civilian authority. The armed forces will be under complete civilian control; the ISI will report directly to me. The defense budget will be audited by the government and that no terrorism will take place from Pakistani soil. You may be skeptic about it. Look at South Korea. It was a military dictatorship between 1961 and 1987 and now it is a civilian led full-fledged democracy. It is emerging as a fully developed nation. Some people may have the doubt whether I can be the boss of the present Army chief. My answer is solid yes. People know that I have suffered at the hands of the military rule. Mushraf was the villain and not the army. The army was controlling the situation in Balochistan, the tribal areas and the erstwhile militant-infected Swat area without any civilian control while the country's largest city of Karachi was controlled by the paramilitary Pakistan Rangers. We will take necessary action to change the situation"

The reporters got important news for the next day papers.

The Dawn proclaimed in the front page

"I am the boss" the lion of Punjab roared

23

PAKISTAN 2014

B JP emerged as the single largest party with 195 seats in the Lok Shaba election held in May 2014. It led the National Democratic Allince to victory. NDA secured 301 seats. It was supported by parties other than RJD, Communists, Muslim League, JD(S) and DMK. Congress won only 98 seats. Narendra Modi became the Prime Minister, Arun Jailtley became the Home Minsiter, Sinha became Finance Minister, Sushma Swaraj became the Foreign Affairs Minister, Jaswan Sing became the Defence Minister and Joshi became the HRD minister. P.M kept the Heavy Industries and Commerce ministries with him. Arun Kejriwal whose party (AAP) won 25 seats, was given the Law Ministry. Other portfolios, like Telecommunication, Railways, Coal, Environments, Surface Transport, Aviation, Housing, Forestry etc were given to coalition partners.

Nawaz Sherrif, though not happy with the result, was ready to do business with Modi and Sushma. He wanted to carry forward the peace inititive started with Manmohan Sing. But the militant groups and Taliban wanted to teach India a lesson for electing BJP government. Therefore they were against any peace initiative with India. Sherrif decided to use the back channel diplomacy to feel the pulse of the BJP government. He used services of Karan Thappar, a well known T.V anchor.

Karan Thappar requested for an appointment with Modi. He, being the favourite of the Media readily granted an appointment at his residence. It was a private meeting without any aide and records. Karan reached Modi's residence exactly at 8 a.m on the appointed date. Modi received him in his study room for a private conversation.

"Tell me Karan Bhai! Have you come as Karan Thappar or Devil's Advocate?" Modi started the conversation jokingly.

"I am here as Karan Thappar, the back room diplomat between India and Pakistan. I assure you that whatever we talk here will be kept confidential. It will not be leaked out without your permission" Thappar assured full confidentiality.

"How is the lion roaring in Pakistan?" enquired Modi.

"So So!. Nothing goes well in Pakistan. Sherrif believes that improvement in Indo-Pak relationship would give him power to take control over the army. Now the army use India card to defend their power. Once there is good relation between India and Pakistan he can downsize the military and the defense expenditure which is the key to implement his development activities. He can take on the militants and Taliban only when the army cooperates with him whole-heartedly. A friendly relationship with India is the Key to solve many problems in Pakistan. So I am here" Thappar explained his mission.

"You mean which Pakistan?. There are so many Pakistan. One is led by Sherrif, another one by the Army Chief, one more by Mullahs and miltants and the last one by Taliban. How can we deal with so many Pakistan?" Modi asked circastically.

'That is the crux of the problem. You should help to make Nawaz Sherif the real boss in Pakistan. Slowly he would bring all the groups including the Army under his control." replied Thappar.

"You want us to pay a heavy price to make Sherrif the real boss. Why should we pay the price? I am not the statesman like Nehru or Gandhi. I am a business man. I want to know what do India gain by making Sherrif as the strong man in Pakistan?. He was the man, who detonated nuclear bombs and the silent spectator of Kargil conflict. I can never believe any leader in Pakistan. Sherrif needs us more than we need him. That is why you are here" Modi spoke frankly without giving any hope to Thappar. He conveyed the failure of his mission to Sherrif. Sherrif was a disappointed man. He did not have any incentive to stop the anti-India speech by the mullahs and militansts. Taliban was happy that they were proved right in opposing India and USA. Sherrif decided to concentrate on improving his relationship with Iran, China and Gulf countries especially with Saudi Arabia. Pakistan depended heavily on Saudi for financial bail out.

On July 7th 2014 there were seven serial bomb blasts in the crowded market area of Hyderabad (India). More than 50 people were killed and 250 were severely injured. Many vehicles and buildings were damaged. Indian Mujahidin claimed the responsibility for bomb blasts. But investigation pointed towards lasker-e-Toiba. Arun Jaitly blamed Pakistan for not curbing the activities of LeT. Modi threatened strong action against Pakistan if it sends it miltant groups to bomb Indian cities. Nawaz Sherrif strongly denied any involvement by Pakistan based militant groups.

Modi called all the DGPs to the capital. When he presided over the meeting he was virtually fuming

"It is shame for India to be at the receiving end at the hands of these uncivilized militants who think that killing innocent people would ensure a place in the heaven. I don't blame them. I hold the police force responsible for not acting proactively to prevent such bomb blast. Therefore I order all the DGPs to create a special cell to collect intelligent information about the suspected militants and their supporters. Every month they should send a report about the number of suspected people interrogated and the number of people killed in the encounter. Don't wory about the courts. Preventing bomb blasts is more important than satisfying courts. They should not wait for a bomb blasts to take action. As a routine work they should detain the suspected people and interrograte them. In future if there is a bomb blast I will take a strong action against the DGP concerned. I ask DGP from Hyderabad to arrest at least atleast 100 suspected persons and the police should kill atleast 10 of them in the encounter. This will teach the militants a lesson" Modi concluded his speech and left in an angry mood.

Next day Hyderabad police arrested 110 suspected militants and killed eleven of them in encounter. All the human rights organizations were up in arms against Andhra Pradesh government. Modi told them to go hell to meet the militants. If they do not want to go to hell, they can console and help the families suffered in the bomb blasts. The common man appreciated the tit for tat approach of Modi.

The tough talk of Modi paid dividends. There was not a single attack during 2014.

24

BIRTH OF A NEW PARTY

Mansoor was not happy about PTI aligning with Religious parties to form a government in KP. Even before the election he opposed the PTI's soft approach towards Taliban. He helped PTI to give tough fight to PML(N) in Punjab. But for the soft approach towards Taliban, PTI could have done better in Punjab. But Imran didn't agree with his view. Mansoor expected Imran to move away from Religious parties and Taliban. But by his move to form the government in KP, he was inching towards Religious parties. Now PTI has to face the menace of Taliban in KP province. The coalition partners ie JI and QWP would not allow PTI government to take tough stand against Taliban. Mansoor expressed his views about the issue in his letter addressed to the Chairman of PTI. Imran Khan felt that Mansoor was an asset in Punjab. Therefore he didn't want to loose him. He invited Mansoor for a discussion.

Mansoor immediately responded to the invitation. He met his Chief at his residence.

Imran opened the topic

"Thank you for your hard work. But for your work we could not have given a tough fight to Nawz Sherrif in Punjab. I know the letter written by you was drafted by your wife. I could see her hands. I could understand her feelings. As a Hindu and a woman it is natural for her to oppose the religious parties and Taliban. But we are doing politics in Pakistan. We have to adapt to the realities prevailing in Pakistan. We cannot practice politics on moral grounds alone. Had I asked my wife Jemina she would expressed similar views. I did not ask her. We have to follow our own path. We should not follow the path of our wives in Politics. Your wife is not our party member. Therefore I have to ignore her views. My party is solidly behind me and they have given me full support in forming our government in KP. It will be suicidal to ignore their support. Therefore we are going ahead and form the government in KP. I have a special assignment for you. You are designated as our special representative to negotiate with Taliban and tribal leaders in PK."

"Thank you for your confidence in me. I started my political carrier based on the advice given by my wife. So far I am following her advice and I will do the same in future too. I feel that she is a wise lady who wants to liberate the women of Pakistan. I cannot disagree with her nor can I decline your offer. As a sincere worker of PTI, I will obey your order and do my best. I accept the responsibility. I want to complete this assignment in three months and submit the report.

Mansoor took the responsibility of making peace with the moderate Taliban. It was not an easy task. Taliban wanted to keep arms with them and implement strict Shariat laws in their territory. Mansoor was ready to make some concessions provided the Talibans lay down arms which they were not ready to do. They expressed that they want self rule for Swat area including some territory in Afghanistan. This was not acceptable to Mansoor. He went to every village and met all the tribal chiefs. They agreed with Mansoor. But they were afraid of Taliban. They said

"Pakistan military cannot protect us all the 24 hours 365 days a year. We have to live with Talban. We cannot go against them. As far as Sharia laws are concerned we have no problem with Taliban. We are already following them. The only problem with them is extortion. If we do not pay money they take away our crops or some times our boys and girls. They return them only after payment of ransom. We have no faith in Pakistani Army that they will behave better than Taliban."

Mansoor lost hope and returned to Islamabad.

He presented his report to the PTI working commitee as follows.

Taliban thinks that they are in a strong position. They are confident that they can take on Pakistan military as long as the civilians support them. Unless our military defeats Taliban decisively it is not possible to make them surrender their weapons. The question is how to defeat them. We have two options. One is to weaken them by isolating them from the civilians. We have tried this option and failed. The other option is to curtail their financial support and make them starve for funds. We should prevail over the military to stop supply of arms to Taliban through the clandestine route. Once the Taliban is deprived of funds and arms they have to come to negotiating table. If this approach too fails the only option available is to take a strong military action against them.

Our military never tasted success so far in any war. They have to prove their credibility by defeating Taliban. If they can't do it there is no use of maintaining such a huge army which spends 26% of our budget.

Let us analyze how our South Asian countries behaved when they faced similar situation.

Take for example India. It is a fighting a war against insurgents in Kashmir, Naga land and Maoist. India always used carrot and stick policy. They have deployed more than half a million troupes in J&K. Without the financial support from Indian government Kashmir government cannot even pay salaries to the government servants. They are fully dependant on central government for survival. Occasionally they make noise against Indian Government. But eventually they fall in line with Indian government.

Sri Lanka fought a civil war for decades and could not win. They never followed a consistent policy towards LTTE. It blew hot and cold. It tried to get help from India to eliminate LTTE. It could neither eliminate LTTE nor please India. Eventually Raja Bakshe decided to go ahead with stick only policy. It broke all conventions and attacked LTTE brutally with all its might and succeeded in eliminating LTTE from Sri Lankan soil.

As a last resort I recommend that Pakistan should follow Sri Lankan policy and eliminate Taliban as early as possible. Our Military should attack the Taliban with its full force and defeat Taliban. Once they are defeated they would lay down their arms and a reasonable agreement could be reached. In this operation we have to accept some civilian casualties as a collateral damage. I recommend that Nawaz Sherrif should consult the Chief of the Army before taking any decision.

This report was discussed by the working committee. The working committee thanked Mansoor for submitting a frank and realistic report. It agreed with the option of cutting the finance and arms to Taliban. But it did not agree with the military action as that would cause civilian casualties. It would send its recommendation to Nawaz Sherrif's government and it is for the Nawaz Sherif's to take a decision in this isse.

Mansoor spent some time with his family in Kuwait.He was not worried about the defeat of his party. But he was worried about the Chairman's lack of direction. In his opinion PTI"s policies are not in tune with the declared objectives. He discussed about his future course in Politics with Santhi.

"I tried to work with PPP. But I could not accept the leadership of Zardhari. Then I joined PTI with the hope he will establish a "Naya Pakistan" But I am disillusioned with his policiy of appeasing the militants and Taliban for selfish reasons. I want to give up politics and I may continue with my social work" Mansoot spoke in a dejected voice.

"Had you told this in the beginning I would have agreed. You have jumped in to politics knowing fully well about the dangers and disappoinments. Now you cannot go back on your journey of serving your nation. I suggest that you should start a paty of your own" Santhi suggested.

"Me! Starting my own party! Are you joking?" Mansoor exclaimed.

"Why not! You are not an intelectual. But you have the fire to serve the nation. You have the common sense better than any of our leaders. Do you know K.Kamaraj!. He was an uneducated common man. He was one of the true followers of Gandhiji. He rose to the level of Chief Minister and ruled Madras state for 10 years. He was considered as the best Chief Minister by the people of Tamil nadu. He rose to the level of Congress president and he was the King-maker too He was the first Congress presiden who asserted his power against Indira Gandhi. In Politics education is not a necessary qualification. You can run this country with your common sense approach. I am always available at your service. Do you know that Kathija, wife of our Prophet Mohamed guided him to become the King? Do not hesitate. You can go to your native place and consult your supporters. I am sure that they will agree with me." Santhi concluded her counseling.

'I respect your wisdom. I wish that you were born as a male. You would have become the Prime Minister of India" Mansoor praised his wife.

"No! No! I don't want. It is the toughest job in the world. Either you will be shot dead or thrown in to the dust bin by the people of India." Santhi said jokingly.

Mansoor started his preparation for his journey to Pakistan.

In January 2015 Mansoor made an open accusation aginst Imran Khan. He accused Imran for forming a collaboration government with the religious parties and for his soft approan on Taliban for selfish reasons. In an interview with press he made a statement.

"Pakistan cannot move forward carrying the luggage of Taliban and militant organizations. PTI is interested only in power and is not willing

154

to get rid of Taliban to retain the support of the coalition partners in KP. Sherrif government too is not willing to use the army against Taliban. He was afraid of his base in Punjab which consists of militants and religious organizations. They may accuse him of towing the line of USA and India. Our military is more interested to keep our internal and external enemies alive to justify its existence. Once we eliminate Taliban, disarm militant organizations and make peace with India we may not need an army of this size. That is the reason why Military hesitates to take action against Taliban and militant organizations. Whenever Pakistan moves forward the peace process either ISI or some terrorist outfits sabotages it. I hold Nawaz Sherrif responsible for this stalemate. I have decided to start a new party."

On 15th March 2015 Mansoor called a press conference to announce his decision

The reporter from Dawn asked

"What is the name of your party?"

"Pakistan Jinnah Party. In short form PJP" replied Mansoor.

"It sounds like BJP. You have started the party in the name of our founder editor's name. It is master stroke. Nobody thought before to start a party in the name of the father of our nation (Quaid-e-Azam). Who selected this name?" the reporter quizzed.

"My wife. I told you that she is wiser than me" Mansoor praised his wife.

"What are your policies? How do you differ from others?" the reporter from the Nation asked.

"Before listing out our policies I want to bring out some historical facts about our Qaid-e-Azam. Today many youngsters know him as the father our nation as Indians know Gandhi as the father of their Nation. The truth is that Gandhi did not create India or Bharat as they call it. India exists for thousands of years as one country divided by territory but united by its culture. But Mohamad Ali Jinnah carved our nation from British India. Once Burma, part of Afghanistan and Sri Lanka were part of British India. British themselves carved out Burma, Afghanistan and Ceylon from India without any blood shed.

Till 1930 Jinnah was a strong advocate of Hindu Muslim unity. After 1930 Jinnah faced many problems with Hindu leaders in Indian National Congress. When Muslim league was formed Indian Muslims did not accept Muslim League as their representative and Jinnah as their leader. Jinnah had to fight hard to win the hearts of Muslims. Even at the time of Independence North West Frontier Province did not elect a single Muslim league candidate. In 1937 Mohammad Iqbal conceived the idea of a separate nation for Muslims and named it as "Pakistan". In 1940 Muslim League passed the "Lahore Resolution" and demanded from the British rulers to carve out a separate nation for Muslims.

Initially Jinnah did not subscribe fully to the idea of Pakistan. He wanted to use it as the bargaining tool to extract concessions from Congress. He was demanding separate constituency and reservation for Muslims. He also wanted reservation in Government jobs and in military. His contention was that Muslims cannot get fair opportunities in Hindu dominated India. In the beginning, his aim was to safe guard the interest of Muslims in India by incorporating suitable provisions in the constitution of India. But in 1945, Hindu leaders like Motilal Nehru, Rajendra Prasad were adamant and refused to give any concession to Muslims. This behavior angered Jinnah and made him to demand a separate nation for Muslim. Gandhi was the only man who opposed Partition.

At no point of time during the freedom struggle Hindus and Muslims asked for partition. It was the politics played by the Hindu leaders and Muslim leaders that led to partition. Even at the time of partition bulk of the Indian Muslims preferred to stay in India. That was why India had more Muslims than Pakistan at the time of partition. The two nation theory failed at beginning itself. 1971 war sealed the fate of Two Nation Theory. In our text book these facts were either twisted or concealed. Our education system portray India is a country infested with wicked people, non-believers and idolaters. This is not true. I have personal experience in Gulf countries, where I had the opportunity to mingle with thousands of Indians. I have not found a single Indian who has animosity towards Pakistanis.

Jinnah was a secular minded person. He never wanted to establish a theological state controlled by Mullahs. On 11 August, 1947 he presided over the new constituent assembly for Pakistan at Karachi, and addressed them,

"You are free; you are free to go to your temples, you are free to go to your mosques or to any other place of worship in this State of Pakistan. You may belong to any religion or caste or creed. That has nothing to do with the business of the State."

On 14 August, Pakistan became independent; Jinnah led the celebrations in Karachi. One observer wrote, "Here indeed are Pakistan's King, Emperor, Archbishop of Canterbury, Speaker and Prime Minister concentrated into one formidable *Quaid-e-Azam*." All the political parties conveniently went against his wishes and made Pakistan as theological state.

Jinnah had bitter experience with Gandhi. Yet when Gandhi was assassinated he said in his statement "Gandhi is one of the great men produced by the Hindu Community"

After Jinnah died, his sister Fatima asked the court to execute Jinnah's will under Shia Islamic law. This subsequently became the part of argument in Pakistan about Jinnah's religious affiliation. Vali Nasr said Jinnah was an Ismaili by birth and a Twelver Shia by confession, though not a religiously observant man. In a 1970 legal challenge, Hussain Ali Ganji Walji claimed Jinnah had converted to Sunni Islam, but the High Court rejected this claim in 1976, effectively accepting the Jinnah family as Shia. Publicly Jinnah had a non-sectarian stance and was at pains to gather the Muslims of India under the banner of a general Muslim faith and not under a divisive sectarian identity. In 1970, a Pakistani court decision stated that Jinnah's secular Muslim faith made him neither Shia nor Sunni" and in **1984 the court maintained that Quaide-e-Azam was definitely not a Shia. Liaquat H. Merchant stated that he was also not a Sunni, he was simply a Muslim.**

Our difference between Sunnies and Shias are much more than that between Hindus and Muslims in India. Had our Quaida-e-Azam lived longer our country would have become a secular state.

We usually avoid even the slightest criticism of Jinnah. Whereas in India people are free to criticize Gandhi. Every book about Jinnah outside Pakistan mentions that he drank alcohol, but this is omitted from the books inside Pakistan. We think that accepting the truth that Jinnah drank alcohol would weaken Jinnah's Islamic identity and by extension, Pakistan's. Why should we hide the truth from the people of Pakistan? Majority of Muslims in the world drink alcohol like any other people. Jinnah was a human-being too. He was not a prophet. He too had some weakness. They do not take away his contributions to Pakistan. Some times truth is bitter. We have to swallow it. We cannot hide our head under the sand and say Jinnah stood for theological state.

Few individuals significantly alter the course of history. Fewer still modify the map of the world. Hardly anyone can be credited with creating a nation-state. Mohammad Ali Jinnah did all three.

By accepting the fact that Jinnah drank alcohol and dressed like Europeans we are not reducing his greatness. All the great people have something negative about them but the world ignores them as inconsequential.

Our party is wedded to his ideals. I know that the religious organizations may brand me as a non-Muslim and they may even demand that a case should be filed against me under Blasphemy law. The public will support me because I speak the truth however bitter it may be.

I am giving the policies formulated by me below. However this is only indicative. The final policy document once approved by our working committee will be released soon.

1. Pakistan will be declared as Secular state. All the religious faith would be treated as equals. People would be free to follow any religion they like.
2. All the citizens of Pakistan will have equal rights guaranteed by constitution. Nobody would be discriminated against because of race, colour, sex, religion, language or wealth.
3. Ahmedias would be accepted as Muslims
4. Every citizen who earns more than 2lakhs per annum has to pay income tax irrespective of his source of income. There will be no exemption. Tax evasion will be made a criminal offence.
5. Pakistan will give up its claim of Plebiscite in Jammu-Kashmir and accept the LOC as the international border. A peace treaty would be signed between India and Pakistan accordingly. We would also agree to the no first use of Nuclear weapon treaty.
6. Azad Kashmir will be declared as the fifth province and it will be known as "Kashmir"
7. Once we sign the peace treaty with India we will cut down our military size gradually. Our target will be to spend only 10% of our GDP on defense.
8. During the peace time the army will be used to build the infrastructure in our country in the way Venizula did.
9. We will sign free trade agreements with all our South Asian neighbors including India and Bangladesh.

10. Pakistan will tender an apology to Bangladesh for the atrocities committed by the Pakistani army in 1971 and will pay a token compensation to all those affected by the atrocities committed by the Pakistan army.

11. Pakistan will invite all countries to start schools, colleges and universities. But 25% of the seats would be reserved for the poor. They should charge the poor a nominal fee fixed by the government of Pakistan. It will provide free education to all the girl children in villages.

12. Human rights organization would be given full freedom and blasphemy act would be repealed.

13. All the languages would be given equal status. Each province would be given a quota in military in proportion to their population.

14. Possession of weapons by individuals or any organization will be strictly prohibited.

     Military will be exclusively used to disarm the militants and Taliban.

15. Pakistan will not interfere in the internal affairs of Afghanistan or any other neighbor.

16. All our text books will be revised. All the falsehood in the text would be removed.

     We will teach our children to love all and not to hate anybody. Any hate material in the syllabus will be removed

17. All the training camps will be closed. All foreign jihads will be sent back. Pakistan will not allow its soil used for terrorist activities.

18. We will continue to maintain cordial relationship with China and USA.

19. All the ministers will be paid only salaries as fixed by NA after deducting taxes. But they will not be provided any perks.

20. We will bring a land ceiling act. The excess land recovered from land lords will be distributed to the poor agricultural labour at a nominal rent. The titles will be transferred to them when they agree to pay the price fixed by the government.

21. Immediate action will be taken to improve the power situation. Incentives will be provided to those who erect wind mills and solar power houses. We will try to maximize power production from the hydraulic sources.

22. To encourage food production we will fix remunerative price for Wheat, Rice and dhal.

23. Rural population will be discouraged from moving to urban areas. They will be provided all the facilities in the rural areas. Top priority will be given to rural development and infrastructure.

24. We will continue the incentive schemes to overseas Pakistanis to attract investment from them.

25. We will not take any loan from IMF or any country. But banks and corporations will be allowed to borrow on commercial terms. Wherever necessary, sovereign guarantee will be provided by the government.

26. Pakistan will not ban any book, website or a film. If anybody tries to harm the interest of Pakistan we will counter them through media. We will accept all criticism sportively. A strong person accepts criticism. Only a weak person protests.

27. As a secular state we will start our parliamentary proceedings without reciting Holy Koran.

   I will form the working committee soon. We will apply to the election commission for registration of our party at the national level and in all the provinces."

All the reporters were stunned when Mansoor read out the policy statements.

The reaction from the media was positive. But some religious organizations condemned the policies of PJP as anti-Islam and anti-Pakistan. Reaction from the parties was muted and mostly they ignored PJP. Probably they didn't want to give publicity to PJP by their reaction.

But a controversy arose when PJP applied to the Election Commission for registration. All the parties objected the use of Jinnah's name by PJP. But the Commission ignored their objection and granted registration. They appealed to the Supreme Court against the decision taken by Election Commission. But the Supreme Court upheld the decision by stating that "Nothing is provided in the constitution which prohibits the use of the name Jinnah by anybody. In fact many institutions, airports, parks, university, trusts use the name Mohamed Ali Jinnah. The claim by the political parties that PJP will derive advantage by using the name Jinnah is not substantiated. If they think so they too can use the name

Jinnah in their party name. Nobody prevents them. Hence the petition by the political parties is dismissed"

Soon the working committee appointed office bearers through out Pakistan. There was membership drive in all the provinces. Within three months PJP had one million members. Most of the members have entered in to politics for the first time. Many honest people who kept themselves aloof from politics were happy to join PJP. Makhdoom Amin Fahim resigned from PPP and joined PJP as its adviser. He refused to accept any post in the party. He wanted to work with Mansoor to make Pakistan a secular democratic state. His presence in the party gave a moral boost to PJP. The working committee wanted to include Santhi as its member. But Mansoor did not accept saying that he was against dynastic rule.

After enrolling one million membership the first public meeting was held on 1st of July 2015 in Rawalpindi. Mansoor presided over the meeting. In his presidential address he said

"I am happy to stand before crowd of half million people. It is a record in the history of Pakistan, a party which was formed only three months ago could attract such large crowd. This shows that our policies are accepted by the people. I expect the staunch supporters of other parties too will join our party. I have no doubt that Imran Khan and Nawz Sheriff are good leaders. But they are not bold enough to initiate changes and afraid to take on the militants and Talibans. We expected the P.M to take full control of military. But it did not happen. Military is so much entrenched in the military establishments it does not want to give up its power to the civilian government. If we come to power we will root out corruption and put the military in to Barracks. I know it is a big risk. But I am ready to take the risk. Only when military is ready to take orders from the Prime Minister our problems would be solved one by one.

During the next three months I will be touring all over the world. I will meet all the Muslim leaders and explain them why Pakistan should be a secular democratic state instead of a Islamic Welfare State. I will also meet the heads of states of USA, U.K. Germany, Russia, France, Switzerland, Holland, Japan, China, Indonesia, Philippines, Korea, Australia, Canada, Bangaladesh, Bracil, South Africa, all the gulf countries, Iran, Iraq, Afghanistan, Egypt and India. I will impress upon them that Pakistan is not a failed intolerant state. It stands for democracy, justice and equality. I will explain them **that PJP stands for, Progress, Justice and Peace.**

Peace, Justice, Progress is our slogan. I appeal to the youth and women of this country to join our party. Our working committee will take care of membership drive in my absence.

Now I request our esteemed leader Fahim to say few words about our policies. As soon as Fahim finished his speech the crowd shouted "Santhi is the architect of this party. We want to hear her speech". Santhi refused to climb the stage. But the crowd continued the shouting which made her to relent. She climbed on the stage with folded hands and spoke

"Me and Mansoor had a covenant before marriage. I will continue to be a Hindu and he will continue to be a true Muslim. Both of us do not believe in conversion. We want to show to the world that a Muslim husband and a Hindu wife can live a happy life as Akbar the great did. In my opinion religion is a private affair between god and the individual. No body has the right to interfere in this freedom. God is one whatever name you call it. Being so, why should we quarrel among us in the name of religion? If secularism can bring peace and prosperity so be it. Pakistan Jindabad! Let us pray that peace should prevail all over the world. That is the meaning of Salaam Alaikum" she concluded her speech in chaste Urdu. The crowd roared in applause. On that night both of them had a peaceful and fruitful sleep.

25

LIFE IN PAKISTAN 2015-16

Later part of 2015 and the earlier part of 2016 proved to be tough time for Mansoor. He was shuttling between the world capitals, Kuwait and Pakistan. He kept in touch with his party executives through email every day. At the same time he never forgot to make his phone call to Kuwait.

His meeting with non-muslim country heads of the states was smooth. Indeed every body congratulated him for his bold stand on religion. Most of the heads of the states looked at him as the future Prime Minister of Pakistan. But when he met the rulers of Muslim countries like Saudi Arabia, Iran, Abu Dhabi who are the traditional supporters of military rule in Pakisatn and Nawaz Sherif, he had hard time in explaining his policies.

He told the King of Saudi Arabia

"When I met the rulers of non-Muslim countries they expressed that Islam and democracy cannot coexist. I told them that I will prove them wrong. I explained them that it is not the Islam that is against democracy but the Muslim rulers are against democracy. Therefore it created a false impression among the non-Muslim counties that Islam is against democracy. Only Islam treats all the human-being as equals. In the mosque the king and his subjects have to pray side by side where as in other religious places people are discriminated in the churches and temples. I do agree with non-Muslim countries that some of the Islamic countries do not treat woman and men as equals. But it is changing. The only way to change mentality of the Muslim men is to educate our women. Once they are educated, there is no necessity for the men to give equal status to women. They will take it from them. That is why I want to give greater importance to woman's education. If you educate a man you educate an individual. But when you educate a woman you educate a family.

When I was living in Kuwait with my wife, I use to see Sun T.V with my wife. I learnt some Tamil by watching Sun T.V. On a Sunday morning I watched an Indian philosopher by name Suki Sivam giving his discourse. Every Sunday he gives speech about various topics in Sun T.V. He told that the food that we eat decides our behavior. He said that our food can be divided in to three categories. He calls them as sathvic (Grade 1) and Rajoistic(Grade 2) and thamasic (grade 3). The grade 1 consists of fruits, vegetables and herbals. Grade 2 consists of grains, dhal, dairy products, fish, spices and nuts. Grade 3 consists of meat, egg, frozen foods, fried foods, polished grains, junk foods and processed foods. He further elaborated that Grade 1 make a person intelligent, calm and creative. Grade 2 makes a person aggressive, greedy, angry and jealousy. Grade 3 makes person sexy, lazy, wicked and selfish. That speech did not make any effect on me. Later when I was contemplating how my wife remains calm, dignified and creative it dawned on me that she is a vegetarian. I want to test the hypothesis that vegetarian food can change the behavior of a person. I started correspondence with advocates of Vegetarianism. I was convinced by their argument. I decided to become a vegetarian. I told my wife that I have decided to become a vegetarian as gift for the service rendered by her as my wife. My wife didn't believe me. She said that I would soon change my mind. But I proved her wrong. Till today I remain a vegetarian and I do not drink alcohol" Mansoor paused to drink some water.

He continued his argument in favour of secularism.

"The religious parties call BJP as Hinduthwa party and it is the enemy of Muslim. BJP chose Abdul Kalaam as president. It was ready to give a second term to him. Congress opposed his re-election. Abdul Kalaam is a true Muslim in his private life and secular man in his public life.He is a bachelor, never drinks alcohol and a vegetarian too. He is considered as the best president India ever had. All the Indians have great respect for him. He is my role model. Indians was so generous to elect three Muslims as their presidents and one as their Vice President. Pakistan would be considered as magnanimous only when we elect atleast one Hindu as our president. I want this to happen in Pakistan. It is possible only when Pakistan becomes a secular country" Mansoor concluded his argue ment.

King wanted to avoid talking about secularism. He wanted divert the topic to a less controvertial subject.

"What is the result of your experiment with vegetarian food?" the King asked.

"It is amazing. My behavior changed a lot. I do not get angry. My health improved. I get wonderful ideas when I contemplate about a problem" Mansoor expressed his feelings.

"You should have started an NGO to promote vegetarianism instead staring a political party" King suggested.

"I wouldn't succeed. Muslims in the Middle East and the Europeans ate meat out of necessity. It shaped their behavior. But Muslims in the sub-continent ate non-vegetarian foods as a culture. The sub-continent was blessed with every kind of food a human-being needed to satisfy the taste buds. You mention a food it is there in the sub-continent. Any person in the sub-continent can live happily without eating non-vegetarian food. The Zoroastrians, when they migrated from Persia to India, changed their food habits. They found that they can live a healthy life without eating too much of meat. For Muslims in India and Pakistan biriyani, kabab, kurma, roasted chicken, mutton, beef and goat are part of their culture. No marriage or any other function can take place without biriyani. Therefore non-vegetarianism is an integral part of Islam in the sub-continent. Gandhi, a pure vegetarian was the first man in the history who shook the largest empire in the world with his simple tool called Ahimsa (non-violence). People in India supported him. The Hindus including the non-vegetarians believe that eating meat is a sin. This belief made them to support the non-violent movement of Gandhi.

The Europeans and the Muslims in the Middle East understood the benefits of vegetarian food. Slowly they are changing their food habits to eat more vegetables than meat. But the Muslims in the sub-continent prefer to eat meat. They go for vegetables out of economic compulsion. I am not a prophet who can change the food habits of Muslims. Democracy means freedom. I have to respect their right to eat meat. They are integral part of the subcontinent's culture. I strongly believe that Allah has chosen me to lead a movement to restore a true democracy in Pakistan. A theological state cannot establish a true democracy. Only a secular state can do it. Islam can flourish in a secular state. India, U.K, USA, and Bangladesh are typical examples where Islam is practiced with full freedom. Prophet Mohamad advocated tolerance with other religions. Islam accepts the existence of Jews and Christians. There is no reason why it cannot accept Hinduism or any other religion for that matter. No religion in the world has the right to say that the people who do not believe in their god are non-believers or infidels or idolators. There were great philosophers who denied the existence of god. They have the right to say so. That is freedom. That is the essence of democracy. I need your moral support to establish a true democracy in Pakistan" thus Mansoor concluded his argument. The King couldn't utter a word against Mansoor. He blessed him success.

Mansoor returned to Pakistan via Kuwait. He and his wife felt very happy after successful completion of his tour of the world capitals. Their happiness received a shot when they learnt from the email that the membership of PJP crossed the ten million mark in one year.

26

PAKISTAN 2017-2018

On January 1ˢᵗ 2017 The membership of PJP crossed twenty million mark. Many more leaders have joined PJP during the year 2016. Some were inducted in to the working committee. The working committee decided to hold its Karachi session on March 15ᵗʰ 2017. They were asked by Mansoor to prepare the resolutions to be passed. They prepared the following resolution.

1. PJP has decided to go alone in the coming election 2018.
2. In case PJP doesn't get an absolute majority it will prefer to sit in the opposition rather than making alliance with parties which do not subscribe its policy of making Pakistan a secular state.
3. Mansoor will be the Prime Ministerial candidate and Santhi will be the star campaigner in the General Election 2018.
4. Two sons of Mansoor will continue to live U.K for security reasons.
5. PJP will not depend on government to give security to Mansoor. What happened to Benazir should not happen again. The security personal selected to give protection to Mansoor will be trained by U.K government. They will be on duty round the clock as soon as the election is announced.
6. The list of the names of all the candidates who will be contesting National Assembly and Provincial assemblies is being prepared by the election committee. It will be released at the end of the session. The objection received from the party members and the public against any candidate will be scrutinized by the working committee. The decision taken by the working will be binding on all the party members including the election committee. Those who seek election ticket on their own will be interviewed

by the election committee and their recommendation would be forwarded to the working committee. Working committee is the final authority to finalize the list. All the selected candidates have to proceed to their respective constituency immediately and start working with the people. They should not leave their constituency without informing the W.C. They should send weekly report about the work done and the response from the public. If any one fails to send report or any adverse report is sent by any member of the party he will be removed from the primary membership. However he will be given a chance to defend himself by the W.C.

7. 50% of the contituencies for NA and provincial Assemblies will be reserved for women. There will be no bar for women to contest the unreserved constituencies. The W.C and E.C. should ensure that all the women candidates are genuine and proxy candidate should not be allowed.

8. All the candidates should obey the election law in letter and sprit. They should not exceed the expenditure limit prescribed by the Election Commission.

9. No two candidates will be allowed from the same family.

10. As far as possible the candidates should communicate with the people in the local language.

Karachi session was held at National Stadium, Karachi. Santhi was not invited for security reasons. Security advisors advised Mansoor to avoid appearing in public places with his wife. The session was presided over by Mansoor. The key note address was given by Makhdoom Amin Fahim.

Two million people gathered. Mansoor spoke in his presidential address.

"My beloved Brothers! Sisters! I welcome you with my humble salaam. I feel that I am dreaming when I see the large crowd gathered here. Now I feel the burden of the responsibility thrust on me by your love and affection. There is overwhelming support from the public to our policies. I have to thank the media without which we could not have achieved this success. I caution our party members not to underestimate the power of the people who are opposed to our policies. You have to work hard to retain the goodwill generated during the last 2 years. There is one more danger against which we have to guard ourselves. When some unscrupulous politicians come to know that PJP is sure to win the election, they may join us to sabotage within. Therefore beware of them. In the lust for power they may distract you from our objectives.

I would request the provisionally selected candidates to go back to their constituencies and work hard and ensure our success. Now I request our esteemed leader Makhdoom Amin Fahim to give his key note address." Mansoor concluded his presidential address.

Fahim began his address

"My dear fellow members of PJP, Women and children! I am indebted to you for the trouble you have taken to come over here and made this session a grand success. I was asked by Mansoor to give this address. But the fittest person to give this key note address is Santhi. She could not come over here for security reasons. To day Pakistan is not a safe country for woman who is bold enough to differ with mainstream political parties. I honestly accept that PJP is the brain child of Santhi. Without her ideas and moral support Mansoor could not have taken this step. Let us pray Allah to give her long life. At every point of time Mansoor consulted me before taking any major decision. I too made my humble contribution to the growth of PJP. I am proud to say this.

I was twice offered Prime Ministership by Benazir and Mushraf. I have turned down the offers for different reasons. When Benazir reached Pakistan she told me that I have to accept the Prime Minister ship after the election. She had a great faith in me. I was loyal to PPP right from her father's time. Had Benazir lived she would have made me the Prime minister and she would have become the president. After the election I expected that Benazir's wish would be fulfilled. But Zardhari hesitated to make me the prime Minsiter because I am a law abiding citizen and would rather resign the post than go against the constitution. Therefore he wanted a Prime Minister who would never go against him under any circumstance. As a loyal party member of PPP I accepted the post of Commerce Minister and contributed whatever possible to improve the economy of our country.

Under Sherrif Government, economy of Pakistan did improve. But the problems posed by the militancy and Taliban remain unsolved. He lacks the boldness and the drive to control the army and take on the militants and Taliban. During his rule for the past four years he could not bring any drastic change what Pakistan is badly in need. His attempt to improve our relationship with India and Bangladesh did not bring the expected result. In short Sherrif could not make any big impact on lives of ordinary citizens. Whatever development he made benefited the rich and the powerfull

Pakistan has become a sick state. Militancy and Taliban are like cancers that may bring slow death to Pakistan. At the right time Mansoor entered in to politics. My question is to you is very simple. There are only two states in the world created on the basis of religion. All other countries declared themselves as secular state. Mansoor says that secularism would change the destiny of Pakistan. Why not give him a chance? Pakistan has lost everything it stood for. It has nothing to loose by giving a chance. I know him personally. He is an honest and straight forward politician. If he cannot deliver the goods as promised he will not hesitate for a moment to resign from the post and order for election. I have more than 50 years of experience in politics. Mansoor is a unique politician probably molded by his wife. She is the symbol of rising women power in the world. If Pakistan tries to swim against the current it may not achieve its goal. I am afraid that it may be swept away by the current." he concluded his address.

The secretary of PJP read out the resolutions prepared by the working committee. The resolutions were passed by the unanimous voice vote.

On 15th May 2018 the general election was announced. The date for election was fixed as 15th July 2018. Many leaders in PTI resigned to join PJP. They hoped to contest from PJP in their respective constituencies. They approached the working committee for tickets. However the W.C did not entertain their application because all the candidates name were fixed a year ago and they were working very hard in their allotted constituencies. They established a good rapport with the people. The public started treating them as their elected representatives even before the election. Most of them were sure of their victory and their victory was a bygone conclusion.

On 15th June 2018 a public meeting was arranged by PJP in Islamabad. Santhi was invited to give her speech. Makhdoom Amin Fahim presided over the meeting. Mansoor did not attend the meeting for security reasons.

Makhdoom in his presidential address stated

"My dear fellow Pakistanis! This is a day of reckoning. People of Pakisatan are standing on the cross roads of the history. They have to decide what type of government they want. It is a fight between status qua and change. It is a fight between theological government and secular government. It is fight between male domination and women's empowerment. It is a fight between fuedalist government and all powerful democratic government. It is a fight between corruption tolerant government and corruption free government. It is fight between old guards and new blood. It is a fight between progress and stagnation. It is fight between liberal values and conservatism.

PJP is standing on one side and all other parties are standing on the other side. People have to choose between the two sides. PJP stands for secularism, women's empowerment, true democracy, transparent and corruption free government, peace loving and anti-jihad government, nuclear free world and humanist government. If you elect the PJP government the image of Pakistan in the international community as an intolerant failed state would be erased immediately. Our rating will go up. Our overseas Pakistanis will pour money in to our country. If Pakistan's image and economy improve we need not beg anybody for aid or investment. They will come to our doorstep without asking for. I see the crowd is restless. They are eagerly waiting to hear Santhi's speech. I do not want to stand in her way. I invite her to speak." Makhdoom concluded his speech.

There was roaring applause from the crowd. The crowd shouted "Come on Santhi! We are here to support you. Come what may"

As Santhi rose to speak, there was a commotion among the crowd. A handful of people were shouting slogans against her. Probably they were planted by some religious parties. There was a scuffle between them and the crowd. Security personnel immediately rushed to the stage and cordoned her. Santhi appealed for calm. Within ten minutes every thing became calm. The miscreants were removed from the crowd. Santhi spoke

"My beloved Pakistani sisters and brothers! Our esteemed leader Fahim spoke whatever I wanted to speak. He left little room for me to contribute. I wanted to start my speech with a story. A rich farmer had thousands of acres of grazing land by the side of a forest. He reared thousands of goats and sheep. He appointed ten workers to take care of the goats and sheep. There was no dearth of demand for mutton in Pakistan. It was a roaring business and he made a very good profit. In the night foxes and jackal used to sneak in to the herd and stole few young goats or sheep for their meals. This was going on for some years. The owner did not bother about it. When people around him asked him to stop this theft he used to reply that the wild animals too have a right to live in this world. He said that any way he is making a good profit. Why should he worry about it? His sons started growing in to adults. The father asked them to work along with the workers to protect the herd in the night. For some time they obeyed their father. They missed watching T.V.serials. They started escaping from their duty and watched T.V in their friend's houses and slept there. Due to absence of supervision the workers too slept without bothering to protect the herd from foxes. The loss of herd went up. At one time the daily loss went up to ten against an average of two or three previously. The owner got worried. He wanted to know the reason for the increase. Their sons did not tell the truth. They blamed the workers. The owner asked his sons to come out with a suggestion to reduce the losses. One of his son suggested that they should put more men on the job. But the owner told that additional salary will be more than the loss. Another son came up with an idea that they should have some ferocious dogs to fight the foxes. Dogs will not demand salary. If we can cut one goat or sheep every day it will be enough for them. The owner hesitated to accept the suggestion. The sons forced their father to accept the suggestion. Accordingly four rottweilers (ferocious dogs) were imported from Germany as per the advice given by a dog expert.

Two of them were males and two were females. They did a wonderful job. The loss of herd stopped completely. After one year the dog population increased to ten. The owner wanted to sell some dogs to reduce consumption of meat. But the sons were so much attached to the dogs; they refused to sell the dogs. They told their father that they have enough income to maintain another hundred dogs. After few years the population of dogs did increase to hundred. The sons were adamant not to sell some dogs. Now they are cutting twenty fine goats to feed the dogs. Finally one wise man visited his home. He told the owner that if he were wise he would not have accepted the suggestion of his sons and your loss would have limited to two or three. Now the loss is not in your control. Your sons are fond of dogs. One day your dogs will eat the entire herd. Better sell dogs and make a good profit.

The owner accepted the suggestion and the sons resisted. This is the story. Now tell me "Who are the dogs?"

"Military and militants" the crowd shouted.

"Who is the owner?"

"The people of Pakistan":

"Who are the sons?"

"Civilain government and religious organizations"

"Who is the wise man?"

"Santhi" the crowd shouted

"No! It is PJP" Santhi corrected the crowd.

I am glad that you have understood the story. The people of Pakistan are the real owners of this land, rivers, mountains, mineral resources, the buildings, parks, the institutions and all the educational institutions. The military and the government are the servants appointed by the people. They are not your rulers. You are the master and they are the servants. If they do not serve you well you can throw them out at your will. No body on earth can stop that. You are the master of your destiny. Act now and make yourselves a proud and courageous people in the world. Tell the world that you have no enemies. You will have only friends and well-wishers if you act wisely. I request the crowd to repeat what I say

"PJP means Progress with Justice and Peace"

The crowd repeated the slogan three times. The shouting shook the whole world and the media.

Next day all the newspaper published her speech in full along with that of Fahim's.

"Indian woman shakes Pakistan" this was the headline published in Dawn

"PJP targets Military and Militants" this was the headline from The Nation.

"Santhi tells people you are the owner" the headline in Pakistan Times

"Santhi calls the military and jihads as dogs" cried one of the newspaper run by the religious organization.

The media surrounded the place where Santhi stayed. She came out and was ready to answer the questions from reporters.

"Are you not afraid of the military and militants?" reporter from Dawn

"No! They are afraid of me"

"Under PJP government, will you be our ambassador to India?" asked the reporter from Nation.

"Why are you trying to separate me from my husband?" Santhi joked.

"It is a novelty that you have chosen to tell a story to drive your point. Where did you learn this technique?" asked a reporter from Current Affairs Magazine.

"It is not a novelty. Jesus, Prophet Mohamed and Buddha used this technique to develop good rapport with people" replied Santhi.

"Are you comparing yourself with Jesus, Prophet and Buddha?" a reporter from religious newspaper tried to corner Santhi.

"No! No! I just wanted to tell the truth that I copied them. They never had a copy right for this technique. So it is not a crime" she retorted.

"How do you get an appropriate story to suit the occasion?" a reporter quizzed.

"I read a lot"

"Do you have a plan to apply for the citizenship of Pakistan?" one of the reporters poked her.

"Citizenship is not a problem for me. I retain my Indian citizenship because as an Indian I can travel to any part of the world without any difficulty. Moreover I found that a sari-clad married Indian woman get great respect from the people all over the world" She shot back at the reporter.

When she retaliated, the reporters became more sober and asked meaningful questions. She answered all their questions patiently for one hour. At the end of the session she asked "Any more question? I take it you have none and take leave. Please excuse me I am waiting for a call from my husband. I end this session. I will meet you soon" she concluded.

"She did not forget that she is a house wife" commented one of the reporters. Every body laughed and disbursed with satisfaction.

Wherever Santhi spoke, she was asked to tell a story. She used the technique of telling a story and asked the crowd the moral of the story by questions. Usually the crowd understood the moral of the story. Some times it looked like a puzzle which the crowd couldn't understand and Santhi had to explain the moral. On one such occasion she told a story in Lahore

There were two brothers living in a village. They lived happily. There was not a single occasion a misunderstanding arose between them. The elder brother protected his younger brother and the younger one respected the elder one. The harmonious relationship cracked when they got married. Both the bahus hated each like enemies. As long as their father lived things were under control. When their father died the problem of partition of assets divided the brothers permanently. The younger one got his share and moved away. After the partition they never met face to face. They used to communicate with each other through some third person. Their wives saw to it that the brothers never met face to face. They were afraid their meeting may change their mind. One day it so happened they saw each other in a market place. Each wanted to talk to the other. But something prevented them from talking to each other. They looked at each other's eyes. One expected the other to speak first. The elder felt that the younger one quarreled and left home and it was his fault. Therefore he has to speak first. The younger one thought that elder's responsibility to behave magnanimously and talk first. Thus they missed the opportunity to break the ice between them. But both wives utilized every opportunity to widen the difference. Both of them tried to harm the other through their enemies. But whenever the elder met the children of the younger he showed his affection and love to them. The younger brother did the same thing. In their heart they could not forget the past golden days when they were together. Probably when their wives die the children from both the families may unite.

Santhi finished the story and asked the crowd

"Who are the brothers?"

The crowd was silent. One young man got up and said "It may be a story from a serial in Indian T.V. We have not seen the serial yet"

"No! It is not a serial. May be you are too young to answer this question? I will give the answer. The brothers are India and Pakistan. I think you can answer other questions now" Santhi waited for the response from the crowd.

"Yes we can" the crowd shouted.

"Who are the wives?"

"Hinduism and Islam" crowd replied.

"Who are the children?"

"Cinema, cricket, trade and music" the crowd replied promptly.

"Who was the father?"

"British" crowd replied without any hesitation.

"It is amazing that the crowd understood such subtle questions even the intelligent find it difficult to answer them." Santhi praised the crowd.

Wherever Santhi spoke she attracted more crowd than any other leader. The reason was that she was not a stereo type leader. She never repeated what she said in one place. Therefore the media showed a keen interest to report her speech in full. Most other leaders including Mansoor and Makhdoom could not compete with her in this respect. Indeed Santhi performed well as the star campaigner for PJP.

On 15 July the general election was held as per the schedule. The election was peaceful. Most of the countries sent their observers. All of them reported that the election was free and fair. The results were announced on 16th July 2018. PJP swept the poll in National and provincial assemblies. It got two-third majority in NA and two provincial assemblies. MQM and PTI retained their strong hold. PJP got only simple majority in Balochestan and Sind. PTI got a decent 20 in NA. PPP and PML (N) suffered heavy losses. Mansoor was elected as the parliamentary leader by PJP. He was invited by the President to take oath on 1st August 2018 as Prime Minister. Due to security reasons Mansoor refused to attend the press conference. Instead Santhi met the press.

"What is the reason for the run-away success of PJP?" reporter from Dawn asked.

"All the major parties were given a chance to rule this country. But they failed to deliver the goods. Therefore they have given a chance to PJP" Santhi replied.

"Some commentators from the western media comment that because of your novel campaign PJP swept the poll. The women were attracted by your boldness and the young were attracted by the juicy stories you have dished out. What is your take on this?" asked a reporter.

"No! It is not true. The truth is that the people of Pakistan have accepted our policies. They want a change which we are ready to provide. More over the people lost faith in other three major parties. In fact it is these parties which brought us to power"

"Some commentators say that the selection of candidates one year ahead of the election helped them to develop a good report with the people. The people had enough time to get to know the merit of the candidates. Is this true?" one reporter asked.

"It is true. People get confused when so many candidates are in the fray. When they are familiar with a face they prefer him" Santhi gave an explaination for her decision.

"What will be your relationship with military?"

"It will be sent back to the place where it belongs"

"What will be your relations with Taliban?"

"Taliban will run for safety in to Afghanistan. It will be left to Afghanistan to deal with them"

"What are you going to do with militants?"

"All the weapons possessed by the civilians would be seized by the military. Without the weapons militant organization would disappear or we will make them disappear" Santhi replied with confidence.

"How are going to improve the relations with our neighbors especially India, Afghanistan and Bangladesh?"

"This is not subject we can discuss in this press meet. Wait for our government to perform"

"What will be your position in the new government?"

"KNPC cannot afford to keep me with them. I will come back to Pakistan. I will serve coffee, tea and biscuits to the ministers who attend the cabinet meeting. That is what I was doing in Kuwait"

"You are the King-Maker. What will be your roll in future?" another reporter repeated the question.

"I will always remain as Home-Maker" Santhi replied.

'Why don't become the home minister instead of home maker" another reporter wanted to pursue the question.

"I am always the Home Minister in our home" Santhi joked.

"Will you bring your children back to Pakistan?" a worried reporter asked.

"No! I will keep them away from Pakistan and politics. I want them to live a normal happy life" Santhi concluded her session.

25th July was the Birth day for Mansoor. He requested the party cadre not to celebrate his birth day because he didn't believe in the culture of celebrating birth days.

But on his birth day there was a big crowd in front of his home to convey their birth day greetings. First Mansoor refused to meet anybody. He wanted to spend the day quietly at home. The crowd became restive and started shouting. Mansoor asked the security to allow the party members one by one inside. Most of the people came with banquette. The security started checking all them with metal detectors and then allowed them. As the time passed, the crowd started swelling. They had to do the checking in a hurry. One man came with a big banquette. The security checked it in a hurry and allowed him to enter inside. He entered and saw Mansoor was sitting in a chair and Santhi was standing by. As he approached Mansoor the telephone bell rang. Santhi went inside to take the call. The man kept the banquet along with other banquette and said "Sal girah Mubarak" he tried to embrace him. But the security person prevented him. A big bomb hidden in the banquette was detonated with loud noise. Everybody was stunned. Mansoor along with 6 securities were in pool of Blood. Santhi came running and saw Mansoor and 6 securities dead. She was so shocked that she stood like a statue for more than hour. She came to senses after an hour. She saw her children and her in-laws crying by her side. No body was allowed inside the house. Security personnel cordoned the house. The news spread all over the world within minutes. Media persons were on the scene.

Forensic experts came and analysed the explosives used. They concluded that RDX was used in the detonator. The man who planted was found to be from Waziristan. On the next day Taliban claimed the responsibility for the assassination. The whole nation of Pakistan mourned the assassination. All the heads of states condemned the cowardly act.

All the newspapers carried chilling headlines

"Assassination culture took away one more precious life" Dawn said.

"It is a great tragedy. It will take a long time to come out of the shock" said Nation.

"The man who wanted to change the face of Pakistan is dead" said Herald Tribune

"God spared Santhi and took away Mansoor" Pakistan Times commented.

"An Indian woman who dared to take on militants and Taliban is punished" Times of India.

"Pakistan is cursed to live with assassinations and military dictatorship" The Hindu commented in its editorial.

"Santhi should not live in Pakistan any more. She should come back to India with her children" Sushma Swaraj invited.

The news of assassination shook the whole world. Makhdoom Amin Fahim was elected as the interim president of PJP by the Working Committee. Within few days after the assassination PJP sent a request to the president to postpone the oath-taking ceremony by a month. Accordingly President fixed 1st September as the date for taking oath by the leader of PJP.

The Working Committee debated on the issue of Prime Ministership. A unanimous decision was taken to select Fahim for the post of Prime Ministership. They could not consult Santhi on this issue as she was in a shocked state. W.C.assumed that she will not object to Fahim to become the P.M. Makhdoom reluctantly accepted the offer. He told the W.C that he accepts the offer as an interim arrangement. He felt that at his age of 80 it is too much of a burden on him. Moreover the objectives set by Mansoor are ambitious. He was not equipped to deliver the goods as expected. He could be a baby sitter till a new leader emerged. The whole world was expecting a leader who can replace Mansoor.

27

EMERGENCE OF A NEW LEADER.2018-19

Santhi was not in state to know what was going on outside her home. The elected PJP members of National Assembly met at the head quarters of PJP and discussed the issue of selecting their Parliamentary leader. Makhdoom too attended the meeting even though he was not MNA.

He told on behalf of the W.C about its decision to elect him as Prime Minister. One of the MNA got up and said

"It is the prerogative of the elected Members of National Assembly to elect their leader. W.C has no right to impose its decision on us". He further said "Makhtoom was a PPP leader till recently and he is not an elected MNA. One of us will be the P.M candidate."

Another MNA got up and spoke "Mansoor gave birth to PJP. But Santhi conceived and nurtured PJP along with her husband. If Mansoor is the father of PJP then Santhis is the mother. Her contribution to our victory is more than that of Mansoor. Therefore we cannot take a decision without consulting her". All MNAs agreed with him. They took a decision to meet Santhi. Few representatives were selected from different provinces to talk to Santhi on behalf of MNAs.

After few days the representatives met Santhi and discussed about the subject of their parliamentary leader. She told them that she was yet to recover from the shock. She suggested that an election may be conducted to elect their leader. She felt that it is the democratic way to elect the leader. But the representative told her that in her absence they would not hold the election. They were ready to wait for her participation. They came back and informed the outcome to other elected MNAs.

PJP party members and women organizations mooted the idea of electing Santhi as P.M.candidate. They have conveyed their feeling to their representatives. Some news paper published the story. As the news spread the support for Santhi grew by the day. There was television debate about Santhi becoming P.M. One of the panelist wondered "How can an Indian woman become the P.M of Pakistan?"

"She was the architect of PJP victory in the election. Being so what prevents her becoming P.M." another panelist argued.

"It is the constitution that prevents her becoming P.M. If she gets converted to Islaam and apply for Pakistani citizenship she might become the P.M." the third panelist suggested. The whole country watched the debate.

After watching the television debate and growing support among PJP party workers Santhi decided to attend the meeting of elected MNAs. At the meeting she spoke

"Neither Mansoor nor I was ever interested in power. Mansoor was friend of my brother. Yet I never thought of marrying him. Only the circumstances forced me to marry him. We had a happy marriage and proved to the world that a Muslim husband and a Hindu wife can live a happy life. The circumstances prevailed in Pakistan forced Mansoor to enter politics. As a dutiful wife I supported him. Beyond this I never thought even in my dreams to enter in to politics. Now I am here. I have fully accepted Pakistan as my country. Pakistanis love and respect me. I have decided to stay here and apply for Pakistani citizenship. I request MNAs to elect their parliamentary leader of NA. I want every one of you to write your choice in a piece of paper and drop them in a box. A box was brought and the papers were dropped by the MNAs. She opened the box and read the names. All the papers carried her name. So she kept silent for a moment and asked the members

"So why do you want me to become the P.M.?"

One of them got up and said

"You are the only person who knows the mind of our beloved leader Mansoor. We are not power mongering politicians. We have a mission to fulfill. We can do that only under your leadership. If you refuse to accept to be our leader we will resign our membership. You can dissolve PJP and go back to Kuwait or India" he spoke emotionally.

Santhi was stunned and didn't know what to say. All the members got up and shouted in one voice "We want you as our P.M" They repeated this again and again till Santhi asked them to stop.

"I sincerely wanted to fulfill the dreams of my husband. I want one of you to become P.M. I am ready to accept the party leadership and assist the P.M" Santhi requested with her folded hands.

All the members got up and shouted

"We want you to be P.M and leader of PJP"

Santhi took a glass of water and took a deep breath and announced

"I accept with humility for the sake of my husband"

All the MNAs stood up and gave a standing ovation by clapping their hands for five minutes. The news was flashed by the media to the world.

Every newspaper carried the story in their headlines

"An Indian woman to become the P.M" Dawn

"Will Santhi bring Santhi to Pakistan?" Hindu

"A revolution in Pakistan" the Nation.

Congratulations poured from the world leaders. Santhi consulted Makhdoom to finalise the list of Ministers. He raised the doubt and said

"The constitution does not allow a Hindu to become the P.M."

"Is it not possible to amend the constitution by an ordinance by the president?. Later we can ratify the ordinance by a constitution amendment bill in NA." Santhi suggested.

"I will talk to the president" Makhdoom agreed.

He did talk to the president. He agreed to proclaim an ordinance to amend the constitution. The media speculated that the president made a deal with PJP. According to the media he will be reelected as President in the coming presidential Election. All the political parties approached the Supreme Court to stay the president from issuing an ordinance. The case was admitted and the hearing was posted on 15th September

In the meanwhile Asma Jahangir organized a big rally of women in Karachi in support of Santhi on 14th September, one day before the hearing date. The interim government lead by Sherrif was not against Santhi becoming P.M. The government allowed the rally and stopped all the transport on 14th to prevent any untoward incident

On the day of the rally Pakistan and the whole world were surprised. A million women gathered. They were all dressed up in saris with bindi (RED DOT) on their forehead. They carried play cards with slogans

"We are ready to accept a Hindu woman as our P.M"

"There is no necessity for Santhi to convert"

"Santhi is a woman. That is enough for us. We don't care about the religion"

"Our ancestors were Hindus"

"If Muslims could become the presidents in India why not a Hindu become the P.M of Pakistan?"

"Santhi is our Savior"

"Men are conspiring against a woman becoming the P.M"

There were many play cards carrying similar messages in English, Urdu, Punjabi,. Sindi and Pastun. On seeing the huge crowd military was called to give protection to the rally.

The rally went through 10 kilo meter route. It took 5 hours to reach the National stadium.

A public meeting was held at 5 p.m. Asma Jahangir presided over the meeting. In her presidential address she said.

"Dear sisters! We are the representative of 50% of the population of Pakistan. So far we remained as dumps and toed the men's line. From today we are going to assert ourselves and take the destiny of this country in our hands. Our sister Santhi showed us the right path. In the past men ruled the world and made it a hell. After independence we expected freedom from the men. But it did not happen. Except for few years men ruled this country and ruined the same. A savior has come in the form of Santhi to save us from men who were corrupt, selfish and inefficient. Allah has given an opportunity to woman to rule this country. A woman from India divided our country. Now a woman from India has come to save us from the clutches of the men.

Santhi made a covenant with her husband that she will remain as a Hindu and he will remain as a true Muslim. If she wants to become the P.M she has to get converted to satisfy the constitution. President agreed to issue an ordinance to nullify the provision in the constitution. But the political parties wanted to prevent Santhi becoming P.M. So they approached the Supreme Court to stop the president from issuing ordinance. This is a conspiracy against women. Tomorrow the hearing would take place. If the Supreme Court decides in favor of the political parties, Santhi will be forced to convert in to a Muslim. A forced conversion is against Islam. Therefore we demand the Supreme Court to dismiss the petition filed by the political parties. I heard from the news similar rallies are arranged through out Pakistan. A commentator estimated that about ten million women have joined the rally in the major cities and towns. So far no politician has opened his mouth against us. They knew that their sisters, wives and mothers are protesting against the men. So they have no choice. Either they have to support us or keep quiet. I hope that Supreme Court will take note of this and pass the judgment tomorrow. Our Human Rights organization fully supports Santhi in the hour of crisis. We appeal to her not to get converted against her will. Let the constitution be changed to facilitate her to become P.M of this nation."

Many speakers have spoken in support. One speaker threatened if Santhi is forced to convert, they will convert all our women in to Hindus by wearing bindi in their forehead.

On 15th September the Supreme Court heard the arguments by the counsels from both sides. It passed the following judgment.

"The supreme court would strictly go by the constitution. As per constitution only a Muslim can become P.M. However if the president decides to promulgate an ordinance for nullifying this provision, he has the power to do so. The learned judges are of the opinion that if a Hindu is appointed as P.M of this country it could only an interim arrangement. The appointment will be become legally tenable only after passage of the constitution amendment bill. The newly constituted National Assembly should take up the bill as its first business and pass the bill. Once the bill is passed the appointment becomes legally valid. So we dismiss the petition"

The judgment was welcome by the cadres of PJP and the women's organization.

Santhi too heard the judgment in T.V. She immediately applied for citizenship. She asked the PJP Working Committee to arrange for a public meeting before taking oath. On 20th September a public meeting was arranged at National Stadium. Heavy security was provided to her by the Army.

Santhi addressed the nation

"My brothers and sisters! I am overwhelmed by the support given by women's organizations and PJP cadres. I do not know how to thank them. I promise that I will discharge my duties to the best of my abilities. I want to inform the nation that I have a duty to perform. When the nation has shown its magnanimity to accept me as its P.M, I too should reciprocate. There are some people who have reservations against me because of my religion. I want to tell them that I was born as Hindu but I was brought up in Kuwait. I know the Muslim world and its culture. Mentally I have accepted all the religions as equal and acceptable. My brother was a secular man. That was reason why he became the best friend of my husband. My relationship with my in-laws always remained cordial. I look at people as human-beings not as Hindus or Muslims. For me religion is immaterial. Therefore I have decided to become a Muslim on my own free will. I hope my husband in heaven will pardon me for breaking my covenant for the sake of our nation. I change my name as Salaami. From tomorrow I will perform five times namaz and observe all the duties as a good Muslim. I request the nation to accept me as a fellow Muslim" she concluded her speech. The crowd raised slogans

"Long live Salaami!"

"She is the embodiment of sacrifice. She sacrificed her religion to please her opponents" a political commentator said.

Every time Salaami spoke it became news. No wonder she is known as news-maker by the media. The media said that she stole the thunder from her opponents before becoming the P.M.

On 2nd October 2018 Salaami took oath as the Prime Minister of Pakistan along with 10 cabinet ministers. She nominated the following women as MNAs under the reservation quota.

1.Mala yousufzai 2. Fahimida Mirza 3. Roshanah Zafar 4. Bilquis Edhi 5. Sherry Rehman 6.Sultan Siddiqui 7. Bushra aitzaz 8. Rabina Feroze Bhatti 9. Ruth Pfan 10.Shazia Marri 11.Ameena Saiyid 12. Jugnu 13. Niger Ahmad 14. Asma Jahangir 15. Souriya Anwar 16. Ghulam Sugra 17.Nighat Said 18.Mukhtar Mai 19.Shandana Khan 20. Farzana Bari 21. Nusrat Jamil

Out of the 10 ministers sworn in 5 were women. Four of the five women ministers were elected MNAs and Mala Yousuf was the only nominated member to become the minister. Asma Jahangir was appointed as the ambassador to India. Hina Rabbani was appointed as commerce minister. The prime Minister retained portfolios of Foreign affairs. MalalaYousuf became the Home minister. Maj.General Shahida Malik was appointed as Army Chief overlooking seniority. Except few ministers, all the ministers were first time entrant to National Assembly.

Salaami met the press next day

"Most of the ministers are young and new to the politics. Do you think experience has no value?" one of the reporter asked.

"If the experience were the criteria I could not have become P.M" she replied.

"Do you think that they can deliver the goods as expected?" another reporter asked.

"The ministers are only policy makers. The government servants implement the policies. So any fresher can do a fine job as long he or she is dedicated and selfless. Knowledge and experience can be acquired. If some ministers are found to be inefficient we have enough talent pool to replace them"

"The appointment of Army Chief is a thunderbolt to the Army Generals"

"We want a general who will obey the civilian government. We found only one General fit for the job"

She answered some more questions and closed the session.

All media praised her women dominated cabinet as revolutionary and inspiring. The world media commented that Pakistan has shown what a woman can do. A western commentator said

"Politics is a game of Chess. In Chess queen is more powerful than the king. Now we understand why it is so"

The prime Minister informed her party members that she could not afford to waste her time in participating in Victory celebrations. She appealed to the party cadres to celebrate the victory with their elected representatives. She further appealed to them not to spend lavishly. Instead she advised them to help the poor. Because of these actions she occupied the front page of the newspapers every day. The jealousy of some political leaders made them fret and fume.

It took three months for the new government to get settled down. All the weapons possessed by the civilians and religious organizations were either surrendered or seized by the army. All the training camps were closed. The foreign jihadis were deported. The prime minister asked the Army Chief to prepare a plan to take on Taliban. She told the Chief that she will negotiate with them once they are defeated and disarmed. Accordingly a plan was prepared by the army. But the general wanted a troupe reduction in the eastern border. She assured her that she will negotiate with India for mutual troupe reduction by half. Army prepared a plan and waited for troupe reduction to start the operation. The operation was code named as "Operation mountain rat"

*   *   *

In India Narendra Modi was the Prime Minister and Sushma Swaraj was the Foreign Minister. Salaami asked Asma Jahangir, the Pakistan ambassador to India to arrange a meeting between her and Sushma Swaraj either in Islamabad or at New Delhi.

Asma had a very good rapport with Modi and Sushma. With in a week Indian government invited Salaami to visit India on a mutually convenient date. Salaami decided to visit India on December 6th 2018.

People of India had forgotten that 6th December 2002 the day Babri Masjid was demolished by the RSS cadre. Now it is on this day Indians eagerly waited to welcome their daughter Salaami. Times of India commented in its editorial

"Salaami conquered Pakistan and comes back as Prime Minister of Pakistan"

The Hindu commented

"Pakistan was saved from self destruction by their beloved Indian Bahu"

Hindustan Times commented

"Gandhiji failed to win the hearts of Pakistanis in 1947. Santhi did it in 2018"

All the media in India went gung ho in welcoming Salaami in her new Avatar as Prime Minister of Pakistan.

On 6th December Sushma personally went to the airport to receive Salaami. She was given a rousing welcome by the people of India. All the T.V news channels in India covered live the visit of Salaami. She visited Rajghat and paid her tributes to Gandhiji. Then she met Modi and the president of India, Lal Krishna Advani. She took their blessings for the successful completion of her mission against Taliban. They assured their cooperation.

Salaami was aided by Asma and officials in her negotiation with Indian government for troupe withdrawal. During the meeting India insisted on a comprehensive settlement between India and Pakistan. But Salaami stated

"Time is not ripe for the comprehensive settlement. At this point of time we cannot offer any concession to India. If I make any concession the political parties in Pakistan would call it as sell out to India. I have to consolidate my position first. Once we defeat the Taliban, we will be in position to settle all the issues between us including Kashmir. More over I have a plan for the whole South Asian Countries which I cannot reveal now. At present I want settle the issue of troupe reduction at the border along LOC. This will help us to move our forces and weapons to Waziristan and FATA areas where Taliban is entrenched. I appeal to India to cooperate with us to win over Taliban. Once we do that I will be strong enough to sit across the table for negotiation with confidence" she made a forceful appeal

After the meeting the following joint statement was issued

"India agrees to reduce its troupes along its border with Pakistan border by half as a good will gesture. Pakistan agreed to instruct its military to stop all infiltrations. Pakistan and India will be in close touch with each other during the operation against Taliban. Pakistan will seek advice from India if necessary. India agreed to help Pakistan in its "operation mountain rat"

The joint statement was hailed as win-win situation by both the countries.

Salaami returned to Pakistan. The media praised her successful mission. They urged her to use this opportunity to eradicate terrorism from Pakistani soil and promote tourism. As soon as she returned she called the Army Chief and said

"I have given you what you wanted. Now you have to give me what I want. I want to defeat Taliban decisively with least civilian casualty. We should not depend on weapon alone to defeat Taliban. We have to wage a psychological war against Taliban. They have brain-washed the people that jihad against USA, India and Israel is the only way to preserve their religion and culture. We have to use a carrot and stick policy. We should make them understand jihad will lead them to disaster. Only education, freedom and economic prosperity would improve their standard of living. Starving people cannot command respect from the international community".

On 1st January 2019 Pakistan started the "Operation Mountain Rat" It started by dropping thousands of leaflets printed in their language. The leaflet said

1. The government will initiate a special program for development of Wazistan and FATA areas.
2. Civilians are requested to isolate Taliban elements. All the peace loving civilians should surrender their weapons within a week or face military action.
3. Any body having a weapon is considered as a Taliban. He will be attacked by the military through air and land. Any body caught

with a weapon will be summarily executed. Those who surrender will be given General amnesty from prosecution.

4. Those who give refuge to the Taliban, will be considered as Taliban and dealt accordingly
5. The government will arrange camps for those who got displaced during the military operation against Taliban.
6. Military will attack the Taliban hide outs by air and land.
7. The NATO forces are waiting in Afghanistan to deal with escaping Taliban in to Afghanistan. So it is better for the Taliban to surrender to our Army rather killed by NATO forces.
8. It is the last chance for Waziristan and FATA areas to get integrated with rest of Pakistan.

The dropped leaflets had a solitary effect. Many people surrendered seeing the writing on the wall. Yet some Taliban decided to fight with Army. The battle lasted for 15 days. On 1st of February entire Taliban was wiped out. None escaped in to Afghanistan. Pakistan government reestablished the civilian rule within three months. Schools, government offices, police stations and hospitals were reopened. Normal life returned to Waziristan and FATA areas.

In May 2019 Indian Lok Sabha election BJP won a clear majority and formed the government at New Delhi on its own. Modi retired from politics. Sushma Sawaraj became the Prime Minister of India. It is widely speculated that he would become the president when Lal Krishna Advani's term expires. Sheik Hasina was going strong as Prime Minister in Bangladesh. Suriya was elected as the Prime Minister of Sri Lanka. Salala Khan was elected as the Prime Minister of Afghanistan. San Suu Kyi was going strong as Prime Minister of Myan Mar. Hillary Clinton was elected as President of USA in November 2015. Angela Merkel was reelected as Chancellor of Germany. Harriat Herrman was elected as the Prime Minister of Britain. Thailand, Brazil, Japan were ruled by Women. It is a coincidence that more than half population of the world was ruled by women. In the previous years the women who entered politics were either wife or daughter of heads of states. Examples are Srimavo Bandaranayaka, Indira Gandhi, Benazir Butto etc. But in 2018 women entered in to politics on their own merit and came to power after a great struggle Examples are Salaami in Pakistan, San Suu Kyi in Myan Mar, Suriya in Sri Lanka, and Salala in Aghanistan.

Most of these women have seen the suffering of the people due to war, poverty, dictatorship and discrimination. They are ready to fight against these evils and make the world a safer place for women and poor.

Salaami wanted to take the lead in uniting the countries to make the world a war-free world. She felt that women and children suffer more in a war-torn country. She wanted to start her work as a crusader from South Asia. She hit the idea of forming a federation of South Asian Nations. She named the federation as UNITED SOUTH ASIAN REPUBLICS in short USAR

Salaami wanted to finalize the structure of USAR after consulting the Prime Minister of India. She felt if India is roped in to USAR other countries would follow suit. She invited Sushma Swaraj to visit Pakistan as soon as she took over as Prime Minister. She accepted the invitation and planned to visit Pakistan in the First week of July

Sushma visited Pakistan on 3rd July 2019. Sushma and Salaami engaged in a personal discussion without any official aide.

Salaami explained

"I have a dream to unite all the South Asian countries under one umbrella. You can give your views. I will discuss with Suriya, San Suu, Salala and Shaik Hasina before finalizing the structure of USAR. We have few models for us to emulate. We have United States, European Union and ASEAN. Which one you like to adopt?" asked Sharmila to start the discussion.

"I do not like any one of them. Each has its own defect. Let us tease our brain to strike a unique idea which no one ever thought of it. First we should decide what we want to achieve by USAR. USAR means beware or caution in Indian languages. This gives me an idea what we should aim at. The whole world should look at USAR as it looks at USA. In short USAR should be an economic and knowledge super power. But it should not be a military super power. USAR should strive hard to eliminate nuclear weapons on the face of earth. The world body should be strengthened in such a way its military power should be in a position to control any military conflict between two nations. USAR should be the leader of third world. USAR should neither oppose nor support any other super power. It should have its own independent policy based on Justice, equality and humanity" Sushma opened the discussion with her views on USAR

"I fully agree with you. I am planning to meet San Suu Kyi, Suriya, Salala and Sheik Hasina one by one and get their views. Then

I will finalize the draft resolution and send them to all six South Asian Countries. Once accepted we will ratify the resolution by signing s treaty" Salaami indicated the course of action.

"One sticky point may be army. I do not know whether all the countries will have their own army or common army. If we have common army who will control the army?. In my opinion this will be the difficult question to solve." Sushma expressed her doubt.

"I am for a common army. Let us hear from others before making a final decision" Santhi expressed her opinion.

"I will consult my cabinet colleagues and send our views on this subject. Till then let your idea be a proposal" Sushma concluded.

Both of them came out of the room. Media persons were waiting outside.

All were eager to know the outcome of the discussion. One reporter asked

"What is the subject of discussion? What is the outcome?"

Salaami smiled and replied

"When normally two ladies meet what do they discuss? They discuss about saris, ornaments, children's education and little bit of politics. That is what we did"

"What is the out come?" another reporter.

"Our discussions were cordial and fruitful" reply came from Sushma.

"Do you have a plan to issue a joint statement?" a third reporter quizzed

"Yes! We have decided to become friends and solve our problems amicably. This is the joint statement" Salaami concluded the session. The reporters were very much disappointed. "Some thing is wrong with our P.M. She never treated us like this before" murmered one reporter.

July 25 was the birth and death day of Mansoor. A meeting was arranged by PJP to pay respect to their slain leader. Salaami was requested to pay tribute to their leader. Makhdoom presided over the meeting. In his presidential address he paid a rich tribute to Mansoor. He said

"Mohamad Ali Jinnah is the father of our nation. Mansoor Ali Khan was our savior. In the past when our beloved leaders were assassinated the nation became an orphan. But Mansoor left his heir Salaami to take care of his legacy and the nation. His absence did not stop his march towards his goal of making Pakisatan a secular state. Let us pray Allah to give peace to his soul"

Salaami rose to speak. There was applause from the crowd. She spoke
"My beloved citizens of this country! One year passed since the untimely death of our great leader. This is the time to take stock of what we have done. So far we have not done much to solve our economic problems. We spent all energy in eliminating the militancy and Taliban menace. I hope that we will be in a position to attract foreign investment.

With our free trade agreement we will be in a position to solve our economic problems soon.

Mansoor, like any other great leader was a simple man. He never spoke a lie. He didn't smoke nor drank alcohol. He looked at all women as his sister, mother or daughter. He was so perfect in his personal life that we never quarreled. He was not an intellectual but he compensated with his robust common sense. It was a personal loss to me. I got on with my life only to fulfill his ambition. I request all of you to take an oath to work hard to honour the promises he made to the people of Pakistan" Salaami concluded her speech.

Somebody from the crowd shouted "We want a story". The crowd started chanting the request. Salaami went to the dais and waved her hands to stop shouting. She spoke

"I know it is not an occasion to tell stories. Yet I feel that it is my duty to satisfy your request.

A husband and wife were walking along the bank of a big lake which was infested with crocodiles. They heard a strange voice "Help! Help!". The husband rushed to spot where the voice came from. He saw a crocodile caught in a net. Somebody has a laid a trap to catch the crocodile. The crocodile asked for help to get releasesd and it told that it would ever be greatfull to him. The husband wanted to help the crocodile. His wise wife told him not to cut net on the headside lest it may catch him. She advised him to cut on the tailside only and let the crocodile come out on its own. Husband took her advice and cut the net on the tailside. No sooner the tail was released, the crocodile did not try to come out of the net but instead it hit the man and killed him. The wife cried for help. People came running to help. They wanted to kill the crocodile. But she stopped the crowd and requested them with folded hands

"My husband will not come back if you kill the crocodile. The crocodile is perfectly justified in killing its prey. My husband did a foolish thing. He was punished by the god for his foolishness. I request all of you not to kill the crocodile but release it without any harm."

The crowd released the crocodile by using some tool to cut the net. The crocodile thanked the women and spoke

"You wise lady knew very well a crocodile's habit is to kill its prey. You should not expect an animal follow your morality. This is a warning to you not to trust people blindly. Lest you will meet the same fate" Salaami completed her story

The crowd listened to the story with a pin drop silence. One man from the asked an innocent question

"I have not seen a crocodile. Do the crocodile speak like human-beings?"

"Yes! They speak in stories" Salaami replied

Some ladies from the crowd sobbed. Some took out their kerchief to wipe out their tears. The crowd dispersed silently without shouting any slogan.

*   *   *

Santhi visited Bangladesh, Myanmar, Sri Lanka and Afghanistan one by one. She discussed about establishing USAR. They gave their views. She was in constant touch with Sushma after every visit and kept Sushma informed about the development. It took three months to complete this exercise. She finalized the draft treaty in consultation with Sushma by the end of October. The essential features of the treaty were listed below

1. The treaty will come to force from 1st January 2020. It will be signed on 25th December 2019 in Dacca.
2. The head quarters of USAR will be in Pune India. The sessions will be held in all the capitals in turn by drawing lots.
3. USAR will have common army with head quarters at New Delhi as European countries have NATO. In addition to this each country will maintain its own army. Each will use its army to maintain internal security. A peace treaty will be signed by all the countries not to attack each other. In case a country violates the treaty the common army will deal with that country. The common army will be known as Military of Asian Security Keeping in short form MASK.
4. All countries will have a common currency and Reserve Bank would be in Dacca with branches in all the capitals.

5. There will be no change in the political system. Each country will ratify the treaty by amending their constitution. The treaty will come in to effect only when all countries ratify the treaty.
6. There will be free trade among the countries. They will sign a separate Free Trade Agreement in the lines of ASEAN free trade agreement.
7. No country will ban a book or a film without the approval of USAR.
8. There will not be any change in sports and games structure. The countries will compete among them as well as with other countries in the world.
9. All countries have the right to run educational institutions without any hindrance within USAR
10. People of USAR are free to travel to its member countries with their passport but without any visa.

The draft treaty was sent to Kabul, NewDelhi, Rangoon, Columbo and Dacca for comments. All countries debated this treaty and gave their acceptance. However it was decided by all the six countries to introduce the constitution amendment bill after the signing the Treaty. The Treaty was known as "Dacca Treaty"

A summit of the leaders of the six South Asian Countries was planned in Dacca. It was planned to be held 25th and 26th December. Most of the countries in the world congratulated the historical Summit. They wished the summit success. They promised to send one of their senior members of their government to attend the summit. CIA sent a secret circular to all the heads of states not to attend the summit. They felt that it is very risky for so many heads of the states to assemble at the capital of a Muslim country. Bangladesh arranged for a five layer securities for VIPs. The government took all precautions to put thousands of suspected people under house arrest. All the flights including helicopters were banned in Dacca. Bangladesh took the help from India for arranging security. On 24th December the heads of states from Pakistan, India, Myanmar, SriLanka, Afghanistan arrived in the charted flights. On 24th CIA reviewed the security arrangements and certified it as the best possible. The heads of the states were lodged in different Hotels for security reasons.

The summit was planned to be held in Bangabandhu International conference centre. The signing of the treaty by the heads of states would take place at 5 o' clock in the evening. A Cricket match between India and Pakistan was arranged on 26th December to celebrate the formation of USAR and to entertain the VIP guests.

At 10 o' clock in the morning Salaami arrived in a helicopter. Sushma arrived in a car from her hotel. Salala and suriya arrived in a single helicopter. Sheik Hasina being the host, stayed at the conference centre on 24th December to oversee the security arrangement. All the delegates were present in the venue before 10 o' clock. Exactly at 10 O' clock the summit was inaugurated by Salaami, the architect of USAR. In her inaugural address she spoke

"My dear fellow citizens of USAR! The heads of states of USAR countries! Respected representatives of all the countries! I welcome one and all to the summit. It is truly historical day in the history of man kind. All the USAR countries are ruled by women. Today more than half the world is ruled by women. In the twentieth century we saw many wars. They were caused by religious intolerance or greediness.

Men always found ways to suppress the women. As individuals they use violence to suppress the women. At the country level they use religion to suppress the women. Why all our prophets and Avatars are men? Why most of the kings were men? It is because they believe that they have born to rule the world and it is the job of women to produce children and take care of them. The education to women is denied. There is gender discrimination at work places. Violence against women is committed all over the world. In the twenty first century things started changing for better. Women have equal opportunity to get educated and work in whichever field they like. Women proved to be better rulers. Even the men started accepting this. Otherwise we would not have won the elections.

In the world many atrocities were committed by men in power. Now the responsibility is imposed on the women to heal the wounds. I sincerely tender my apology to Bangladesh on behalf of my country for all the atrocities committed by the Pakistani army in 1971. I apologize to India for the barbaric behavior of Pakistani army personnel mutilating the dead bodies of Indian solders. Now Pakistani army is headed by women. I am sure that such thing would never happen again.

The objectives of forming USAR are as follows

1. To preserve our culture from the invasion of western culture
2. To achieve 100% literacy in USAR countries
3. To improve the standard of living and Human development index in USAR countries.
4. To eliminate nuclear weapons from USAR Countries.
5. To encourage free trade without barrier
6. To set up joint research institutes in all fields
7. To reduce the military strength of USAR countries to the bare minimum
8. To promote our culture and arts
9. To change the food habits of our people for better health and eliminate the influence of MNCs to change our food habits
10. To change the education system from western oriented to eastern oriented and to promote education through mother tongue.

I request the representatives of the countries who have assembled here to take cue from this summit and form of their own union of nations to eliminate wars completely from the face of earth. If money spent on wars is used in eradicating poverty, nobody on earth would go hungry. I appeal all the citizens of the world to unite, reduce army sizes, reduce weapon, eliminate all the barriers and treat all the human-being as equals. With this I conclude my speech. Thank you for listening me patiently" she concluded. Standing ovation followed.

After her Sushma, Salala, Suriya and San Suu Kye spoke on the same lines. Sheik Hasina gave the vote of thanks. All the representatives came to Dias and congratulated the six heads of states. The summit was over by 12 O' clock. All of them returned to the places of stay. The media from all over the world covered live this historical summit. It was estimated that 3 billion people saw this summit live, the largest ever in the history of mankind.

Exactly at 5 p.m all the six heads of states assembled again to sign the treaty. India signed first. Pakistan, Bangladesh, Srilanka, Afghanistan and Myanmar followed suit. At 5.15 p.m the signing ceremony was over. All the heads of states felt relaxed and chatting with each other forgetting they are the Prime ministers. At that moment a great tragedy occurred. A rocket carrying a nuclear head hit the podium. There was a huge explosion and fire. Nobody understood what was happening. Electricity and communication links were cut in the entire Dacca city. Dacca plunged in to darkness. The whole world was kept in dark about what happened in Dacca. The humanity met the worst disaster ever happened in the history. This is a warning to the people who wanted to change the behavior of men. God save Pakistan!

END

DAUGHTER
OF THE ENEMY